Welcome Tavern. Enjoy your Visit!

VERMIN

THE VERMIN SERIES

ARDIN PATTERSON

Ardin Patterson (signature)

Loose Roof Books

VERMIN
ARDIN PATTERSON

https://loveknotbooks.ca
An imprint of DAOwen Publications

Copyright © 2021 by Ardin Patterson
All rights reserved.

Vermin / Ardin Patterson
Edited by MJ Moores and Douglas Owen

Cover art by MMT Productions

ISBN 978-1-928094-74-6
EISBN 978-1-928094-75-3

10 9 8 7 6 5 4 3 2 1

For Vanessa

1

Wind slithered in through the cracks between the walls of the snow-covered barn. The pair of bedraggled teens shivered helplessly, huddled together.

"I'm hungry," a voice mumbled from underneath the damp, tattered blanket. "When's Micah coming back?"

A gentle kiss silenced Nicholas. He rubbed it from his cheek and frowned. Raising his head slightly, the youth gazed into the sleepy brown eyes of his sister.

"I know you aren't feeling well." Suzanna patted his head gently. "But you shouldn't complain."

He wrinkled his nose and glared at her. "We haven't eaten all day."

"You've had more to eat than anyone else," she said firmly. Suzanna tossed her long, tawny hair over her shoulder and tugged at her small turtle-shaped earring. She'd managed to hide it and the tips of her ears beneath her thick mane.

"*Iya Nasei...*" Nicholas whispered, trying to hold back a cough. He licked his lips as his ears perked up at the crunching of snow beyond the barn and crawled out from under the blanket. The door creaked open.

"Nicholas, come back here." Suzanna eyed the figure stepping through. She jumped to her feet and grabbed Nicholas by the arm, pulling him back behind the wall of hay.

A horrible stench filled the air.

"Zana," Nicholas choked out. "Where's Micah?"

Suzanna hushed him, forcing him to lay back down. She inched out of their hiding place, glaring at the man by the door.

"Hey there, pet," the man chuckled, waving a gun in his hand. "Be good now. Don't go biting anybody."

Nicholas shivered, holding his breath.

"What are you mongrels doing in my barn?" he asked.

Four others entered. Two of them dragged Micah by the collar of his jacket.

"Micah!" Suzanna raced toward him. She hesitated, looking at the group of men. "W-what's that smell?" Smoke drifted in from beyond the men. "What have you done to my brother?"

The bearded man glared at her. "We're building a fire."

Micah spat blood onto the man's shoe and smirked, flashing his dull fangs. "You don't think our kind will hunt you down?"

Nicholas' hands shook; he pressed them to his chest and held his breath. *How did they find us? We were careful. Weren't we? I have to do something. What if they catch up to the others?*

"Shut up, you damn animal!" the bearded man growled, smacking Micah across the back of his neck.

Micah winced and let out a nervous laugh.

"Grab the girl," the man with the gun ordered.

Micah struggled against his binds. "Don't you dare lay a finger on her!"

Suzanna backed away from the men and reached for the knife in her pocket.

The man with the gun aimed it at her brother, grinning. "How's about you put that down, pet. Don't want any trouble now, do we?" He snickered.

"Since you're such a pretty pet"—the bearded man chuckled—"maybe we'll give you to the doctor as a gift."

Suzanna clutched her knife and glanced over at the wall of hay where her younger brother hid. "I-I don't want to hurt anyone." Her hands trembled.

A cry rose from the outside. "The fire's ready!"

Micah yanked himself out of the men's grasp, knocking one over as he dashed toward his sister.

"Come on."

"But what about—"

"There's no time!" Micah told her, dragging her out the barn doors.

"Why didn't you shoot?" the bearded man asked.

"No need." The one with the gun grinned. "We've got twelve outside. Those two beasts won't stand a chance."

Nicholas shivered. Suzanna screamed. His stomach turned. He forced himself up onto his feet and stumbled out of the hiding place toward the laughing monsters before him. His pupils narrowed as he latched onto the gun the man held.

"Well, what do y'know?" The man smirked. "You mongrels just keep poppin' up."

Nicholas glared at him. His chest tightened.

"You're not stupid, kid. Let go of the gun," the bearded man snapped.

"He said let go, you dumb animal!" cried the man Micah had knocked to the ground.

Nicholas flinched. His keen hearing amplified the shouts from the humans outside. He jerked the gun out of the man's hand and raised it up.

"Look at his face," the bearded man murmured. "He's got the fever. Just beat him, and let's go find that girl before someone kills her."

"Cato and I will go after her," the smaller man said.

The dark haired one nodded, and the two of them hurried outside.

The remaining three men inched toward the sickly boy, grim smiles on their faces.

Nicholas' eyes blurred over as he pointed the gun at the remaining three men.

"No one steals from the doctor," the bearded man snapped. "And no one lets your kind just roam around freely. Tavern is a human only zone. Your kind ain't welcome here."

"If you give us back the gun"—the soft-faced man knelt in front of the boy—"we'll leave you alone."

"What about my friends?" Nicholas cleared his throat and sniffled. He scanned the face of the man carefully. Heavy smoke swam through his nostrils. He winced, trying to keep focus.

The whisper came low and harsh. "That older boy is going to be burned, and that young girl will be used to pay for the damage he did to the doctor's home."

Nicholas shook his head.

"We'll let you go free." He held out his hand, green eyes glimmering.

Nicholas gulped up some air and trembled.

"That fever is going to get much worse. We won't need to kill ya." The bearded man smirked.

"What's your name?" the soft-faced man asked.

"Nicholas. Nicholas Slayden."

"Hello Nicholas." The man smiled. "I'm Vincent Gray."

Nicholas glared.

"It's pretty hard to kill a man if you know his name. Those kinds of memories can haunt a man for ages." Vincent raised his brow to emphasize the fact.

Nicholas lowered the gun. His throat tightened.

"Why don't you give that here?"

Nicholas shook his head, raising the gun up at them again. Hands shaking, he staggered toward the barn door.

"Come now, Nicholas, there's no need to hurt anyone." Vincent crept toward him. "Be a good boy and give me the gun."

"Move," Nicholas forced out.

The men eyed him, then turned to Vincent.

"I said move!" the boy screamed.

"As you wish." Vincent smirked, stepping out of the way.

"Zana!" Nicholas shrieked, racing out of the barn. He stared at the horror before him, then shut his eyes. The world swayed along with his body, and he collapsed.

The three men hovered over the boy as he lay in the snow. The man who had the gun spat on him and kicked him in the side. "Stupid animal."

"Here's your gun." The bearded one chuckled, prying the weapon from the boy's hand.

"Thanks. Hey, Vince, that was a good move, tryna outsmart that beast."

Vincent sneered and shook his head. "The poor thing reminded me of my old man's dog." He looked down at the boy's body and sighed, shoving his hands into his jacket. "Let's leave him here. He won't survive much longer."

The two men nodded.

"I'm heading to the pub." The bearded man laughed, putting an arm around the others' shoulders.

Nicholas kept his eyes squeezed shut and his body still as he listened to their footsteps fade into the distance. When only the crackling of the fire remained, he propped himself onto his elbows and crawled away from the scene. A lump grew in his throat as he thought of his siblings. For all he knew, they were both dead. Now, he was truly alone. No pack. No family. No one. He rolled onto his back, gasping for air.

"Zana, Micah...I'm sorry."

Roland's niece clung to his arm. "Look, they have new books!"

He glanced at the large sign in the bookstore window and turned to Rose. "So, they do. Want to go in and look?"

Rose nodded. "Yes, please." Her brown curly bangs flopped against her forehead.

Roland led his niece into the shop and waved to the owner. "How are you, Mr. Timmins?"

Mr. Timmins gave a light chuckle. "Fine. Thank you."

Rose strayed from her uncle's side, the heels of her boots, clicking happily against the wooden floor as she waltzed over to a table filled with the newest releases. Her round, blue eyes sparkled. "Which one should I get?" She turned to her uncle. "There are so many to choose from."

Mr. Timmins and Roland made their way over to the young girl and eyed the books on the table.

"These ones over here'll give you nightmares," Mr. Timmins warned. The old man adjusted his glasses, pointing to the cover of a book with a contorting, grey sea-creature. "And the ones in the middle are for boring folks."

"You mean those who like to enrich their minds with a stimulating, and highly advanced read." Rose giggled, shooting a glance at her uncle. She hovered over a book with a picture of a horse on the front. "This looks interesting."

"What's wrong with an educational read?" Roland asked.

"They turn your brain to mush." Rose teased. "That's why my teacher is so boring and dull."

"Young lady, just because its your birthday doesn't mean you can talk badly about others," Roland scolded. "And just so you know, I quite enjoy those educational books."

"That's because you're boring, Uncle." Rose winked. "I like this one with the horse. It sounds like it's packed with adventure and romance."

Mr. Timmins shook his head. "What does a young thing like you know about romance?"

"Nothing really." Rose shrugged handing him the book. "Just that it makes people's brains turn to mush."

Mr. Timmins let out a laugh and went over to the cash register.

Roland followed, removing his gloves, while Rose continued to check out the display of books.

"That niece of yours reminds me so much of your brother," Mr. Timmins said softly as Roland pulled out his wallet. "Does she ever talk about them?"

Roland hesitated for a moment then shook his head. "No. Not since she got sick."

"Well, I suppose it'd be a complicated conversation to have, given the circumstances."

"Circumstances?" Roland peered up from his wallet. He examined the expression on the older man's face, catching the glint of fear in Mr. Timmins's eyes. He couldn't believe after all these years, the people of Tavern still looked at him like that. It was the way his mother had looked at him at his brother's funeral—confusion, hatred, and pity swam in their eyes. *How else would they look at me?* Mr. Timmins shifted from side to side, adjusting his glasses again.

Roland pulled the money from his wallet. "Yes, well, when Rose was sick, it was very hard on all of us."

"That bloody fever, it's killed another six people, you know."

"I heard." Roland sighed, paying Mr. Timmins. "I'm thankful I was able to afford her medical care."

"You *should* be thankful, Mr. Crispin." Mr. Timmins grinned. "With all that money, you could probably get anything you want."

Money. What money? Roland smiled shyly. "I hate to leave like this, but our driver is waiting, and Rose is getting a little too friendly with those books of yours."

Mr. Timmins laughed. "You take care now."

Roland tugged on the wide, fluffy hood of his niece's jacket, handed her the book, and ushered her out of the shop. "I have a meeting in a few hours. Do you mind finishing the guest list for your party without me?"

Rose shook her head as the two of them got into the backseat of the stately car. Rose gazed out the window, likely daydreaming about owning a beautiful horse of her own. They used to own several, but times were lean.

A small grin crept over her lips as they headed down the country road. "I wish we lived on a farm," Rose whispered, looking at the snow-covered barns outside.

Roland glanced at his watch. "Mmm?"

"Isn't the snow pretty?"

Roland looked over at his niece. "Did you say something?"

Rose rolled her eyes and leaned toward the window. "Mr. Leon, stop the car!"

Their driver glanced up into his mirror and waited for Roland's command.

Rose grabbed onto the car door. "Stop the car!"

"Rose, calm down. What's the matter?" Roland grumbled.

"Someone's lying in the snow!"

The vehicle halted, and the young girl raced out into the cold, the skirt of her dress gathering snow as she forged a path.

Roland hurried after her, his feet sliding on a patch of ice. "Rose, wait!"

The two of them stood over the body and trembled.

"H-he's breathing," Rose whispered. She took off her jacket and wrapped it around the boy. "He should see a doctor. We can't leave him here. He'll die."

Roland stared at the boy and swallowed hard. *How long has he been out here? There's sweat running down his forehead...This is bad. He needs to get inside.* "We'll take him with us. It looks like he's got the fever." He picked up the boy and brought him to the car. Roland laid the young man down in the back seat. "Rose, sit up front with Mr. Leon."

Rose nodded and rubbed her arms over her long red sweater.

Roland crawled into the back and watched the boy's chest rise and fall as he struggled to breathe. "You'll be all right," Roland said gently.

His niece stared at the boy from the front seat, her blue eyes filling with tears.

"He'll be all right." Roland drew in a deep breath and forced himself to gulp it down. Taking care of an invalid, let alone a stranger, meant he'd have to try and get his hands on more medicine and find somewhere for the boy to stay. Two months ago, dealing with Rose's sickness while keeping his nephews out of trouble had drained the twenty-four-year-old. What would another young soul do?

Roland sighed. "We'll do whatever we can to help him."

2
———

Roland raced up the stairs to the nursery carrying the shivering boy in his arms. At his heels followed his niece, two nephews, and the children's nursemaid, Lisa.

Their driver, Mr. Leon, was tasked with calling for the doctor.

"I'll fill a bowl with warm water." Lisa disappeared into the nursery's bathroom.

Roland laid the boy down on his old bed, wrapping the sheets around him. "We need to keep him warm."

Caspian hovered over the bed. "What kind of person doesn't wear a coat in the winter?"

"Be quiet," Rose grumbled. "Let's go find him some dry clothes."

Her younger brother folded his arms and pouted. "He's probably going to die."

"Caspian"—Roland shot the ten-year-old a glare—"please leave the room."

Caspian wrinkled his nose and turned on his heels. "I hope Dr. Gray has to give him a huge needle!"

Roland recoiled at his nephew's remark. *I wish that boy would act his age. He's been spoiled rotten...oh, who am I kidding? I'm just as much to blame.*

"Get out of here, you annoying pest!" Rose pointed to the door. "Julius, go get one of Uncle Roland's long shirts."

Little Julius stared up at his sister, then looked at the stranger lying on the bed. "Um, can you come with me?" he asked, rocking back and forth.

"You two are so..." Rose glared at him for a moment, tugging at the white ribbon in her hair. She drew in a deep breath. "I'll do it. Have Tabby make a warm snack."

"Okay," Julius whispered. He eyed the boy and pouted. "Maybe he needs another blanket, too."

Roland dashed for the door. The boy groaned. Roland whipped his head from the child to the hall. "Is someone coming to help us?" he hollered from the top of the staircase.

Mr. Leon shook his head, calmly making his way up the stairs. "There's something I need to inform you of."

Roland glanced back into the nursery and nodded. "Let's do all we can for the boy first."

"As you wish, sir." Mr. Leon pulled his hat off and pushed back his grey hair. "Peter and Dianna are going to be stopping by after your meeting."

"After? The meeting!" Roland turned from Mr. Leon and cursed under his breath. "I forgot about that."

"Do you think Lisa will be able to care for the child on her own, sir?"

Roland shook his head. "He needs medical attention."

A scream erupted from the child's lips. Roland flinched. The two men glanced at one another before hurrying back into the nursery.

"What's wrong?" Roland eyed his trembling niece and nursemaid.

Lisa pulled Rose closer to her. "Master Crispin, sir, the boy's terrified of me."

Roland inched toward the boy. "You need to let her help you," he said softly. "No one is going to hurt you."

The boy's eyes filled with tears. "Stay away from me!"

Roland nodded. "I'll stay over here, but you need to let these two ladies assist you. You're bleeding and very cold." Roland backed away from the boy and gave him a gentle smile. "We just want to help."

The boy's eyes grew heavy as the young nursemaid approached him. His leg twitched as she rolled up the bottom of his pants.

"Zana," he called hoarsely.

Rose held the blankets for Lisa to work. "Try and relax."

"I have to find Zana," he moaned.

Roland let out a sigh of relief as the boy's eyes shut.

"Sir, your meeting." Mr. Leon tapped him on the shoulder.

"Right, the meeting. Rose, have Tabby come upstairs and help Lisa. I don't want you or your brothers getting sick. I should be back in about an hour."

"Okay," Rose mumbled, laying the blankets down on a chair. She kissed her uncle goodbye and watched him hurry on his way.

"Rose, dear, could you pass me that bowl of water?" Lisa rubbed her hands together to avoid startling the boy with cold fingers.

Rose nodded. After handing the bowl to her nursemaid, she hovered over the boy. "He isn't going to die, right?"

"I hope not." Lisa pressed the wet cloth onto his leg. "There's no time to get Tabitha. He's shaking again. Dab his forehead."

Rose picked up a cloth and dipped it into the warm water. The young girl concentrated on the boy's half-opened eyes. Her heart pounded as she gently brushed the cloth across the stranger's forehead. She pushed the boy's long, wavy, dark brown hair away from his face causing the ends to curl against his neck, and cheeks.

He kept weary eyes on her.

"How did you hurt your leg?" Rose asked.

The boy's head flung back as he let out a wracking cough. His eyes glazed over. He placed his head back on the pillow and held out his hand to Rose.

"Gimme that," he ordered.

Rose cautiously handed the cloth to him.

"I'll be right back. I'm just going to get him some pyjamas," Lisa said.

"All right." Rose frowned.

The boy groaned as he tried to sit up. He gripped his stomach, gritting his teeth. His eyes rolled back.

Rose reached out to him, but he pulled away and flung himself off the bed onto the floor.

"Are you mad?" She watched him drag himself across the hardwood. Rose hurried over to the door and called out. "Lisa, come quick!"

The boy gagged violently as he threw himself onto his back. His eyes watered.

Rose knelt down next to him. "Calm down," she hushed. "You'll only make it worse."

The boy swallowed a few large gulps of air and glared at her. "I have to s—" His body shook, lips trembling. "Zana. Suzanna." He gasped. Tears sprang from his eyes.

Rose glanced away shyly and placed a hand on his shoulder. "Whatever it is, can wait. You need to rest now."

The boy brushed the stray tears from his face and nudged her hand away.

Lisa tumbled into the room and eyed them. She shot Rose a worried glance then relaxed her shoulders and placed the pyjamas on the bed. "We'll let you dress. I'm going to see if we have anything for your leg."

Rose got to her feet and gazed down at the hem of her dress. "If we leave, he might—"

"He'll be perfectly all right. Now come along, dear, Tabby's made some snacks."

Rose caught the boy's gaze as she nodded, then left. "Okay."

Nicholas eyed the room. The boy struggled to rise onto his elbows and flung the cloth at the door. Pain pierced Nicholas' stomach again as he tried to sit. Tears welled. With gritted teeth, he forced them back. The pyjamas rested neatly on the bed, Nicholas's eyes widened. Never in his life had he seen such clothes given to someone like him—a vermin.

He crept toward the bed. The corners of his lips rose as Nicholas's hands brushed against the soft silk. It wasn't long before he'd changed into the lovely red pyjamas. If only Micah could see him. Wouldn't that be a treat? He swallowed the lump in his throat.

"Micah *Iya*...I—"

Nicholas tugged on the long, silk sleeves recalling the nice gentleman's hats and coats worn by the classy, rich humans he'd seen when living in Dinara. He eyed the wet grey sweater lying on the floor. It used to be his brother's.

Nicholas glowered.

Micah was most likely dead. The thought of his brother's body burning turned his stomach even more. He pulled himself up onto the bed. *What am I going to do?* Nicholas had never been hunting on his own and could barely keep up with his pack. Now that he was alone, he didn't have a clue. For all he knew, the humans could be preparing a bonfire for him.

A quiet knock rapped the door. The knob shook. Nicholas glanced over at it as two women bickered outside.

"Are you dressed?" Lisa asked, entering the room.

Nicholas nodded.

"I brought some tea to warm you up." The older, shorter woman smiled, placing a tray on the nightstand.

Nicholas had never had tea before, but he kept his mouth shut. He decided it would be safer to play along.

"My name is Lisa," the first lady said sweetly as she tied back her platinum-coloured hair. "That there is Tabitha, the greatest cook in the world."

Tabitha giggled. "Oh stop."

Nicholas rubbed his eyes.

"This should relax you," Tabitha told him, handing him a cup. "What's your name?"

Nicholas glared at her.

"He's very hostile at the moment." Lisa turned to her. "Snapped at Master Roland he did."

Tabitha shook her head and kissed her teeth.

Nicholas took the teacup into his hands and pursed his lips. He watched the two women stare at him. *Maybe it's poisoned.* Humans were cunning. It wouldn't be the first time their kind used poison on a vermin. When he was little, he'd heard tales about the humans in Lytel poisoning a well used by the pack there. Those who drank from the well foamed at the mouth and trembled, their eyes rolling back in their heads. Nicholas had nightmares about the story for a week.

"Something the matter?" Lisa crouched before him.

Nicholas eyed her.

"Please drink it," Tabitha begged. "You look so cold. Your lips are practically blue."

Nicholas sighed. "I'm not thirsty."

"Just a sip then. To help you sleep."

Nicholas looked at her. He didn't feel threatened, and the warm drink smelled sweet like honey. He loved honey. He pressed the cup to his lips and took a sip. His throat burned. "I-it's hot!"

The two women rushed to his side. Tabitha took the cup while Lisa grabbed Nicholas some water.

"Drink this," Lisa said.

Nicholas shook his head. *Deisso. Does she think I'm stupid? These human drinks are Verjik!*

Lisa eyed him. "It's cold. Drink it."

Nicholas grabbed the cup from her and drank cautiously. He smiled as the cool water eased his throat. "Thanks."

"I didn't think it was going to be that hot." Tabitha pouted. "Were Rose's senses off like that, too?"

"She was dizzy a lot. Never hungry." Lisa placed a finger on her chin in thought.

Nicholas lay back on the bed and shut his eyes. He drew in a deep breath.

"Are you tired?" Tabitha brushed her hands over her apron.

Nicholas nodded.

"We'll leave your food here for you, just in case you get hungry later."

"Um...okay."

The two women glanced at one another and headed out of the room, leaving the door open.

Nicholas ran his fingers along the delicate, warm blankets. His hands tingled. *How can something be so soft?* He pressed his cheek against one of the pillows, which was fluffy and plump, unlike the dingy ones back in Dinara. *I'm in Tavern...it's a human only area.* His elation soon faded. "But if they find out I'm a vermin, they'll kill me."

———

Roland Crispin sat in the lecture hall, forcing his mind not to wander while he drummed his fingers along the skull resting on the seat next to him. The group presenting was nearly finished, and unfortunately, he could barely sit still. He gritted his teeth together whenever he thought of the feverish boy back at the house. Roland shouldn't have left his staff and family to deal with the situation, but his friend and colleague, Peter, had bailed on him last minute. This meeting needed to go well.

"Next up, we have Roland Crispin and Peter Rissing, who will be speaking to you about expanding vermin research here in Tavern," the Master of Ceremonies said.

Roland gulped and rose from his chair, grabbing the skull and his script. Many of the university's vermin studies students glared at him as he stood behind the podium. The microphone picked up rustling paper and his deep, uneasy breath.

"Mr. Rissing is regrettably unable to be here today, so I will give the presentation without him." He cleared his throat, hands shaking. "There are many vile creatures living in our society."

A few of the audience members perked up.

Roland steadied himself, gazing into each face. "They are dangerous, said to be killer beasts. Sadly, these animals are hard to track. My partner, Peter Rissing, and I require funding to continue and expand our research on the vermin. They already know too much about us, and many of us can only seem to capture one or two at a time, only to have them end up burned for trespassing. Now, to get an entire pack—well, ladies and gentlemen, imagine what we could learn about their habits, strengths, weaknesses. More research is needed to be able to protect ourselves from this threat. The data my partner and I have collected from second-hand accounts simply isn't enough."

"Why do two rich idiots like yourselves need money?" A voice snarled the slur.

Not again. Roland frowned and looked over at the students. "All the money I have goes into caring for my family. I don't have the funds to—"

"Family, ha!" another spat. "Your family is so bloody rich you could lose everything and still be able to afford those fancy suits."

"If I can redirect your attention over to this skull," Roland said, taking a deep breath as he held it up. "You will notice that although it resembles a human's, the vermin are missing two of their top incisors, indicating that they are able to pierce into their prey and tear its flesh all in one action. The research my partner and I have done is limited to bones and stories. The only way we can learn more about these creatures is if we start capturing them alive. In order to do so, we'll need muscle. And we'll need money to purchase the necessary equipment."

"Why not just kill them?" Another student chuckled. "Then you can profit from their death the way you did with your father and brother."

"That's enough!" the Master of Ceremonies yelled.

The student sank down into her seat.

Roland clenched his teeth, gripping his notes. He opened his mouth to respond, held his breath, and shook his head. *Say something. Damn it, why did Dianna have to come back today? Why couldn't someone else pick her up? Peter knows how important this is. People* like *him! They hate me. I swear, if one more person makes a comment about my family, I'll*—He drew in a deep breath and lowered his head.

"I think it's a great idea, Roland," Mrs. Eloise Taylor-Hood called out. The mayor's wife made her way up to the podium and placed a hand on Roland's shoulder.

His eyes widened. *What is she doing?*

"This young man and his friend are talking about finding a solution to these disgusting, violent animals. I don't know if I should be saying this, but"—she looked into Roland's eyes and pouted her lip—"there was a vermin attack here in Tavern today. Those monsters injured and killed a group of our local farmers. If no one else will fund you, I will beg my husband to help, but I feel that all of the citizens of Tavern need to work together to stop tragedies like this from ever happening again. The only way we can do that is, as Mr. Crispin said, by expanding our research."

Roland gave her a gentle grin and raised his head. "Thank you, Eloise." He turned to the audience. "As Mrs. Hood said so beautifully, it is up to *all* of us to find out what we can about these creatures and put an end to the bloodshed." He lowered his head and gathered his notes. "That concludes my presentation. Thank you for your time."

Eloise squeezed his shoulder and walked with him back up the aisle and out into the hallway.

Roland sighed. "You didn't need to do that."

"I couldn't stand listening to them cut you down." Her face paled. "Especially when they started accusing you of killing your brother."

Roland nodded and drew in a deep breath.

"Don't listen to them, Roland. Lawrence was always kind, dedicated, and hard-working." Eloise scanned the hallway before placing a kiss on his cheek. "Just like you."

Roland eyed her and swallowed hard. "Thank you. I think I'll head home. I've got my hands full lately."

Eloise nodded and backed away from him. "Peter is picking up Dianna Warren, isn't he?"

"Yes." Roland glanced away from her. News always travelled fast in a small town.

"Sometimes we have to do things for the benefit of others...even if it does leave us feeling miserable."

Roland mustered up a smile. "I'll see you around."

"I'll be sure to stop by with Thompson sometime soon."

"That would be nice." Roland retrieved his coat from the nearby hanger. "Take care, Eloise."

3
_____

Roland pulled his scarf up over his mouth as the thick snow blurred violently around him. He squinted to see the old, black, 1930s Chevrolet master deluxe parked across the street waiting for him. It's whitewall tires and chrome grill, barely visible in the storm.

Mr. Leon waved to him and opened the door. "How was it, sir?"

Roland pulled his scarf down. "As I expected. Terrible." Roland got into the back of the car and waited for his driver to join him.

"Should we head home, sir?"

Roland gazed out at Eloise as she made her way down the frozen street to a brand new '48 Aston Martin. "I guess so."

The older man nodded. He glanced back at Roland. "About what I wanted to say earlier..."

Roland let out a deep sigh. "Mmm?" He thought back to the unruly students.

"The boy we picked up, he...well I believe he could be a—"

"How dare they interrupt my presentation!" Roland growled, slamming his fist into the backseat. "This is why I begged Peter to do it. Now I have to try and get this boy cared for, plan Rose's party, and entertain our guests instead of tracking down leads and finding solid funding for our work. And to make matters worse, Dianna will be around."

"Sir, I don't mean to cut you off, but there's something you need to know," Mr. Leon snapped, gripping the wheel.

Roland's cheeks burned. "I-I apologize. Continue."

"I was talking to Tabitha," he began, lowering his voice. "She received a telephone call from dear Mrs. Farley, the farmer's wife. Farley, her husband, was almost killed today by a vermin."

Roland's eyes widened. "Eloise said something about that earlier."

"Well, where it happened isn't very far from where we found that boy." Mr. Leon swallowed. "So, I didn't call Dr. Gray because I believe the child might've been involved."

"Are you suggesting that he's a vermin? He looks nothing like the sketches I've seen."

Mr. Leon remained silent. He kept his eyes on the road. Roland had never seen a vermin before, only read about their fierce brutality.

"If...if he is, I left my family alone with a monster. A wild animal."

"It's hard to tell the difference between us and them," Leon said. "I wasn't that old during the war, but I never forgot how they decorated those ears of theirs. Then again, nowadays, most of the vermin in Riversburg are all mixed blood. You could pass one on the street without any idea."

"I honestly didn't get a good look at him. All the necropsy reports I've studied say their teeth are a dead giveaway. Plus, the books in Tavern are extremely outdated. Some depict these creatures with horns and tusks, and claws. This is exactly why Peter and I want to capture a few for..." Roland's eyes lit up. "This...if you're right, this may just be exactly what we need." Roland rubbed the back of his neck. "I-if the boy really is a vermin, we could attempt to domesticate him."

"Not to overstep my boundaries, but if I'm right, you don't want to be charged with harbouring a vermin. Remember the woman that was hung for it a few years ago?" Mr. Leon glanced back at him. "I think maybe you should speak to Mr. Hood and the sheriff. To protect yourself."

Roland pinched the bridge of his nose, shaking his head. "They'd burn him."

"Discuss it with Peter then," Mr. Leon said firmly.

"For now, keep this from the others. Especially the children."

"As you wish, sir."

Roland hurried up the steps to his front porch and collected the key from his jacket pocket. His hands shivered as he unlocked the door, heart pounding so heavily it might have bruised his ribs. He wasn't sure what to expect and did his best not to think of the possible terror that threatened the lives of his family. Yet, at the same time, a small part of him hoped Mr. Leon was right—dubious as it was.

He propped open the door, and his heart nearly stopped at the utter quiet. "Hello?" he called out into the empty hallway. With Leon following close behind, the pair made their way to the coat rack. Slowly, Roland removed his jacket and slipped off his shoes. If someone were to attack, he could use the coat rack to hold them off. However, he wasn't sure if a wooden pole would be able to protect him from a dangerous predator—especially a predator known for being unpredictable.

"Roland, how did the presentation—"

Roland grabbed the coat rack and spun around, lunging. His face grew hot as he lowered his weapon. "Peter." He cleared his throat and loosened his shoulders. "You startled me."

"I can tell." Peter pointed to the rack. "Lisa let us in."

"Wh-where's Dianna?" His stomach turned as he caught a glance of a figure standing behind the piano in a long wool coat.

"Sir, I believe there was something you needed to discuss with Mr. Rissing." Leon took the coat rack from his employer.

"Oh, right. Peter, could you meet with me in my office for a moment?" Roland whispered, walking down the hall. "Leon, could you go and check on the children?"

Mr. Leon nodded.

"Wow, Rolly, did the presentation really go that badly?" Peter teased as they rushed past the sitting room.

The two men entered the small office. Roland shut the door and paced back and forth in front of his desk.

"You don't look so good." Peter eyed him. "Is everything all right?"

"Everything could be great or worse or..." He stopped and turned to Peter. "What if I told you that I may have possibly found a vermin?"

Mr. Rissing grinned. "I'd ask why you're still breathing."

"I think I found a vermin, or at least Mr. Leon believes it could be a vermin." Roland stared at his friend.

Peter's jaw dropped. "H-how are you—"

"Apparently, their kind have been affected by the fever as well."

"Did you tell the sheriff?"

Roland shook his head. "Nobody knows but you, Leon, and me. And we're not even certain yet. It looked nothing like the ones we've studied. Could just be a scared boy."

Peter ran a hand through his wavy, dirty blond hair. His eyes widened.

"The best and most nerve-racking part is that this potential creature is currently in this house, sleeping in the children's nursery."

"Wait. You have it here?" Peter chuckled. "This is the craziest thing I've ever heard. Okay, well, not the craziest, but it's a close second."

"So, this is what I was thinking. If Mr. Leon is right, we try and domesticate the creature. That way, we'll be able to study it."

"If people realize you're keeping a vermin here, they'll be

outraged." Peter paced in a tight circle. "Maybe we should come up with a better plan."

"We could always try talking to Mayor Hood. With him backing us, no one would get in our way."

Peter nodded. "Do you plan on telling the others?"

Roland shook his head. "My workers, yes, the children...I don't want to scare them." "Maybe Rose depending on how things play out."

"All right, so how do we get it to cooperate?"

"At the moment, it's terrified of me. I guess we'll have to do our best to act as if we're not afraid of him while we investigate."

"You know, while she was living in Riversburg, Dianna developed a strange compassion for the brutes."

Roland raised his brow.

"She was brainwashed by some man she met while she was away at school. To be honest, I think you've got some competition. She hasn't stopped talking about him."

"Her experience with the species may be a great asset." Roland stroked his chin and stared up at the ceiling toward the nursery.

"Unless she tries to free the creature."

"As much as I hate to say it, I think we should discuss this with her." The last thing Roland wanted to do was spend any kind of time in that woman's presence. But, based on the meeting earlier, desperate measures were akin to sane rationalization. "If everything goes well, and it turns out the boy is a vermin, we'll arrange for a meeting with the mayor." Roland shrugged and inclined his head toward the sitting room.

"What if the mayor doesn't side with us? If they try to harm the creature, there's no doubt in my mind Dianna will do something regretful. She's always had somewhat of an adventurous spirit. I love my cousin. I really do, but sometimes she scares me," Peter muttered as the two of them left the room. "I don't get what you see in her."

"Saw," Roland snapped. "You don't get what I saw in her."

Peter inched a few steps in front of him and furrowed his brow. "Do you think she'll help us?"

"If I beg on my hands and knees." Roland pushed away the ill thoughts of his youth. Some things were best left behind, and Dianna Warren counted among them. He spotted Mr. Leon atop the stairs, shrugging his shoulders and shaking his head. They needed an expert to assess the boy. Roland gave Peter the nod.

"Dearest cousin, we have a favour to ask." Peter danced around the bundled and irritated-looking young woman standing abandoned in the sitting room.

Roland stopped and glanced back at her.

Dianna pressed her lips together until they lost their colour. As she folded her arms over her chest, she gazed up at the two men, making sure to shoot a threatening look at her cousin. "What do you want?"

Peter took hold of her shoulders and led her to the piano stool. He smiled and knelt beside her. "Dianna, since you're so wonderful and kind, and smart—"

"Stop with the flattery and get on with it." She glanced over at Roland and sighed as she stood. "You look as though you've seen a ghost."

Roland tried not to meet her eyes. "It's been a long time."

"Yes, it has. So, what can I do for you two?"

"You took vermin studies while you were in Riversburg, right?" Roland asked.

Dianna raised her brow. "Yes, I did."

"Well, since Riversburg has a vermin problem, Peter said you might be able to help us determine if someone was a vermin."

"It's true, Riversburg has a fairly large vermin population. It can be a bit tricky if you don't know what to look for." Dianna removed her black beret and gloves. "But I can tell most of the time. Why?"

"There's a sick child upstairs in the nursery, and he might be one," Roland said softly.

Dianna's eyes grew wide. "Might be? How is it that you aren't able to tell when the two of you have been studying them almost five years now?"

"He was a kid who needed help. I didn't take the time to analyze him. Plus, Tavern is a vermin-free town. It's not like anyone expects to just find vermin just lying about. Besides, I had to get to the presentation and—"

"Also, we've never had the chance to encounter one." Peter groaned. "They tend to avoid Tavern. Besides, the ones that wander into town usually end up dead within minutes."

"We need your help." Roland stared into her deep green eyes, an act he used to lose himself in, and steeled himself as she nodded slowly.

"You have to promise me that you will protect this vermin from being harmed," Dianna insisted.

"I promise the staff and children will be civil."

Dianna glared at him through partially squinted eyes.

"And Peter and I will behave."

"All right. Take me to him."

Roland led them upstairs, being sure to keep his voice down as they made their way to the nursery. "It has the fever. Try not to get too close. I don't want anyone getting sick."

Dianna and Peter watched as Roland turned the knob cautiously. He propped open the door, and the two of them huddled in behind him.

Roland examined the sleeping creature as he tiptoed into the room.

"Poor thing," Dianna whispered. She bit her lip. "He looks awful. We should try and get him some medication first thing in the morning."

Peter swallowed hard, watching his cousin as she sat down next to the youth. Roland's nerves had also gone into over-protective mode.

Gently, Dianna nudged the boy. She gave him a warm smile as his weary eyes forced themselves to open.

"Zana?"

"Hello," Dianna said gently. "How are you feeling?"

"W-who are you?"

"My name is Dianna Warren."

Roland eyed him carefully as the boy sat up.

"Can I ask you some questions?" Dianna brushed back his hair. A small white feather hid beneath it.

Nicholas winced as her fingers grazed the pointed tip of his ear. His heart raced. "W-what kinda questions?"

Dianna glanced over at the two men then turned back to him. "You feel pretty warm. We'll see if we can get you some medicine. Okay?"

The boy slid away from her, gripping the blankets.

"I won't hurt you, sweetheart. What's your name?"

He cracked his knuckles. "Nicholas."

She blinked but didn't respond to the harsh noise. "Nice to meet you." Dianna smiled. "This is my cousin Peter and his friend Roland."

Nicholas nodded.

She eyed his ear again and bit her lip.

"Your leg's all wrapped up?" Roland waved a hand toward the bed.

"That lady, Lisa, cleaned it." Nicholas covered his shaking hands with the blanket.

"Aren't you hungry, *Kokinok?*" Dianna asked, looking at the tray of food on the nightstand.

Nicholas furrowed his brow. "What?"

Dianna scanned his face. "Aren't you hungry?"

"*Nei*...no...no." Nicholas dug his fangs into his lip and looked away from her.

Peter and Roland glanced at one another.

Dianna smiled at Nicholas. "*Todelya?* Are you sure?"

"W-why are you...why are you using those words?" Nicholas stammered.

"What words?" Dianna asked, patting his head gently. "*Danya Hoten Nelich Morin,*" she said, looking at his ears again. "Hard to see under all this hair."

Nicholas' eyes widened. His shoulder's tensed as he dug his nails into his palm, trying to stop himself from shaking.

"Dianna," Peter said, inching toward her. "What are you saying?"

"His ears are nice, aren't they?" She turned to him, brushing Nicholas's hair back. "The little pointed tips at the top are perfectly hidden by his hair."

Nicholas grabbed her by the wrist and glared at her.

"Why hide such nice ears?" Dianna asked, ignoring his hostile behaviour.

"*Iigen Bliesso Daknovosa, Seiina,*" Nicholas snapped, pulling her toward him.

Dianna yelped. Her eyes widened.

"H-he speaks their language," Peter choked out, slowly creeping toward them.

Dianna nodded. "He's a vermin, that's why."

"What did he say?" Roland eyed the boy cautiously. *The vermin might hurt her if we get closer.* glanced around the room. *If only there was something to distract him, maybe he'd let her go.*

"It wasn't very nice." Dianna frowned. "But like I said, I'm not going to hurt you."

"You're lying." Nicholas squeezed her wrist harder.

Dianna flinched. "I-I promise. I'm a friend. *Daknov Frudach.* Your friend."

"You're not my friend," Nicholas spat as her wrist cracked. "Y-your gonna kill me."

Dianna paled.

Roland floundered toward them. His heart stopped. "D-don't—"

"You little brute." Peter glared at the boy, making to pry the animal off his cousin.

"It's okay," Dianna said quickly. "Nicholas, I won't hurt you. I promise."

"Why should I believe you?" The boy glowered.

"You speak our dialect fairly well," Peter said, likely to distract the boy.

Nicholas glared at him.

"Your kind usually travels in packs. Does yours know where you are?" Dianna asked, trying to work her hand free from his grip.

The boy shook his head. *"Nei."*

"We heard some farmers were attacked close to where we found you." Roland crossed his arms to keep from wrenching the animal's hand off Dianna. "Were they members of your pack?"

Nicholas let Dianna go and covered his ears. *"Stai!"* His eyes flooded with tears. "Leave me alone."

Dianna wiggled her fingers and placed a hand on his shoulder.

Roland wished she'd move away, not closer. An old ache needled his chest, but he squashed the sensation.

"It's been a tough day. You should get lots of rest. Tomorrow, we're going to do our best to help you feel better."

Nicholas sulked, brushing her hand away.

"Let's go." Roland opened the door. "We'll see you in the morning, Nicholas. Call Lisa if you need anything. Her bedroom is just next door."

Nicholas shivered as the humans left the room. His heart threatened to burst through his chest. He shut his eyes and let out a deep, shuttering breath. For some reason, he was alive. He didn't know why and for now, it didn't matter. Being alive meant he could find Suzanna, and the two of them could go home. He licked his lips and ran a hand through his dark hair.

"My pack," he whispered to himself and stared up at the ceiling, willing the tears to drain back where they came from. Slowly, he crawled underneath the soft, warm covers. "Why would they ask about my pack?"

4

"You're all probably wondering why I called this meeting." The next morning, the master of the house gazed around the nursery at all those gathered. Nicholas buried his nose under the covers.

The cook and the nursemaid glanced at one another and shook their heads. The driver tipped his hat toward Dianna and Peter as they entered the room.

Still in bed, Nicholas shivered. A cold sweat swam down his neck. He blinked hard, trying his best to keep his composure.

"I'd like you all to be formally introduced to our guest, Nicholas." Roland gave a grim smile.

The women waved politely, but the older man and Peter stood quietly near the door.

"This is my home. You already know Tabitha and Lisa. This gentleman is my driver, Mr. Evan Leon, who I don't believe you've been introduced to yet."

"Hi," Nicholas whispered, gazing up at them.

"Yesterday, you met Miss Warren. And you also spoke briefly with Peter."

Nicholas nodded.

"It is my duty to tell you Nicholas is a vermin. He's been affected by the fever, and he will be staying here until he recovers. I'm going to request a meeting with Mayor Hood, asking for Nicholas to have special protection while under my care."

"A wild brute in this house?" Tabitha shrieked.

"The children are not to know about this," Roland growled. "And until I've spoken to Mr. Hood, I had better not hear anything about this floating around town, either. Do I make myself clear?"

Slowly everyone nodded.

Nicholas lowered his head.

"He's a child, not a brute. We all need to treat him with respect." Dianna glared at Tabitha.

"Respect this...this thing? You've got to be joking." The older woman snorted. "He's a filthy animal."

Lisa shuffled her feet. "Tabby, he's a little boy. Don't say such cruel things."

"*Iya Shcrein Yet Arii,*" Nicholas mumbled.

"Pardon?" Mr. Leon stepped around the three women and eyed the strange boy.

"I'm not a child. I said I'm fourteen years old. And I'm not filthy, you *Doksot.* I washed this morning."

Tabitha's cheeks burned red. "W-what did you just call me?"

Peter opened up his bag and pulled out his notebook. "Fourteen years old?" He scribbled into the little book. "Is this in human years or vermin years?"

"Are they different?" Lisa asked.

"No," Dianna said low, shaking her head.

"How would you know?" Peter pointed the end of his pencil at her.

"I've gotten to know a few quite well."

Nicholas looked over at Roland and pouted. The young gentleman's irritation radiated off him with the way he looked skyward and rubbed his neck.

"Do human packs do this a lot?" Nicholas asked.

"We're not packs," spat Tabitha. "We're groups."

"It's basically the same thing," Dianna said.

"I refuse to have some rude girl speak to me in such a tone." Tabitha placed her hands on her hips and turned from her.

"Oh, *I'm* being rude?" Dianna threw her arms up.

"That's enough!" Roland barked, slamming his hands against the edge of the bed. "You were simply told Nicholas' species for your own well-being." He eased his tense shoulders and headed for the door. "When the children come home from school, do not speak a word of this to them."

"Okay." Dianna pressed her lips together.

Roland opened the door. "If you need me, I'll be in my office looking over my niece's guest list."

Nicholas watched as the young master trudged out of the room.

"I can already tell that Dianna and I have overstayed our welcome." Peter gave Tabitha and Mr. Leon an apologetic smile. "Tell Roland that I'll give him a call tomorrow around one."

"Will do," Mr. Leon said.

Peter nodded and led his cousin out.

Nicholas eyed the three workers as they stood by the door.

"Evan" –Tabitha turned to Mr. Leon– "Roland is out of his mind. Addi would have never—"

Mr. Leon shrugged. "Adeline isn't here. We were to stay and work with Master Crispin until our retirement."

Tabitha opened her mouth then shook her head. "I don't like this. He doesn't understand. He doesn't know what they're capable of."

"I know." Mr. Leon frowned. "However, Roland isn't a child anymore. He's our boss. We need to respect his decisions."

The two women nodded.

"The poor dear." Tabitha gazed out the open door after Roland. "Falling in love with such an awful girl. I'm glad they broke it off."

Lisa's eyes widened. "She's the one?"

Tabitha gave a knowing smile. "That was many years ago."

"Young love," Mr. Leon chuckled. "It's only fun for a little while. Well, I'd better go pick up the children."

Tabitha glanced over at the clock. "I'll get some snacks ready. The boys will be hungry."

"If you don't mind, could you also prepare some tea?" Mr. Leon gave her a grin. "There's an awful chill outside today, and these old bones will need some warming up."

Tabitha laughed. "Of course."

Nicholas crawled toward the edge of the bed and pouted. "Um... I-I'm hungry."

"And?" Tabitha growled, raising her brow.

"Can I have a snack?"

"Not unless you use proper manners," Tabitha snarled. "Unbelievable. Julius is five and knows better."

Nicholas sighed deeply. "*Stabima*...I mean um..."

"Make yourself something, you disgusting creature." With that, Tabitha stormed from the room.

Lisa's cheeks flared red.

"I'll be off then." Mr. Leon put his hat back on.

Lisa nodded. As the driver left the room, Lisa inched toward Nicholas with caution. "Tabitha didn't mean to insult you...well, she did." Her face flushed a deeper scarlet. "She wants you to ask nicely for things."

"I did ask nicely," Nicholas grumbled.

Lisa stepped back and swallowed hard. "Try saying 'May I please have a snack,' next time. She'll be happy to serve you if you use good manners."

Nicholas nodded. "May I please have something to eat? I'm hungry."

Lisa gave him a gentle smile. "Of course. I'll bring some food up for you in a couple of minutes."

"*Dar Danya*," Nicholas whispered.

Lisa raised her brow in confusion. She forced a smile watching Nicholas sink into the sheets and headed for the door.

Roland Crispin sat at his desk with a furrowed brow and a hand under his chin. His eyes wandered down the guest list, but his mind drifted. *Was it a good idea to get Dianna involved? That boy could've seriously hurt her. Maybe I shouldn't have left the others alone with him. I don't even know what I'm doing.* He glanced down at the list for the party again. *I don't know how I'm going to afford all of this... and now we'll need to purchase medicine for the vermin's fever...* With a deep breath, Roland reached for the phone and called Mrs. Hood. Sighing, he put the phone to his ear.

"Hood residence. Thompson Hood."

"Could you please give the phone to your mother?" he asked Eloise's teenage son.

"Might I ask whose calling?"

"Roland Crispin."

A moment later, that familiar melodic voice sang into the phone. "Roland, darling. How are you?"

"To be honest, I'm a bit stressed. Eloise, could Peter and I stop by to meet with your husband sometime this week? It's very important."

"He should be available on Wednesday. Did you see Dianna?"

"I did." Roland craned his neck.

"Yes, yes, of course you did." Eloise laughed. "I was just about to take Tom out to buy a new suit for Rose's party. He's very excited."

"Oh, well, I'll let you go then. Thank you, Eloise. Enjoy your afternoon."

"Anytime, darling."

Roland stared down at the list as he hung up the phone. "I guess Tabitha and I will need to order a lot more food and hire a couple extra hands." He leaned back into his chair and moaned. "The girl invited the entire bloody school!" Roland sat up straight as Lisa knocked on the door.

"Sorry to bother you, but I was just wondering if you wanted some tea?"

Roland nodded, laying the list down on the dark mahogany desk. "That would be nice."

Lisa entered with a tray of teacups and a few small desserts.

"For the children?" Roland said as she poured his tea.

"For Nicholas," she whispered. "Milk?"

"Yes, please." Roland gazed up at her. "Did you tell Tabitha this when you grabbed the cakes?"

"I took them while she was absent." Lisa blushed. "She's not exactly fond of the boy."

"No, she isn't. She was a little girl during the war. She has her reasons." Roland eyed the mint green wallpaper, deep in thought. "He'll be trained in no time. I'm sure."

"Sugar?"

"Yes, please." Roland rubbed his neck.

"So, Miss Warren was your sweetheart?"

He winced, pinching the bridge of his nose. "Did Tabitha tell you?"

"Both her and Leon."

Roland shook his head and gave her a sad grin. "Figures...they also probably mentioned what a big mistake that was."

"Hmm. I once loved a boy named Stephen McGregor. Then I found out he was married. It was a mistake, but some good came from it."

"Like what?"

"Well, I had Alicia, and I ended up working for you. Although it would be nice to not have so many people ask why I work for such a strange man."

Roland chuckled. "People find me strange?"

"Yes. Especially me." She laughed. "At your age, you should be out having fun, not worrying about work. You hired me to make your life easier. You sitting here looking so glum makes me feel as if I'm not doing my job." She placed a cake on his saucer and brushed back her platinum-coloured hair.

"Aren't you younger than me?" Roland teased.

"Barely, but I have fun, Mr. Crispin. I'd better sneak these upstairs." She giggled, hurrying from the room.

Roland eyed the cake and sighed. "Maybe I should try having more fun." He stuck his finger into the icing and put it into his mouth. Fun used to be running around West Tavern with Peter, Charlotte, and Dianna. They were always finding something to do, whether it was harassing the staff at the Taylor's Hotel or having one too many drinks at Roland's father's pub. As a teenager, fun always seemed to lead to trouble, and when everything around him started to crumble, fun turned into empty bottles of liquor. *I don't know how to have fun anymore.* He stuck his finger into the icing again.

"Uncle Roland, did you read over the guest list?" Rose skipped into the room. She eyed him. "What are you doing?"

Roland took his finger out of his mouth and cleared his throat. "The icing is delicious."

"Tabitha's cakes *are* the best in Tavern." Rose removed her hat. "So, have you looked over the list?"

"Yes, and I see you've put down a lot of people."

"I thought I should invite all our friends and neighbours."

"Rose, I don't think we need to invite the entire school."

"My teacher would be insulted if I didn't invite him. Oh, and I have to invite some of Caspian and Julius' friends. I don't want them to be bored."

"They can invite their friends to their own parties. Plus, most of Julius' friends are fictional." Roland got up from his chair and made his way over to her. "Your friends only, all right?"

"If it's only my friends, then why did you invite Thompson?" Rose placed her hands on her hips.

"You know why."

"No, I don't."

"Yes, you do."

"Is that boy feeling any better?" Rose wondered, watching her uncle sip his tea.

"Nicholas? Yes, he's feeling a bit better. Anyway, don't change the subject you—"

"That's good to hear. I've got something to give him."

"Rose, maybe you should wait." Roland swallowed his tea hard and set his cup down.

"No, I'd rather give it to him now before I go help Tabby prepare dinner," she said sweetly. "I'll fix the list later." She started out the door then glanced back. "Oh, and enjoy your snack."

"I will," Roland mumbled. His chest tightened as she skipped back out of the room. He prayed Lisa was still in the nursery with the vermin boy.

5

Rose crept into the nursery, holding behind her back one of her many treasures. As she turned her head in the direction of the bed, a swift figure threw the blankets up and wrapped themselves within. Rose stared at the two dark eyes gleaming at her from the make-shift window of the large fabric cocoon.

"I-I'm sorry, I didn't mean to frighten you," she said softly.

The eyes flickered as she glanced over at the treats on the nightstand. "You don't need to hide from me." Rose giggled, sitting on the bed on the other side of the door. "I'm not a monster."

Cautiously, the boy let the blankets slide off his head.

A small smile crept onto Rose's face. "I brought you something." She revealed the treasure from behind her back. "It's a lovely story. I read it when I was sick. I thought you could borrow it until you feel better."

He scanned the book and nodded.

"Lisa's going to have a fit if she sees what you've done to your bed."

"I can fix it." He raised his tired eyes and shivered. "What's your name?"

"Rose." She held the book out to him. "And yours?"

"Nicholas." He pushed his hand out from underneath the blanket.

Rose gave him the book and grinned. "Maybe we can read it after supper?"

"S-supper?" Nicholas bobbed his head up and down.

"You can start reading without me." She laughed. Rose furrowed her brow and watched as Nicholas' eyes rolled back. His body swayed to and fro as sweat ran down his forehead. She dashed out of the room. Her heart pounded as she stumbled into her uncle's office.

Roland raised his brow and groaned, placing his cake down on the table. "Yes Ro—"

"Uncle Roland, come quick!"

Roland jumped up onto his feet and grabbed her by the hand. "Is everything all right? You aren't hurt, are you?"

"No." Rose choked back a sob. Her eyes widened as a loud crash came from the nursery. "Nicholas." She pulled away from her uncle and fled back upstairs.

Roland chased after her, his legs heavy on the steep steps. "Rose, slow down!"

In the nursery, the two stopped over Nicholas' body. Their faces paled.

"His eyes went all white," Rose whispered. "We should call the doctor again."

"No," Roland snapped, sitting the boy up. He patted the vermin's face gently and eyed him.

Nicholas opened his eyes and let his head drop down to his chest.

"Are you all right?" Roland asked firmly.

Nicholas glanced up at him. "*Ha.*"

Rose knelt next to her uncle and gave Nicholas a stern look. "You need to rest. Stay in bed and don't move unless you absolutely have to."

"What she means is, the only way you'll get better is if you get lots of rest." Roland frowned. "Do you need help getting up?"

Nicholas shook his head, grabbing onto the nightstand for support.

"How long have you been sick?" Rose questioned, getting to her feet.

Nicholas shot Roland a threatening glare. "Why do you people keep pretending to be nice me?"

"What?" Rose rubbed her hands together and blushed. "I-I wasn't pretending."

Nicholas sat on the edge of the bed.

"Don't worry about it, Rose. Nicholas is just being rude."

"I'm not being rude," he murmured. His eyes darted about the room. He squinted, then buried his face in his hands.

"Are you okay?" Rose tugged at the orange ribbon in her hair, the same colour as her dress.

Nicholas trembled and drew in an uneven breath.

Rose looked at the redness in his face as he began panting.

Roland crossed his arms, examining the boy. "Rose, go assist Tabitha in the kitchen."

"Okay." She hesitated. *Tabitha's not the one who needs help right now.* She balled up her fists and headed for the door.

***

Roland stood over the vermin and shook his head. "She doesn't know."

"Doesn't know what?" Nicholas snapped.

Roland glanced out into the hallway, making sure his niece was no longer in sight. "She doesn't know you're a vermin."

Nicholas looked up at him. "She doesn't?"

"None of the children do. Until I can convince the mayor to let you stay here, no one but Peter, Dianna and my employees will know your secret."

"*Dar Danya*," Nicholas said. He pulled the blankets toward him.

"Pardon me?"

"Thank you," the boy repeated. "I'd be dead if you hadn't stopped to help me."

Roland tilted his head. "You're welcome."

"I've had this fever since the leaves fell."

"And you're still alive?" Roland rubbed the back of his neck. "Rose had it for only a week, and she...we didn't think she'd make it."

"This *Bloka* fever's caused me a lot of trouble."

Roland nodded. "Watch yourself. Using words like that is a dead giveaway to your species. Plus, Tabby won't hesitate to give you a good scolding if you swear like that."

"A scolding?"

"It's what happens when you do something wrong. You get them, especially when you're young."

Nicholas smirked and rubbed his eyes. "Yeah, well, I think I'll get some shut-eye."

"All right." Roland smiled. "I'll leave you be then." *Since the leaves fell, that was a month ago.* He left the room. *The fever must work slower on vermin. Whatever I do, I have to keep him alive. He's my only chance at redemption.*

"He should be punished for his crime!" the rookie officer cried, pointing at the vermin as they walked toward the jail cell. He glared at the creature and wrinkled his nose. "I don't care if he claims to be a bloody mutt. Let's burn him."

"And what would we do if this Slayden boy somehow manages to get in contact with his father? You do understand this creature claims to be Theodore Wolfe's son." Vincent Gray looked into the creature's eyes. "If we kill him, Nev, we could be locked away for the remainder of our lives."

"And if we don't, the whole bloody town'll be furious. My

grandfather fought against these brutes forty-four years ago. He lost his leg."

"Sounds like you two have a tough decision to make," the vermin chuckled hoarsely as they shoved him into the cell. The lanky bundle of muscle toppled onto the cement floor and glared at them.

"Keep your trap shut, you bloody animal!" the officer barked, aiming his gun at the creature's head.

"Pull the trigger, and you'll regret it for the rest of your life," Gray snapped. He looked down at the vermin and smiled. "Now, if you cooperate, we can make sure that no harm comes to that lovely sister of yours."

"If you lay one finger on her, I'll—" the vermin scowled as the two men laughed. His face grew pale. "What did you do to her?"

"Nothing yet," Nev taunted. "But I'm sure she'll be all right as long as you do your part."

"You damn, disgusting—"

Vincent kicked the vermin over and grinned. "Nev, close the door. Apparently, this brute doesn't realize he belongs with the rest of the filth in this world."

Nev nodded and gave a cruel smile. "I don't care who your father is, you're a dirty animal, and you always will be."

Nicholas sat up in bed as the girl crept into the nursery and shut the door. She turned on the lamp and smiled at him. He stared back.

"Have you had a chance to start the book yet?"

Nicholas shook his head.

"That's all right. We can start it together." She took the book off the nightstand. Rose hesitated, eyeing him. She ran a finger down the spine of the book, a puzzled look on her face.

Nicholas watched her cautiously. His pupils narrowed as she approached and took a seat next to him on the bed. He leaned away from her as she opened up to the first page.

"Chapter one. In the deepest part of the forest, it is said that light never shines, still the girl wandered in. She followed the shadowy figure, keeping her eyes locked on him, listening to the voices of the forest calling out to her."

Nicholas watched the small letters on the page come to life as Rose spoke. His eyes gleamed as she held her hand out and whispered. "Even the worst of things can be beautiful." *Was that true? Could something bad also be beautiful?* Nicholas' ears twitched as she read. Each word made them tingle. He tried to subtly brush more hair over them, eyeing her lips as she spoke. Most of her teeth were round and flat. Her ears the same.

Human teeth aren't edged, Micah had told him. *They're dull like an unsharpened blade. Can't cut anything.*

He ran his tongue along his teeth, following the ends of his fangs. Micah and Zana had a human father. Their teeth weren't very sharp, and their ears were a lot rounder, but nothing like this human's. Nicholas was faster than Micah, but Micah was still the better hunter. Nicholas had never managed to kill anything he caught. He'd always begged his brother to do it. And he hated hunting with the pack. They always mocked the way he squirmed whenever they bore their teeth into their prey.

Nicholas rubbed the sweat from his forehead onto the blanket and laid down, listening to Rose's voice. *I could try and escape.* He thought to himself. *She's a bit smaller than me.*

Rose smiled at him, turning the page. "Are you okay?"

He nodded shyly. *I don't want to hurt her, she's kinda nice.* He winced. *The humans in Dinara weren't mean, but this is Tavern, not Dinara. It sounds like a nice place, but it isn't. People are different here.*

Rose stretched out her hand and felt his cheek. "You're still really warm. Do you want the window open?"

Nicholas slid away from her, his heart racing. "I...um...."

"When I was sick, I had the window open all the time. The

medicine will help, though. My uncle said he's going to get you some."

"Y-your hands are—"

Rose blushed. "Sorry, they're kind of sweaty."

"Mine too."

The pair sat quietly for a moment.

Nicholas's cheeks burned—and not from the fever.

"W-where was I...." she asked, skimming the page open on her lap.

"Even the worst of things can be beautiful."

"Right...even the worst of things can be beautiful, he told her. He pressed his hand against the dangling vines and smiled. Welcome to Midnight Garden."

When the clock in the hall sang out, the two looked up from the book and gasped. An hour had slipped by completely unnoticed.

"It's getting late. I'd better get to bed. Goodnight, Nicholas." She climbed off the bed and handed him the book. "We can read again when I come home from school tomorrow."

Nicholas nodded. "*Nor*...I mean...Night, Rose."

Rose grinned, stepping out into the hall and waved goodbye.

Nicholas opened the book up and frowned. Tiny black symbols ran across the page. He couldn't read these words. *It doesn't matter. We'll just finish the book tomorrow.* Nicholas crawled underneath his covers and tucked the book in beside him. His eyes fluttered shut as he faded into a deep sleep. A small grin crept onto his face as he snuggled into the warmth of the blankets.

6

Roland wrapped his scarf snug around his neck and pushed his way through the blur of snow before him.

Peter chuckled putting an arm around him. "There you are. I was starting to think the little brute ate you."

"Can we please go indoors?" a familiar voice whimpered. "My toes feel as if they've been numbed to the very bone."

Roland groaned as his eyes fell on Miss Warren. "Why is she here?"

"I'm sorry. She's very persistent," Peter grumbled.

"Does my presence disturb you, Mr. Crispin?" Dianna grinned like a child playing a cruel joke.

Roland tried his best not to furrow his brow in frustration. He did that far too often these days. Of course, it disturbed him whenever she was around. After everything she'd done, how could it not? A short time ago, just the thought of Dianna made him sick to his stomach. Still, no matter how he felt about her, she always managed to find a way to seep back into his thoughts. Always.

The trio soon made their way to city hall, where they hoped to meet with the mayor.

"Before we enter, remember your promise to me about the boy," Dianna said quietly behind the two men.

"I remember promising that no one in my house would harm him."

Dianna latched onto the arm of his coat. "Roland."

Peter eyed them.

"No harm whatsoever is to come to him," Dianna glowered. "Promise me."

Roland yanked his arm away.

"We don't have time for this." Peter stepped between them as his cousin attempted to grab at Roland again. "Dianna, it's a vermin." He fended her off.

Roland shoved his hands into his pockets and shrugged. "Fine."

Peter and Dianna turned to him. Peter's jaw dropped.

"No harm whatsoever. Now, can we go?"

Dianna nodded slowly.

Peter glanced at her then turned to Roland as he removed his hat. "Are we really going to do this?"

Roland nodded. "We can't afford not to."

The three stood silently, side by side in front of the stately doors.

Slowly Dianna reached for the handle and pushed the door open. The two men winced. "Let's go then."

Roland held his breath as he spotted the plaque outside the mayor's office. *Kurtis Hood.* He pressed his lips together and removed his scarf. His skin chilled as Peter led him toward the receptionist's desk and out of the blast of weather.

The young woman gave the two men a friendly grin, then gazed over at Dianna with a knitted brow. "Good morning, gentlemen."

"Good morning." Peter tipped his hat. "We're here to see Mayor Hood."

"Names, please."

"Roland Crispin and Peter Rissing."

The receptionist grimaced as *Crispin* left Peter's mouth. She eyed

Roland cautiously then tried to plaster the grin back onto her face. "W-wait right here. I'll let him know you've arrived."

Both men nodded and watched her dash across the hall.

Peter chuckled. "Lovely smile. Maybe I should invite her out to dinner?"

Roland smirked, shaking his head. "I think it would be best to wait until you two become more acquainted."

"Well, the two of us can get acquainted over a nice meal."

Dianna stared at Peter and shook her head.

"Mayor Hood is ready to see you." The receptionist returned to her desk.

"All right then," Roland said hoarsely. "Let's...let's—"

"Let's try not to get ourselves hung," Peter whispered.

Roland shivered, watching the colour fade from his friend's face. He swallowed the lump in his throat. "Yes, that sounds like a good plan."

Dianna followed the two men into the office and eyed them carefully.

"Come in, have a seat." The mayor shut the door behind them.

Peter sat down and glanced up at Roland.

"Dianna, would you like to—"

"I'm quite fine standing." Dianna shot Roland a threatening glare.

"Oh...well, all right." Roland took a seat next to Peter. It was bad enough they were about to reveal a crime without Dianna giving him nervous energy, too.

Mayor Hood stared into the faces of the men and frowned. "Is everything all right? You boys look terrible."

"We may as well be dead in the next hour if this backfires." Peter wrung his hands.

Roland let out a nervous laugh, and he rubbed his neck.

"Mr. Crispin, you look ill. Should I have Cora bring you a glass of water and send for a doctor?" the mayor asked.

"No, thank you. I'm feeling quite well." Roland cleared his throat and stared into the older man's face. "As you know, Mr. Rissing and I have been trying to gain more knowledge about the vermin for the benefit of Tavern. So that we can be better equipped at defending ourselves against their attacks."

"Yes, yes, of course. My wife's been attending your seminars." Kurtis Hood took a seat across from them.

"Well, recently, I came across a young vermin boy. He's got the fever, sir...and we'd like to try and domesticate him in order to further our research."

Peter nodded quickly. "We wanted your permission before we did anything, as we know having one of these creatures so close to town is a threat to civilians."

"A vermin boy," Kurtis whispered, running a hand through his dark curls. "How do you plan on domesticating him?"

"It would be like...breaking an untamed horse. We'll be firm," Roland assured him. "And the vermin seems to already have some understanding of proper human behaviour. He's even dressed presentably."

"He's in need of medical attention." Dianna stepped up beside them. "Without it, he may die, and these men will never be able to gain a firm understanding of the species to help resolve future issues."

The mayor gazed at her. "You realized that the people will be furious."

"Yes, sir." Roland drummed his fingers against his knees. "That's why we are asking you to allow us to domesticate and study the creature. Without your word or protection from the sheriff, we may find ourselves in serious trouble."

"I'm intrigued by your proposal. I think it has merit. I'll give you three weeks. That should be enough time for the boy to gain back his strength." Kurtis leaned back in his chair. "I'd like to meet him then... to be sure you've been training him. For the time being, he must remain on the Crispin estate. I will make sure that Doctor Gray and the sheriff know absolutely no harm is to come to him."

Roland smiled. "Thank you, sir."

"If at my meeting with the beast, I feel that he's still a danger, he will be terminated. And if he places anyone in serious danger while under your care, you two will be held responsible."

The men nodded.

"Well then, I guess this concludes our meeting, gentlemen. Good luck to you both." Kurtis rose.

Dianna opened the door and hurried out of the room. Roland and Peter waved to the mayor before chasing after her.

Outside the building, Dianna paced back and forth between two piles of shovelled snow. She gazed at the men nervously. "I-if anything happens to that boy or my cousin"—she marched up to Roland—"I will make sure they put a rope around your neck!"

Roland glared at her. "The man was generous. He could have had us arrested then and there."

"I'm going to do everything in my power to make sure you two don't get yourselves killed," Dianna spat. "You...you bloody idiots!"

"Dianna, you're causing a scene," Peter grumbled. "Come, maybe a drink will help you calm down."

Dianna drew in a deep breath. "I just can't bear the thought of those children losing the only family they have left, all because the two of you have completely lost your minds."

Roland took a step back and eyed her.

Dianna sighed, rubbing her hands together. "You know what, Peter, I wouldn't mind a drink."

"To the pub then." Peter grinned, linking his arms with her. "Roland, let's drink to another day of this wonderful thing called life."

"You know I haven't had a drink in years." Roland watched the sky. "Liquor's never calmed me."

"It'll be fun," Peter pestered. "Like old times."

"Oh, shush. If the man doesn't wish to go, then leave him be. Besides, it wouldn't do his health any good," Dianna snapped.

Roland glowered at her. "My health is perfectly fine, thank you, and has been for some time."

"Come now, you two. Don't start a brawl outside city hall." Peter tugged on his cousin's arm.

"If you're in such good shape, then you won't mind joining us for a few rounds," Dianna smirked.

Roland clenched his fists. "You're impossible."

"No, I just have common sense!"

"I honestly can't stand being around you."

Silence hovered in the air for several minutes. The three stood below the steps of city hall, glaring at one another.

Dianna drew in a shaky breath and nodded. "I'll be going then. Enjoy the pub."

Roland bit his lip as she turned to walk away. "My ride is here." He gestured to the old, black car parked across the street.

"Then farewell," Dianna whispered.

Peter shot Roland a dirty look then shook his head. "I hope you can put aside your personal feelings for the sake of our research. Especially since you and I both know that you're in desperate need of money."

Roland nodded.

"We'll begin training the boy tomorrow."

7

Nicholas' eyes shot open. Two men hollered as they forced him from his bed.

"N-Naska Iigen Ana?" he wondered, glancing back and forth between the men, his heart racing.

"Starting now, no vermin words," Peter said firmly. "Every meal, we will work with you on proper table manners." Peter plopped Nicholas down into the chair by the window. "Breakfast is an important meal. It gets you going in the morning."

"At the table"—Roland laid out the bowls on the small table in the room—"you may only speak when spoken to."

"But why? And why do I have to learn how to eat?"

Peter shook his head. "You're learning to be polite while eating at the table. We're not teaching you how to shove food into your mouth."

"Since you're not well, we'll be having porridge," Roland told him. "Now, from this moment, until given permission, you cannot speak. This is with the exception of an emergency. Do you understand?"

"Um..." Nicholas grimaced and lowered his eyes. "Yes."

"Good." Peter took a seat. "Tabitha, you may come in now."

"Good morning, Master Crispin," Tabitha said with a warm smile. In her hands, she carried a small pot. "Good morning, Mr. Rissing. Lovely day isn't it?"

"Yes, it is. A bit warmer than yesterday."

Roland helped make room for the pot on the table.

"Nicholas, I hope you had a goodnight's rest," Tabitha muttered through gritted teeth.

Nicholas hesitated. He looked to Roland, who gestured for him to speak. "Th-the...it was good." He swallowed past a lump in his throat. "The night...that is."

"Try not to mumble or stutter," Peter said firmly. "Speak with confidence."

"But think before you speak," Roland added.

Cautiously, Nicholas turned to Tabitha. "You didn't have to make breakfast for me. It's not fair to make you do all this extra work."

"These are heated leftovers." Tabitha snarled. "I'd never think of going to the lengths of feeding a stray dog like you."

"A dog?" Nicholas glared at her. "I'm much better than some dog, you *Schlubai*."

Tabitha glared at him. "What did you call me?"

"I called you a *Schul—*"

"Nicholas!" Roland shouted. "No vermin words. Now please apologize to Tabitha for your tone."

"She should apologize to me," Nicholas snapped. "I was trying to be nice."

Peter struck the vermin across the cheek. "Apologize."

Nicholas' hands shook as he glared at the man. "I'm not gonna do anything if you're just gonna—" Nicholas' glazed eyes looked up at the hazy images of the men before him. The cook hurried from the room.

"Jeez Peter...you didn't have to hit him," Roland said softly.

"We'll take him and lock him in the guest house. He'll stay there until he's willing to cooperate."

"You're monsters!" Dianna cried. Nicholas opened his eyes. A soft hand gently ran along his forehead. "He's feverish and most likely starving, and you're threatening him with not being perfect?"

"Dianna, the creature needs to do as he's told," Peter said bitterly. "It's bloody cold, Roland. Could you close the door?"

Slowly, Nicholas sat up. He looked at Dianna and pouted. "Please don't leave me alone with them."

"I don't plan on it." Dianna cupped his face in her hands, turning his head from side to side, inspecting him carefully. "You've been hurt. Who did this to you?"

Nicholas glanced at Peter but lowered his eyes and let out a sigh. "I wasn't listening, Miss. I um...where am I?" He looked around the room, eyes wide.

"You're in the guest house." Roland knelt down beside him. "You'll be staying here until you're willing to cooperate. No more outbursts."

"The door locks from the outside." Peter leaned against the wall, picking at his thumb. "And if I were in your current position, I wouldn't dare think of trying to escape."

"You're caging him like...like an animal!" Dianna cried, rising to her feet.

"Is he not an animal?" Peter questioned. "Because I believe you're confused, dear cousin. A child is a child and should be treated as such. An animal," he spat. "Is an animal and should be treated as such."

"Peter, please..." Roland gazed up at his friend. "She's already upset."

"I've decided that I'll be supervising you while you domesticate Nicholas." Dianna's face grew red, her tan freckles fading in colour.

"Oh, my dear cousin, people don't need domestication. However, animals do." Peter grinned. "Shall we buy your new pet a collar, then?"

"Peter, that's enough." Roland held up his hand then ran it through his messy dark hair. His eyes met the vermin's as Dianna gripped the edge of her skirt.

"Rehabilitate him. Conform him! Bend him to your perception of what's right," Dianna yelled, thrusting her arms above her head. "Whatever it is, I won't let you treat him like this!"

"Mind your business!" Peter grabbed her wrist.

Nicholas flinched. *Did I hurt her when I grabbed her like that?* His stomach turned.

Dianna yanked herself free from his grasp and glared at him.

"It's a small bruise." Roland scanned the purple mark along Nicholas' cheekbone. "It should heal soon."

Nicholas nodded, his eyes on the sullen cousins.

"Now, you will remain here until you learn to hold your tongue." Roland frowned, glancing at Dianna. "What you say can sometimes get you into a lot of trouble. We advised you to think before you spoke. Clearly, you need practice."

Dianna drew in a deep breath. "I think you two should leave."

Peter smiled at her. "Are you suggesting that we leave you alone with this beast?"

"Yes. Now get out."

"As you wish, Miss Warren." Roland rose. "Thank you for volunteering your time."

"Stop trying to flatter me. You're no better than my cousin." Dianna turned away from him.

As the two men left the guest house, they muttered between themselves, speaking ills about Dianna. Nicholas heard them clearly, even if the lady didn't. He held back his fury until both men shut the door.

"*Feiv Doksot! Iya Naskit Sorna!*" he cried.

Dianna sank to her knees and lowered her head. "They're rich men who were spoiled rotten as children."

"Spoiled rotten...like fruit?" Nicholas tilted his head. He glanced around the room again, noting the dust-covered furniture and dead plants.

Dianna smiled. "Not exactly. What I mean is that they were given whatever they wanted when they were young, and it has tainted the way they see the world."

Nicholas nodded. "Thank you for staying with me."

"*Duvya Yomonch.*"

Nicholas eyed her. "Why do you know Valdin Zungta?"

"A friend in Riversburg taught me. Nicholas I...I'm really sorry. The other day, I didn't want to trick you, but...it's better if I know you're a vermin. That way, I can keep you safe."

"Why would you keep me safe?"

"My friend is half-vermin. It wasn't until I actually lived in Riversburg that I realized humans are the evil ones. Keeping vermin as slaves, not letting them vote in elections, forcing them out of their homes —all over some senseless war that happened long before I was born."

Nicholas nodded.

"Was your pack forced to leave their home? Is that how you ended up here in Tavern?"

He looked away from her. "Yes, but it wasn't the humans who did it...it was another pack. Not that it matters. Either way, I don't have a home anymore." Nicholas shivered, remembering how his small pack of twenty-two were ambushed. They should've merged with one of the other packs when they had the chance. Zana had to leave her mother's locket behind. It was all they had left of her—a wedding gift from their father. Nicholas tried to go back for it, but the elders wouldn't let him. *Cowards.*

Dianna glanced away from him. "I'm so sorry."

Nicholas raised his head. "Will you ask Rose to bring the book to me?"

"What book?"

"I don't know the name. She read it to me the other night."

"I'll ask her about it. But let's not mention this to Mr. Crispin. He's very protective of her and her brothers, and we need to make sure she doesn't fall ill again."

Nicholas nodded.

"Do you have any brothers or sisters?"

Nicholas shrugged shyly. "A brother and sister. Well...I was raised by their grandmother. I don't have anyone I'm actually related to."

"No family at all?"

"No, my father left me with her when I was a baby."

"I don't understand. The vermin that I met were very big on family and community," Dianna said.

"Men in my pack never mate with a single woman."

Dianna's eyes widened.

"There were many elders at one point, and so the men were forced to mate with women outside of our pack. Then, they would bring the children to live with us. Many of us ended up being abandoned unless a woman offered to nurse us."

"That must've been difficult for you...not knowing your mother or father."

"I've never really thought about them." And it was true, he hadn't. His pack was his family. They took him in and raised him. Everything he knew about the world, he learned from them. He'd only spent a year of his life in Ferine before being brought to Dinara for the remaining thirteen. Who his parents were was never of any importance to him or to the family who adopted him.

Dianna brushed her hair behind her ear. "As I've gotten older, I've begun to wonder if love actually exists...You know, I was very foolish when I was about your age."

"Foolish?"

"I got attention from a boy and fell in love...or at least I thought it was love."

"Oh..." Nicholas scanned her. She didn't look much older than his brother, but the expression on her face made his chest hurt.

"Nicholas, do you think your parents loved each other?" Dianna wondered.

"*Nei.*" Nicholas gave her a slight grin. His cheek stinging. "Do you love the stars in the night sky or the sound of the birds chirping during the season of birth?"

Dianna nodded, eyeing him.

"Love is the way the grass brushes between your toes or the way rain falls onto your face. Like the night sky or the birds chirping. It's never the same sky. The grass, it can be soft or prickly. Rain can be warm or cold, and it might be a different bird each season." He smiled, his sharp fangs peeking out from between his lips. "Love exists. It just...simply changes."

Dianna stared at the boy in awe. Never had she expected someone so young to say something so profound. Especially on the subject of love.

"You're a smart boy. An incredibly smart boy."

Nicholas blushed. "I heard Nyla say something like that to Micah."

"Who?"

"Nyla, my grandmother."

"So...Micah is your brother then?" Dianna questioned.

"Ha."

"Yes." She nodded. "You don't need to be domesticated." She pulled the blanket up under his chin. "You're more civilized than both my cousin and Mr. Crispin. They simply need to learn to listen to someone other than themselves."

Nicholas laughed.

Dianna smiled. "You should rest. I'll prepare something for you to eat. I believe the doctor will be arriving shortly."

Nicholas froze. "Doctor?"

"Yes. He'll prescribe the medication needed to help with that fever of yours."

Nicholas looked away from her. "Will you be here when the doctor comes?"

"Of course. I don't trust anyone else to make sure no harm comes to you."

8

Nicholas glowered at the doctor. He followed the man with his gaze, clenching his fists tightly.

The doctor carried a strong resemblance to one of the men from the barn. Even smelled like him. Whenever the doctor smiled at him, the tips of Nicholas' ears twitched.

"The wound on his leg should heal soon if he doesn't put too much strain on it." The doctor looked over at Roland. "As for the vermin's fever...well, I think rest is the best thing for him."

"Shouldn't you be giving him some sort of medication?" Dianna prompted.

The doctor glanced at her then turned his attention back to Roland, who smiled apologetically.

"I'm not sure if I can or should be prescribing medication to him...I mean, I went to school to study medicine for people, not animals."

"Are you suggesting we have a veterinarian take a look at him?" Peter asked.

The doctor blushed and cleared his throat. "It might be the best thing to do."

Nicholas gritted his teeth and leaned forward in his chair. "You remind me of someone I met recently." He shot the doctor a threatening glare. "Say, I didn't catch your name."

"Oh, I'm sorry. I'm Dr. Gray." The doctor inched away from him. "Y-you speak well for a-an animal. Of your species, I mean."

"Dr. Gray!" Nicholas roared. Everyone in the room jumped. "No one steals from the doctor, eh? Ain't that right, doc?"

"Nicholas, calm down." Dianna placed a firm hand on his shoulder.

"Have we met?" Dr. Gray questioned, getting to his feet.

"Your friends took away all I had left in this world!" Nicholas screamed. "It's *Doksot's* like you that should be burned alive! If you have a problem, deal with it yourself, don't send your damn goons!"

"I-I'm sorry, but I don't know what you're talking about." Dr. Gray stumbled back, clutching his bag. His eyes wide.

"My brother is the one that stole from you."

Roland and Peter stepped between the vermin and the doctor.

"Nicholas, calm down," Dianna repeated gently.

"I had nothing to do with your brother being arrested. And I understand how scared you must be right now, but yelling and pointing fingers isn't going to change anything." Dr. Gray pressed his lips together.

Nicholas let out a deep sigh and lowered his head. His eyes burned. "Micah's alive?"

"Yes, my son placed him in jail."

"Vincent Gray..." Nicholas murmured, raising his head, eyes narrowed.

"Yes."

Nicholas jolted up from his seat and lunged toward the man, screaming as he tried to claw at him.

Peter grabbed onto him. His eyes widened as Nicholas broke free from his grasp and sprinted toward the doctor.

"Nicholas, stop!" Dianna shrieked, jumping to her feet.

Nicholas turned to her and drew in a deep breath.

"He's innocent," she said calmly, stepping between him and the doctor. "He's not the one who hurt you."

Nicholas gulped as he stumbled away from the ghostly-looking man. "*Iya Nasei,*" he whispered. "I'm sorry."

Dianna took him into her arms and held him. "It's all right. No one's going to hurt you."

Roland eyed her.

Dianna met his gaze briefly. He suggested Peter and the doctor step outside for a few minutes. After they left, Roland gripped Nicholas by the shoulder and spun him around, so they faced one another. His blue eyes were hard as if he'd strike the boy any second.

Nicholas stared at him blankly.

"I sent Mr. Rissing out so that you wouldn't get a beating. Don't you *ever* let yourself act so...so feral again. This is the whole reason we brought you out here—to stop nonsense like this."

Nicholas glared at him.

"If you wish for me to treat you like a person, then you need to control yourself." Roland looked to the heavens, releasing his grip. "Now, do you promise to be on your best behaviour?"

"I hate doctors," Nicholas replied bitterly.

"And how many doctors do you know?" Roland teased.

Nicholas pursed his lips. "Dr. Gray."

"I know a fair few, and all they want to do is help people. Now, because of your outburst, you'll be given a punishment."

"Roland..." Dianna glanced toward the door. "You've already forced him to stay in this cage."

"As part of your domestication, you will work for me. That is when you're feeling better," Roland said firmly. "You must do what I ask without any complaints."

Nicholas nodded his head and let it fall against his chest as he sank to his knees, exhaustion taking him.

Roland grabbed onto him and dragged him back to the chair where he'd been sitting.

"The poor thing." Dianna pressed her hand to her face, her green eyes fixated on the bruise running across Nicholas' cheek. "Especially after what you barbarians put him through today."

"We're barbarians? Miss Warren, I'm not sure if you noticed, but this boy being as sick as he is, had enough strength to pull away from a grown man."

Dianna pouted, folding her arms across her chest. "It's called adrenaline."

"He may have been brought up with half-breeds, but he's still wild," Roland reminded her. He glanced over at the boy. "I'm curious about what happened between him and Vincent, though."

Dianna nodded. "If he ran into Vincent and the sheriff, why didn't they kill him?"

"I don't know. Stay here with him. I'm going to bring Peter and Dr. Gray to the main house."

Dianna sat down next to Nicholas and nodded as Roland left.

———

"As they walked, the wet grass squelched beneath their feet," a familiar voice said gently. "The birds sang out cheerfully as the sun rose up into the sky."

Nicholas raised his head and gazed at Rose, who sat on the chair beside him, reading aloud from the book. He sat up straight and rubbed his eyes.

"Where's Miss Warren?"

"Upstairs. She's cleaning the bedroom for you. My uncle is worried that you'll get someone else sick."

Nicholas nodded. "What are you doing here?"

"Reading to you, of course. Miss Warren asked me to."

Nicholas glanced toward the staircase. "That's not what I meant. Never mind. Is the doctor still here?"

"Dr. Gray? Oh no, he left hours ago." Rose chuckled. "Mr. Rissing is really upset with you. I heard you got quite the lashing."

She eyed him and shook her head. "Well, I'm glad it's not that bad of a bruise."

"Rose, you're Mr. Crispin's niece...right?"

"Yes, I am."

"So, shouldn't I call you Miss Crispin?"

"That's too formal. We are practically the same age." Rose closed the book. "Just call me Rose."

Dianna came down the stairs, her hair a mess, spilling out of her ponytail. She wiped her hands on a pair of work slacks. "You wouldn't believe how filthy those windows are. Your uncle should take better care of this side of the property."

"I've barely ever been this far away from the pond." Rose tugged at the blue ribbon in her hair. "My uncle doesn't like coming here."

"Why not?" Dianna rubbed her hands together. "It's near the trail. We all used to go through there up to the creek back in the day."

"Well...this is Grandmother's favourite spot."

"Where is Mrs. Crispin anyway?" Dianna placed a hand on Nicholas' forehead and sighed. "I'll get you a cool cloth."

"We don't really talk about it." Rose hugged the book close to her chest. "But my uncle visits her often."

Nicholas noted the way she twisted her frown back into a smile as she squeezed the book into herself.

"Hmm. Your uncle doesn't seem to enjoy talking about anything," Dianna muttered before heading into the kitchen.

"I'm really worried about him." Rose glanced at Nicholas. "He's become...very distant. He wasn't like that before...."

Nicholas' ears twitched as her voice shrank. He gave her a smile. "Will you read some more to me?"

"I'd like to, but I've got to help plan for my birthday party."

"You're having a party?" Dianna asked, re-entering the room. She placed the wet cloth on Nicholas' forehead and smoothed back his untamed hair, careful not to reveal his ears in front of the girl.

"Yes, my uncle and I are still planning everything." Rose got to her feet. "Would you like to come?"

"I'm not so sure your uncle would want me there," Dianna said sweetly.

"Why not?"

"We have...history."

Nicholas looked up at Dianna. "I've never had a party."

"Well, maybe if you build up some strength, you can go to Rose's." Dianna smiled.

"I'd better get going." Rose stood up, brushing out her skirt. "I don't want to get into trouble." She placed the book gently into Nicholas' hands and gave him a warm smile. "I'll come by as often as I can."

Nicholas forced himself to meet her eyes. "Goodbye, Rose."

9

As Mr. Leon pulled the car up to the entrance, Roland's hands trembled. He cautiously looked upon the large stone building and gulped, pushing open the door of the Chevy master deluxe. The older vehicle had seen him through the worst of times. Roland's hand lingered on the narrowed hood, the warmth of the engine giving him courage.

"When should I come pick you up, sir?" Mr. Leon asked, glancing back at him.

"In a half-hour." Roland slammed the door shut and made his way toward the gate. *This place is like a prison.* The gate creaked open. He'd listened to its sound for four years, and it still made the hairs stand on the back of his neck. The cold weather gave it a howling wail as if the gates themselves cried out in pain.

"Good morning, sir." The young man at the gate tipped his hat. "How are you today?"

"I'm quite well, thank you." Roland forced a smile. "I'm here to see my mother."

"Name?" The young man shut the gate and led Roland up the stone steps and into the building.

"Crispin. Adeline Crispin."

The young man flinched, averting his eyes.

Roland held his breath, as the other man caught sight of a nurse walking through the hall and waved her over.

"Ah, Ms. Stuart. Do you mind taking this gentleman to see his mother?"

The nurse beamed. "I'd be happy to." She took Roland by the arm and looked up at him. "What's your mother's name?"

"Adeline Crispin. She's been moved to one of the rooms upstairs, I believe."

"Ah, yes, Mrs. Crispin, the marvellous painter. She's such a gifted woman."

Roland was surprised the nurse didn't flinch in the same way the young man did. He'd become used to hearing *Crispin* spat from the lips of the townsfolk as if it were a curse. Instead, the nurse gave him a warm smile. He struggled to return it.

As she led him up the stairs, a woman shrieked. His stomach turned. The shrill of her voice drew his shoulders to his ears. It was difficult to resist peering into the rooms, but he found the people in the mad house strangely enticing, even though they made his skin crawl.

When they arrived at Mrs. Crispin's room, the nurse released Roland's arm and knocked on the door. "Mrs. Crispin, may we come in?"

"Yes."

Roland entered first, drawing in a deep breath before he looked upon his mother. She sat by the window, a frail woman with a dazed expression, gazing out at the lonely garden.

"You have a visitor," the nurse said sweetly.

Adeline turned to face the nurse and smiled gently. "Would you like to join me for a bit of tea, Freya?"

"I'd love to, but I already promised to have tea with young Sylvia later."

Adeline glanced over at Roland and wrinkled her brow. "Excuse me, young man, but are you new here?"

Roland shook his head, shoving his hands into his pockets. "I've been here often. Don't you remember me visiting you last week?"

Adeline scrunched up her face as she eyed him. "You brought me sweets last time you were here."

Roland smiled. "Yes, I did."

"I didn't recognize you. You're wearing a different coat."

"Yes, I usually wear this coat when the wind is bitter." He forced himself to sit down in the chair beside her. "You must miss the flowers."

Adeline chuckled. "I had a rose bush outside my kitchen. My boys used to play there when they were little. I got so upset whenever they walked through my flower beds. So upset. Those two were a real pair. Despite their difference in age, they got along very well." Adeline turned to the nurse and smiled. "Freya, did the boys send me any letters?"

The nurse glanced at Roland and cocked her head. "Mrs. Crispin, do you know this man's name?"

Adeline smiled to herself. "I'm afraid not."

Roland held his breath and placed his hand on hers. "You know it. You're probably just a bit tired because you've been sitting in the sun for so long."

Adeline stared at his hand, silver tears sliding down her face.

Roland pulled away and reached for his handkerchief. "Here, use this to dry your eyes."

Adeline took it and held it carefully between her frail fingers. She thrust it back at him, her face red with anger. "I can't dry the tears I shed for the ones I love!" She shot out of her seat and stormed over to her dresser, where she picked up a small portrait. "I want to go home to my husband and my boys..." She pressed the frame to her chest and wept. "Why haven't they sent a letter? Do they hate me? Their own mother!"

The nurse inched toward her. "Mrs. Crispin, this man is your—"

Adeline chucked the portrait across the room and screamed. "I want to go home!"

Roland ducked as it whipped past his head. He turned around, looking down at the small cracks in the glass that ran across his twelve-year-old neck. *They look like a noose.* He wrapped his handkerchief around his hand and picked up the broken frame.

"Mrs. Crispin, do I have to get the needle?" the nurse asked firmly.

Roland gazed out the window and watched the snow drift down. "I brought a message from your son," he said softly.

Adeline quieted herself and sank to the floor. "W-what did he say? Which darling had you bring this message?"

"Roland." He kept his eyes on the snow. "He said to tell you that he's feeling well and that Tabitha has been taking good care of him in your absence. He also asked me if I could bring one of your paintings home to hang up in his room."

A large grin crawled across Adeline's lips. "Tell him that I'm so happy to hear from him." She raced over to a painting leaning up against the wall. "Give him this one." She held it out to him.

Roland looked at the painting of his brother's horse and bit his lip. "It's beautiful...h-he'll love it."

Adeline nodded. "This is Lawrence's horse, Dusty. My eldest raised it from a colt. He's a fine horse. Lawrence used to ride all over town and race with his friend Gilbert. My little Roland adores Dusty. I never let him ride, but I thought maybe this painting would be nice...R-Roland adores Dusty. He adores him." Adeline handed him the painting and stumbled toward her bed.

"Mrs. Crispin, are you all right?" the nurse asked.

Adeline laid herself down and squeezed her eyes shut. "That man. Send him away."

The nurse gave Roland an apologetic look and guided him out of the room. "I'm sorry, she's been very emotional lately."

Roland leaned up against the wall and exhaled, letting his cheeks puff up. He looked at the nurse, shaking his head as he tried to speak, but no words came out.

"I'll walk with you." The nurse said. As they headed outside, the nurse took him by the arm. "Before you go, I wanted to say thank you. Many of the patients never get any visitors, and rarely do they hear from their families. You visiting your mother like this really makes her happy, and her health improves with every letter you write."

Roland stared at her as she squeezed his arm gently.

"I understand that it's hard to see her like this, but I and the rest of the staff admire your strength."

"T-thank you," Roland whispered. He turned from her and shuffled his feet.

The nurse patted him on the back and smiled. "Have a wonderful day, Mr. Crispin."

He nodded and looked over his shoulder as she left. Roland headed toward the entrance and waited for Mr. Leon's return. Pacing back and forth, he clung to the painting, muttering to himself the preparations he still needed to make for his niece's party.

Thinking about the party put him at ease. Birthdays were normal. Fun. *It was bad enough I had to go to a meeting on her actual special day. Then we found Nicholas...That isn't the way anyone should spend their thirteenth birthday. The party has to be perfect.*

Roland stomped his feet, looking out at the road. His heart stopped. *Wendy and Lawrence would've decorated the entire house with streamers and had a cake ready. All we did was buy a stupid book.* He glanced at the painting again. "I'm sorry for selling your horse, Laurie. I needed the medicine for her...I hope you'll forgive me."

Mr. Leon pulled up beside him. "Sorry, I didn't realize you'd finish early today."

Roland jumped, coming out of his daze.

"It's a good thing. The boy's fever's getting worse. He's been hallucinating."

Roland banged off his boots and slid into the back seat of the car. "Did you call Dr. Gray?"

"He's afraid to go near the boy." Mr. Leon glanced back at the painting in Roland's arms. "Where did you get that?"

"Mama," Roland said softly.

"How was she?"

"More alert than usual..." Roland stared out the window, pressing his lips together. His eyes burned as he held back unwanted tears.

"How about you?" Mr. Leon pestered.

Roland tilted his head. "Pardon?"

"How are you today?"

Roland gazed down at the painting and sighed.

Leon frowned. He wouldn't get an answer.

10

Rose hovered over her uncle's shoulder as he jotted down a list of food needed for the party. She rocked back and forth on the balls of her feet, waiting for him to finish. Once he put his pen down, she threw her arms around his neck and grinned.

"Uncle Roland"—she batted her lashes—"would it be all right if I invited Miss Warren and Nicholas to my party?"

Roland winced. "I'd rather you didn't."

"But Nicholas seems so lonely out there in the guest house. A bit of company might be good for him."

"Do you want him spreading disease to your guests?" he snapped.

"No, but I don't want him to feel left out."

"The answer is no. Now, if you'll excuse me, I have to give this list to Tabitha."

Rose let go of him and pouted, folding her arms across her chest. "What about Miss Warren?"

Roland pressed his lips together. "I don't think so...no. The answer is no. We've got more than enough mouths to feed."

Rose wrinkled her brow as her uncle left his office. She pulled a chocolate from her purse and smirked. "None for you then." She laughed, popping it into her mouth.

"Hello?" Julius' small voice squeaked. Her youngest brother pushed open the door and smiled. "Hi Rosie. Where's Uncle Roland?"

"He went to speak with Tabitha."

Julius entered the room and took his sister by the hand. "Will you play with me?"

"Later. I promised to go..." Rose paused and knelt down beside him. "Can you keep a secret?"

Julius nodded quickly, a huge grin sliding onto his face.

Rose smiled and breathed into his ear. "I'm going to visit Nicholas."

"The boy outside?" Julius exclaimed.

"Shh!" Rose glared at him. "No one is allowed to know. I promised Miss Warren I wouldn't tell."

"Can I come too?"

Rose twirled the black ribbon tied into a neat bow at the side of her head. "Well..." She gazed into Julius' round hazel eyes as he gave her his sweetest smile. "I guess. But you have to be quiet, and you have to promise you won't get too close to him. Nicholas is really sick, and he isn't well enough to play right now."

"Okay, Rosie."

The two put on their coats and boots and headed out the kitchen door. Rose led her brother down the path, past the frozen pond, to the little house hidden behind the trees. She knocked on the door and glanced down at her younger brother, who decided he should knock as well.

The door creaked open, and Miss Warren invited them inside.

Rose removed her jacket. "I brought Julius along with me."

"Where's Nicholas?" Julius' gaze darted about the room.

"Laying in bed." Dianna wrung her hands together. "He's been hallucinating...please don't over-excite him. It's lovely you're here but do keep your distance."

Julius cocked his head and furrowed his brow before throwing off his coat and dashing up the stairs. He looked at Nicholas, who peered at him through sunken eyes.

"Do you 'member me?"

Nicholas shook his head.

"I'm Rosie's brother. I saw'd you when you came."

Nicholas raised his brow and sat up, turning his attention to Rose.

"I am so sorry," Rose whispered, opening her purse. "Here, I brought you some chocolate." She placed the treats on the coffee table and sat down. "Did you manage to get any rest?"

Nicholas rubbed his temples and groaned.

Julius looked at his sister. "Do I get any candy?"

"Not right now. The rest of it is back at home."

"I hope you didn't take those from your uncle." Dianna sat down in the chair next to Nicholas. "Peter once tried to steal a treat out of Roland's lunch while we were in school, and Roland hit him over the head with a rock. I don't know what to expect if he discovers you've given away his treats."

"Actually, I got them from a boy named Thompson. It was part of my birthday gift."

"I want candy for my birthday." Julius pouted. "But it's not till a really long time."

Dianna smiled at him.

"What...what do these taste like?" Nicholas pointed to the chocolate.

"It tastes like music!" Julius shouted. "It's so yummy. I want some too!"

Nicholas wrinkled his nose. "You're telling me that this tastes like music?"

"He's five." Rose ruffled her brother's curly blonde hair. "He says silly things whenever he's excited."

Nicholas took one of the chocolates from off the table and handed it to the bright-eyed little boy. "You can have one."

Julius' jaw dropped. "Thank you so much!"

"Maybe you'll be quieter while you eat." Nicholas groaned. He grabbed himself a piece of chocolate and sniffed it.

"Just try it." Dianna laughed.

"Why are you sharing part of your gift?" Nicholas asked, turning to Rose. He glanced at Julius as the young boy forced the entire chocolate into his mouth.

"Tom gave me way more than I can handle. If I eat every piece, I'm sure it'll make me sick."

"He must really like you," Dianna teased.

Rose frowned. "Our families wish to see us married."

Nicholas leaned forward and eyed the chocolate. "This smells very sweet, but it looks like dirt." He looked at Rose. "Are you sure it's okay to eat?"

Rose laughed. "Yes. It's perfectly safe."

"Does your uncle want you to marry this gentleman, or was it the wish of your parents?" Dianna asked.

"It's my uncle's wish."

"I have a hard time believing that," Dianna said softly.

"I don't. I doubt he's the same man you knew." Rose fiddled with a heart-shaped piece of chocolate in her hand, digging her nails into it.

"What is this?" Nicholas cried.

Rose and Dianna shot their heads in his direction.

"This is delicious!" Nicholas rose to his feet. "Never in my entire life have I tasted something so...so wonderful!" He picked up another chocolate and tossed it into his mouth. "Why is this so good?"

Julius smiled. "I told you."

Nicholas spun around in a circle, stumbling about. The sugar from the delicious treat filling his head. He giggled. "Miss Warren, you really need to try some!"

Roland lifted his gaze as his niece, and a young man passed his office. He rose from his seat and made his way out to the main hall. "How was school today?"

"It was all right," Rose said softly, turning her attention to him. "Thompson Hood came home with me."

"Good afternoon, sir." Thompson removed his hat.

Roland gave him a gentle smile. "My, you've grown."

Rose kept her gaze on the floor. "If you'll excuse us for a moment, Tom and I are trying to find Julius."

"Would you like to join us for dinner?" Roland asked.

Thompson scratched his head. "I don't want to be a bother."

"You know that you're always welcome here."

Rose balled her hands into two tight fists until the whites of her knuckles appeared. "Pardon me," she spat. "I need to get something from the kitchen."

Roland and Thompson shot each other worried glances as she stormed off.

"I'm sorry about her behaviour." Roland cleared his throat, shoving his hands into his pockets.

"She's young." Thompson shuffled his feet shyly.

Roland scanned Eloise and Kurtis' boy. He'd grown a lot since he'd last seen him. His shoulders had broadened. Roland couldn't help but picture Thompson as a baby. He remembered the first time he held him; the infant's hair black like his father's, almost the colour of a crow's wings. His eyes, exactly like his mother's, a warm blue.

Roland smiled at him. "How old are you now?"

"Sixteen, sir."

"Any plans for furthering your education?"

"My father would like for me to study politics." Thompson looked in the direction of the kitchen. "However, I'm more interested in travelling."

Roland nodded. "Have you been anywhere outside of Tavern?"

"Yes. My mother and I took a boat from East Tavern to the little island Luciole. The scenery was breath-taking, and there were so many amazing creatures." As Thompson spoke, his voice became soft —just above a whisper—as if this place, Luciole, was some great secret.

Roland glanced over the young man's shoulder. "The last time I was in East Tavern, I was a little older than you. Seventeen maybe? I haven't been there in...I guess it's been seven years." He clamped his hands together and cleared his throat. "Where has my niece run off to?"

"She and I had a bit of a disagreement earlier. I'm afraid I've offended her."

"Rose can be very forgiving. Rose!" he called, gesturing for Thompson to follow him. "Rose, where are you?" Roland glared at the kitchen door as he pushed it open.

Tabitha jumped, twirling around in the direction of the two men. "You...you startled me!"

"Sorry about that. Did you see Rose come in here?"

"Yes, I did." Tabitha brushed back the loose strands of her greying hair. "Miss Crispin put on her jacket and headed out back." She gave Thompson a warm smile. "Why, Mr. Hood, you're all grown up."

Thompson nodded, then looked to Roland, who grew uneasy.

"I'll go after her." Roland pressed his lips together. "I have a funny feeling she and I need to have a bit of a chat."

"I'll aid Mrs. Gibson then," Thompson said.

"Thank you." Roland hurried out the door ignoring Tabitha as she nagged him about not wearing a jacket and forced his way through the thick snow. He spotted his niece, crouched beneath a tree.

"Rose!"

She raised her head and glowered at him.

"Is there a reason you decided to come out here?"

Rose let out a sigh. "I wanted to speak with Miss Warren...but, unfortunately, I somehow lost my glove." She eyed him. "Where is your coat?"

"Flower,"—Roland knelt beside her—"have you been going to the guest house often?"

Rose shook her head, avoiding his eyes.

Roland held out his hand to her. "Thompson told me that the two of you had a slight disagreement."

Rose placed her hand in his and nodded.

The two of them walked back to the house hand in hand, looking for her missing glove, as she described the conversation between herself and young Mr. Hood.

"We were discussing how a lot of people can't afford the medication to treat the fever. I believe that it should be given out for free, but Tom thinks it would be unfair to the people that created it because they would lose out on profit. But there are a lot of people dying from a fever that could easily be treated by a few spoonsful of medicine a day."

Roland squeezed her hand gently. "Both of you are correct. So, there's no need to get upset over something like that."

"What upset me"—she growled, pulling away from him—"is that he thinks he's right simply because he's older than I am. He talks down to me as if I'm an idiot." She drew in a deep breath. "I don't appreciate being treated like a child."

"But you're still a young girl. Thompson's a young gentleman. I don't think he's trying to upset you."

"Yes, he is." Rose snapped. "He's only three years older than I am. He doesn't need to act as if he's my superior."

"You're starting to sound like Dianna." Roland groaned, recalling one of many arguments between the two of them before she'd left for Riversburg.

Rose stared at him. "What is that supposed to mean?"

Roland gave her a weary grin. "Rose, have you been spending a lot of time with Miss Warren?"

"What does that have to do with anything?"

"This conversation is over. Let's go back to the house. I don't have the energy to argue with you right now."

"I'm going to the guest house to see Miss Warren. I won't be long."

"Stay away from the boy."

"His name is Nicholas," Rose said sullenly. "Oh, and don't worry, I won't get too friendly with Miss Warren since you seem to hate her so much."

11

Roland turned his attention away from his plate and over to the small grandfather clock near the hutch in the dining room. His niece still hadn't returned from the guest house. *What if that feral beast harmed them? If she gets sick again, I'll lose it.* He forced down the lump in his throat. "Stop it!" he mumbled to himself. "There's no need to worry."

Lisa entered the room with her daughter and gave him a gentle smile. "I'm going to get Alicia ready for bed."

Caspian and Julius looked up from the table and waved.

He nodded. "All right. I'll send Julius up when he's finished."

"Night," Caspian said, sliding his younger brother's plate closer so that he could help him cut his meat.

Lisa curtsied, then exited the dining room.

Thompson scanned the room with his blue eyes. "Did Rose not want to come to dinner because of our argument?"

"Probably." Caspian grinned, stabbing his fork into Julius' chicken.

Roland sighed. "I also upset her."

Caspian rolled his eyes.

Thompson smiled shyly. "Well, it's more likely that she'll forgive you over me."

Roland pouted as he knit his brow. "It isn't like her to be late... Maybe I should go see if she—"

"R-Roland!" Dianna stumbled into the room, both Rose and Lisa behind her.

Roland looked at them as he rose from his seat.

"Nicholas..." Dianna choked out. "He...he's..."

"Spit it out," Roland growled.

"He's barely breathing," Rose said, tumbling into the room beside Dianna.

Caspian's hands shook. He set down the knife and fork, turning to his uncle.

Roland staggered back and slapped his hands onto his face, sliding them down from his brow to his jaw.

Thompson gazed up at Rose, meeting her gaze. He hurried to her side and took her into his arms.

She shoved him back as tears sprang to her eyes.

"Boys," Lisa said gently. "Why don't we head upstairs and get ready for bed."

"It's not bedtime yet!" Julius cried. Tears automatically bubbled forth as he watched similar ones slither down his sister's cheeks.

Caspian rose from his seat. "Shut up."

"But I'm still hungry."

Lisa took him in her arms while her daughter stood in the doorway. "Why don't we have a picnic upstairs in your room?"

Julius nodded.

"I'll call Dr. Gray." Roland sighed. "So that he can collect the body and dispose of it properly."

The children's eyes widened.

Dianna glared at him. "Nicholas isn't dead."

"Not yet."

Rose shot him a dirty look.

"Dr. Gray is the reason this happened. You realize what this

Roland furrowed his brow. "So, you're somewhat sane. Um...have you had chocolate before?"

"No, but I really liked it."

"You barely had a pulse a minute ago...I'm surprised you're awake." Roland took in a deep breath.

"I don't know what you mean."

"A pulse is like...when your heart is beating. How fast it's going."

"My heart...it makes the sound of a drum."

Roland nodded, smiling grimly at how the boy seemed almost drunk from his fever. "Just for tonight, I think you should sleep in the nursery."

"But I thought—"

"Only for tonight."

Nicholas nodded.

"Come along then. Let's tell everyone you're not going to die on us."

Nicholas pouted and got up onto his feet. "Will Miss Warren be staying in the nursery with me?"

"At your age, it's a little odd to have a nursemaid. Don't you think?"

"What's a nursemaid?" Nicholas asked as they headed outside.

Roland's eyes widened as he looked at the boy's bare feet. "Where are your boots? Aren't you cold?"

Nicholas nodded. "I don't know where they are."

Roland groaned. "It's a short walk. Do your best to move quickly." He removed his jacket and handed it to the vermin doing his best to navigate the dark path back to the main house.

When the two arrived, Dianna embraced the boy, kissing his frozen cheeks.

Nicholas flinched and shivered as she and Lisa took him upstairs.

12

Unease washed over Nicholas the moment he returned to the nursery. He glanced about the room as a cold sweat ran down his back. He recalled his first night at the Crispin estate. Though he'd been frightened then, he was less afraid of the humans now and more afraid of his life slipping away.

Nicholas glanced at the door as he listened to Rose's brothers playing in the hallway. He drew in a deep breath and hacked violently. His eyes watered as he brought his hands to his lips and gagged.

Mr. Crispin had said he'd be here for one night. However, one night soon turned into a week as Nicholas' condition worsened. Nicholas tried his best to hold on. He needed to get back to his family.

It was clear that the humans were curious about him. Both Roland and Peter constantly wrote things in their journals, while Dianna kept a close eye on them. Nicholas didn't mind it when she asked him questions. She seemed nice. The other two were *Doksot's*.

Nicholas struggled to swallow. His mouth was dry, and his lips were chapped. He sighed gently, resting his head on the back of his bed, his body tired and hot. Removing his blankets would help; however, he feared he'd start shivering again. Nicholas listened to the sounds of the house: Tabitha's haughty laugh, Caspian's high-pitched whines, Lisa's cheerful humming.

His ears perked up with a thunderous plunk. His eyes grew like large brown saucers and his brow knit together. *What an awful sound.*

Plunkity-plunk!

Nicholas wrinkled his nose in disgust and threw his legs out over the edge of the bed. He cleared his throat and rubbed his temples.

Bang! Dong! Plunk! Plunkity-plunk!

With a groan, he forced himself out of bed and stumbled into the hall.

Roland told him not to go downstairs, to stay out of sight. However, the noise came from the main floor. It kept blaring in his ears, and the curiosity gnawed at him.

Nicholas tiptoed toward the stairs, running a hand along the smooth dark railing. He peered down into the parlour and spied Julius and another small child sitting on the stool of the grand piano, banging their hands on the keys. Nicholas shook his head. It made him dizzy. He sat down on the steps, head in hands.

"That's enough of that," Roland grumbled, coming out of his office. He glared at the two children and shooed them away from the piano.

Julius took the little girl's hand and lead her away from his uncle. "We were making music."

"You were making a racket. How many times must I tell you not to play around with this?" He ran a finger along the bench. "The piano is not a toy."

"It's an instrument." Julius beamed. "A big, loud one!"

Nicholas grinned, relieved that someone had finally put an end to that unearthly sound. He rose to his feet and grasped the railing tightly for balance. As he looked down, Mr. Crispin took a seat on the black bench and placed his fingers on the ivory keys. To his amazement, the man's hands danced across the instrument. Nicholas swayed as he listened to the gentle melody that sailed up to the top of the ceiling and rang out into the rest of the house. He shut his eyes and drew in a deep breath.

"I once knew a bonnie lass, whose eyes were bluer than the sky," a voice sang sweetly. "She asked if I liked to dance, then asked if I wished to fly."

Nicholas forced his way back into the nursery and laid himself down on the bed. He smiled to himself, humming the tune until he fell asleep.

As a young boy, Roland Crispin took delight in music. His mother often bragged about his soft, angelic voice and encouraged him to pursue the arts.

Darius, Roland's father, did not deny that his son was talented but took no interest in his musical abilities. Throughout the majority of his childhood, his father took no interest in him at all. Lawrence was the favourite. His father's pride and joy. Roland was simply a child who lived under the same roof and called him "Papa."

It was his mother who convinced his father to purchase that damn piano. "The boy should be happy while he's alive. He has no friends. At least let music be his companion," she'd said.

Roland soon got a piano teacher, Dr. Gray's late wife, and when he was feeling well, he'd sit and play for hours. His family grew to appreciate the music that filled the quiet house until Roland began composing his own.

For the first time, his father struck him and ordered him to never go near the piano again.

Roland had sung about his first love: a freckle-faced girl named Dianna Warren.

13

R oland sighed deeply as he paced back and forth. Over the past week, he'd struggled to juggle the new dynamic in the house. Dianna moved into one of the guestrooms upstairs —without his permission. He didn't even try to fight her on it. He'd watched from the parlour as she lugged a suitcase upstairs while he drank his tea. It was the last moment of peace he'd had since. Nicholas wasn't getting any better and the worse he got, the more agitated Peter became.

When Roland wasn't running between the office and the nursery to check in on Nicholas, Dianna complained to him about Peter or Peter ranted about Dianna. To top it off, his niece continued to evade him whenever he tried to talk to her about going around Nicholas. Every time he started, she claimed she was either on her way to school, doing homework, or adding to her long list of party demands.

Roland drummed his fingers along the railing as he made his way up the stairs, reviewing his points over and over as he prepared himself for the confrontation.

"Rose." He knocked on the door. "We need to talk." He waited for his niece to open the door. He glared at her and folded his arms as she came out into the hall. "I believe you have some explaining to do." He cleared his throat.

Rose searched his face. "I'm afraid I don't know what you mean."

"Really?" Roland groaned, pressing his lips together. "You've been around the...that thing. Boy. Nicholas."

Rose grinned. "Does this have to do with when we were looking for my glove?"

"Yes."

"I've been visiting him with Caspian and Julius. Don't worry, we don't stay long and besides, last time I got sick was because—"

"No."

"No?" Rose furrowed her brow. "No what?"

Roland placed his hands on her shoulders and gripped them tightly. "Rose, I don't want you three going near him anymore. His condition is getting worse...his face is pale, and he's become very weak. I can't afford to have any one of you fall ill." He lowered his voice as his niece's lip quivered. "Peter and I fear that unless we can get him some sort of medication, he'll die."

Rose turned from him. "He'll live."

"Flower...we were all hurt by the loss of your mother and father." Roland glanced down at his feet. "But this boy is a stranger. He won't last much longer. Don't let yourself get so attached to him." He turned her face toward his gently and smiled at her. "I have enough to worry about right now, and I want you to have a wonderful time at your party. Please, just avoid coming into contact with him."

Rose nodded and pulled away. "Why is it that you can't get any medication for him?"

"He attacked the only doctor in West Tavern," Roland said bitterly.

Rose laughed. "He's a very rough boy. It's funny watching him around Julius. He's not sure how he should act with small children."

Roland nodded. "Miss Warren tells me that he has a lot of nightmares."

"About his brother and sister," Rose said softly.

"Did he tell you this?"

She shook her head. "He talks in his sleep." Rose pulled her braid over her shoulder and grinned. "I'm hoping that when he's better, he can stay here with us."

"Stay away from him. For once in your life, listen to me. I'm trying to protect you."

Rose lowered her head. "Excuse me. I have to get ready for my party." She slipped into her room and shut the door.

Roland groaned. "She's her father's daughter." He headed down the hall to where the vermin stayed and knocked on the door.

"Are you up?" he asked. Roland waited and listened to the sounds from the other side of the door. "Nicholas?" he called, opening the door. He tiptoed into the room and glanced over at the creature.

Nicholas laid sprawled against the bedsheets, his hands over his face. "Mr. Crispin," he said hoarsely. "My head won't stop pounding."

Roland inched toward him. *He looks terrible.* "I'm going to assume you've been having trouble sleeping."

Nicholas whimpered.

Roland leaned over the vermin and frowned. "Are you all right?"

"I guess," the boy sobbed.

Roland looked him over, inching closer. "Do you need anything?"

"I need to get better."

"I know."

"Tell me that I'll get better," Nicholas whispered, revealing flushed cheeks.

Roland took the boy's hand and squeezed it gently. "I don't feel comfortable giving you false hope."

Nicholas began to tremble. He cried.

Roland shut his eyes. "Hush now. There's nothing to fear."

"I'm so tired. I'm so tired."

Roland let go of his hand and sighed. "You must promise not to say a word to anyone about this. I have something that will help you get to sleep, but if I give it to you, you have to promise that you'll be good, and you'll do what Mr. Rissing and I ask you to do."

Nicholas nodded. "I-I just want to sleep."

"I'll be back in a few minutes." Roland cursed under his breath and left the room.

Nicholas raised his head to look up at the man and let out a miserable moan.

"Here." Roland handed the vermin a shot glass full of amber liquid. "Drink it quick, or it'll burn your throat."

Nicholas looked at the yellowish liquid and wrinkled his brow. He sniffed it. "Spirits? You're giving me spirits?"

Roland nodded. "It'll relax you for a short while."

Nicholas shrugged, took a deep breath, and pressed the glass to his lips. In one gulp, he drank down the bitter liquid. He shook his head and stuck out his tongue. "That's absolutely terrible."

"It is, isn't it." Roland took the glass from him. "Now, you may be aware of this already, but we are going to have company over."

"For Rose's birthday party."

"Yes. You'll remain in your room. I don't want to hear one peep from you, is that understood?"

Nicholas nodded.

"Do your best to relax. The spirits should put you to sleep in a while."

After Mr. Crispin left the room, Nicholas placed his head onto his pillow and drew in a deep breath, He squeezed his eyes shut as the room began to spin and swallowed the vomit rising in his throat. Nicholas rolled onto his stomach, burying his face into the warm, soft pillow. Hot tears slid down his face.

"Zana, Micah, please come find me," he whimpered. "I'd rather be with Nyla and..." Nicholas held his breath as the door to the nursery creaked open. He kept his face hidden and sniffled.

Dianna placed a hand on his cheek and bit her lip. "You're burning up again." She hurried to the large window on the other side of the room and propped it open just enough so that a bit of fresh, cool air might seep in.

Nicholas grinned at the cold biting into his warm flesh. He rubbed his face onto the pillow and turned to look at Miss Warren. She smiled at him wearily.

"I'm afraid that Dr. Gray won't treat you…However, there's a town nearby with a pharmacy. I'm going to try and persuade Mr. Crispin and my cousin to go there to get some sort of tonic that might cure you."

Nicholas' fangs peered out from between his lips in his daze. "What's a pharmacist?"

Dianna laughed and covered her mouth. "It's a person who gives different types of medication to people…and sometimes animals."

Nicholas bit into his sleeve briefly, wrinkling his nose. "I'm tired."

"You look tired. You've got awful circles around your eyes."

Nicholas gagged and wheezed heavily.

Dianna frowned. "Oh, Nicholas…" She sat down beside him and patted his head. "Sweet little Nicholas."

Nicholas shut his eyes and smiled as Dianna smoothed back his hair.

"Tell me a story," he asked hoarsely.

"I don't know any good ones."

"Tell me about yourself then. Just talk to me."

Dianna sat quietly for a moment, knitting her brow. She pursed her lips together and sighed. "Well, when I was a bit younger than you, I admired this pretty, older girl at my school. Her name was Charlotte. She had beautiful curls that fell just past her shoulders, and she always got to wear the loveliest dresses. She was just a beautiful person. Perfect in every way. You know, she kind of reminded me of one of my dolls." Dianna smiled to herself. "My cousin was absolutely in love with Charlotte. All the boys were. I always felt so silly and childish when I was around her. I'm not sure why she even bothered speaking to me. My cousin and his friends always teased me because I used to wear my hair in two long braids... especially Roland. He'd pull them out to the sides and say that they reminded him of a jump rope. He called me *Pigtails* for the longest time..."

"My sister had pigtails," Nicholas muttered, looking up at her.

"You know, you've got long hair. You could probably have pigtails yourself. Your hair is nearly past your neck."

"I'm growing it until my birthday. When I cut it, I'll start looking for a mate."

"You're only fourteen." Dianna chuckled. "You should wait until you're a little older."

"But if I don't mate with someone, the pack will..." Nicholas wrinkled his brow. "Micah is eighteen, and he's never mated."

"Exactly. They should wait, and so should you. It isn't easy finding the right person. Love takes time and should never be rushed."

"Were you ever in love?" Nicholas asked, tilting his head to the side.

Dianna hesitated. "I was...when I had pigtails."

"I've never been in love. Nyla says it's special, though. That you only know what it's like when you have it."

"She's a very wise woman."

Nicholas nodded.

"She must be so worried about you." Dianna let out a gasp as she noticed the boy's expression darken. "Oh Nicholas, I-I'm so sorry. I should have—"

"It doesn't matter," Nicholas spat. "She's probably dead."

Dianna took him by the hand and looked him in the eye. "If she and your siblings are alive, wouldn't you want them to know that you're safe?"

"Of course. But I doubt they're doing any better. We got separated from our pack during the migration...Nyla was slowing us down. She said she'd catch up with us. I knew we shouldn't have left her." Nicholas swallowed hard and gazed at Dianna as tears ran down his face. "Now she's probably dead..."

Dianna wrapped her arms around him. She held him close and rocked him gently. "I'm going to see if I can find out about your family. Then you'll be able to know for sure."

Nicholas sniffled. "I've been crying a lot lately." He managed a small grin as he drew in an uneven breath.

"That's all right. You shouldn't hold in all of your emotions. It isn't healthy."

Lisa entered the room and blushed. "Pardon me, but Mr. Rissing and Master Crispin are requesting you meet with them downstairs."

"Thank you, Lisa. I'll be down in a minute." Dianna brought her attention back to Nicholas and ruffled his hair gently beneath her fingers. "You'll be good for Lisa, won't you?"

"Yes." Nicholas chuckled. He rubbed his red cheeks and wiggled his nose.

"I'll bring you a treat later." Dianna winked.

"Let me get you a handkerchief for your nose. Or a wet cloth," Lisa offered.

Dianna smiled, handed the flustered Lisa a cloth from the nightstand, then dashed out of the room.

Lisa thanked her before dipping the cloth into some water. Her hands shook as she inched toward the boy.

Nicholas furrowed his brow. "Are you all right, Miss Lisa?"

"Me? Oh yes, I'm fine," she said, wiping his nose. "It's just...the fever is contagious, and you see, I've got a little girl." She tried to smile at him. "Master Crispin and I are concerned about the children catching it. So many people have died from it in town already. Five more as of this morning. Most of them were quite old...the one woman had six children. Six! I can't imagine the pain she must've felt leaving her little darlings."

Nicholas tried not to listen to her. Instead, he admired her platinum-coloured hair. It was such a pale shade it made her grey eyes appear like ice. She was very fair and looked strange compared to his olive colouring. He could barely see her eyebrows; they were so fine.

"How old is your daughter?" he asked.

"She's four."

"Why are you so pale?" Nicholas blurted. His face reddened. "What I mean is...why don't you look like Mr. Rissing or Mr. Crispin?"

"I moved here with my daughter. I'm from a small fishing village way up north, near Belleridge. We get a lot of snow and rain there, so the sun's barely out. Not like in Tavern." Lisa raised her brow. "There aren't any vermin where I'm from. You're the first I've met. To be honest, I can't tell the difference between humans and vermin. You look like a regular little boy—act like one too."

Nicholas wrinkled his nose as she said little. "Well, I've lived with half-breeds my whole life, and they aren't able to see as well as I can. I've got better hearing too."

"But I don't see any actual indicators that say you're a vermin." She scanned him. "I'd think you were a farm boy."

Nicholas smiled at her. "It's because my hair's long enough to hide it, and I don't show my teeth when I smile." He gave her a big grin. Her eyes went wide.

"I-I should let you rest before the guests arrive," Lisa said softly, her eyes drifting to his sharp fangs.

Nicholas laid down and shut his eyes.

The two men glowered as Dianna entered the office. Roland turned to Peter and sighed. The men mirrored each other by folding their arms.

Dianna shut the door behind her and drew in a deep breath. "You wanted to see me?" She lingered near the door. *Peter looks like he's about to kill someone, and Roland*—she examined his expression carefully—*Roland looks exhausted.*

Peter glared at her. "Have a seat, dear cousin."

Dianna lowered her head and took a seat in the chair next to Roland.

"Your precious little brute isn't making any sort of recovery, and we're running out of time."

Roland turned to Dianna and gave her an apologetic look. "We understand that you fear pushing the boy will only make him worse, but we don't know what else we can do. Waiting around isn't getting us anywhere. We have a deadline to meet, or the boy might not be the only one to suffer."

"Can't you ask for more time? He's doing exceptionally well for someone without any medication. The fact that he's been living with it for nearly two months is astonishing."

"Dianna, our necks are on the line here." Peter leaned his head back and groaned. "Look, we've decided that starting tomorrow, we're going to work on domesticating the animal. It doesn't matter how good or bad he's feeling."

Dianna nodded and pressed her lips together. "I was thinking, maybe we could get him medicine from a pharmacist in Riversburg."

"In Riversburg? The place is crawling with crooks." Peter scrunched up his face, squishing the freckles on his nose.

"I know, but if we can get Nicholas the medication he needs, then we can get him domesticated much faster. He might have a stronger immune system than humans, but he's getting worse, not better."

Roland and Peter turned to one another.

"One of us could stay here while the other goes to Riversburg," Roland suggested.

"I'll be fine making the trip on my own."

"There've been a lot of robberies in that area. Even my father wouldn't travel there alone." Roland chewed on his lip.

"I have family and friends there. I'll stay with them."

Peter shook his head. "I don't like the idea of you going alone. What would our parents think if they heard you'd been killed by some desperate—"

"I won't be killed. I lived in Riversburg for years. There are many good people there. I'll be leaving tomorrow."

"Please let me come with you," Peter said.

Dianna groaned. "Will going alone worry you that much?"

"Yes. I would rather you gave me the address for the pharmacy so that we could have the medicine mailed here."

"It would take two weeks to get here. We can't afford to wait that long." Dianna shook her head. "I can take the train and have Phoebe and Uncle Scott pick me up. The pharmacy is only a few blocks from the station."

"You just got back from their place last week."

"What does that matter? Besides, you two keep going on and on about how you need to domesticate Nicholas. Going with me would only delay you further. That is, unless you two want to go to Riversburg while I domesticate him. I'm sure I'd do a much better job at it anyway." Dianna grinned.

"Doubt it," Roland muttered.

"Pardon?"

Roland smirked. "If you go by car, it will only take an hour. Why don't I have Leon drive you?"

"That would be much easier," Dianna said softly.

"Then it's settled. Now, enough vermin talk. The guests will be arriving soon. The last thing we need is for one of them to overhear. You know how people in Tavern like to gossip."

14

───────

"Julius, sit still. And stop slouching." Roland fixed his eyes on his young nephew until the boy readjusted himself on the couch and folded his hands neatly onto his lap. Roland then focused his attention on his other nephew, Caspian, who seemed as though he were up to something. The ten-year-old was known for pulling pranks. Roland shot him a threatening look that chased the smirk off the boy's face.

"What? I'm not doing anything."

"Watch your tone," Roland said firmly. He gazed over at Rose and her guests, who circled around his niece with gifts in hand.

"How scary," one petite girl in a striped sweater blurted out as another girl breathed into her ear. The two of them gawking at Roland.

The other girl nodded, her curls bouncing about her head. "It's true. My mother almost didn't let me come. She said he...well, you know."

Roland's eyes widened as the girl slid her hand across her throat and stuck out her tongue.

"Could you please pass me that?" Rose asked, turning to her classmates.

Roland noted the shakiness in his niece's voice as she wrapped the ribbon in her hair tightly around her finger. She mustered a laugh as the girl in the sweater nodded and handed her the gift box beside her.

"Thanks, Barbara." Rose gave her a smile.

Roland's eyes grew heavy as Rose excitedly held up another dress. *How many dresses does a girl need?* All of a sudden, he found himself being drawn to the bright red gown of Eloise Hood. His face flushed pink as he cleared his throat.

"May I sit here?" Eloise asked sweetly, tucking a strand of hair behind her ear.

"Yes, of course." Roland slid closer to Julius. However, Roland tried to avert his gaze; his eyes wandered, entranced, over to the bright red of her dress. He wasn't the only one staring.

"Why, Mrs. Hood, what a lovely gown," Rose said softly, her eyes sparkling.

Eloise gestured for her to come near.

Rose made her way over to the couch.

"I thought very long and hard about what to give you." Eloise took the girl by the hand. "I know how much you love to read."

Rose nodded.

Roland managed to direct his gaze to Mayor Kurtis Hood standing at the other end of the room. A knot tied in his stomach. *Maybe I should've cancelled the party? Having so many people at the house with a vermin here was a stupid idea. What if something goes wrong?* He swallowed the lump in his throat. He drew in a deep breath and held it, praying Nicholas would remain quiet in the nursery.

"Oh, Uncle Roland, did you hear? Mrs. Hood got me the play version of Midnight Garden!"

Roland furrowed his brow and watched his niece wrap her arms around the woman. *All these dolls and dresses, and she's excited about a book?* He grinned. Maybe he was rubbing off on her after all.

"Oh, thank you. How did you know that was my favourite novel?"

Eloise and Roland gazed at one another before Eloise smiled. "It was your father's favourite as well."

Roland rose from his seat, his stomach contorting itself. He thought he might vomit on his way into the kitchen. He leaned up against the counter and let out a deep sigh.

"Are you worn out already?" Tabitha chuckled.

Roland turned to her and grinned. "You know that I'm not a huge fan of parties."

"Liar." Tabitha held out a plate of cookies. "When you were a little boy, you loved going to parties with your mother."

"I loved the food, not the parties." Roland laughed. "I miss being a child. Everything was so...simple."

"You look a bit flushed. I've been worried about you spending so much time with that *thing*. Aren't you afraid of catching the fever?"

Roland shrugged. "I'll be all right."

Tabitha folded her arms and glared at him. "I know you as well as your own mother. You can't hide anything from me."

"You know me better than my mother." Roland looked away from her, his long, dark lashes shading his eyes. "You practically are my mother."

Tabitha shook her head. "You need to forgive her."

"How can I? She doesn't even know who I am?"

Tabitha frowned at him. "Stop looking so gloomy and have a cookie."

"I don't want anything to eat."

"You're turning down freshly baked shortbread?" Tabitha eyed him carefully. "You look tired, Roland."

"I'm fine. Do you need help carrying these out into the dining room?"

Tabitha shook her head. "I've got extra hands." She got up onto the balls of her feet and felt Roland's cheeks. "You're a little warm. Why don't you go lay down for a while?"

Roland brushed her hands away. "Because I don't want the children, or Peter and Dianna, to know that I'm not feeling well."

Tabitha slapped his hand and glowered. "You had better be in bed by eight or—"

Roland's eyes widened. "Is it appropriate to hit your employer, Mrs. Gibson?"

"No, it isn't," Tabitha said softly. "And if I could've, I would have beaten that father of yours for how he treated you."

Roland wrapped his arms around her.

"I can't stop picturing you as a little boy." Tabitha chuckled. "You were such a little darling."

Roland snuggled close to her and kissed her cheek. "I'll be in bed by eight-thirty at the latest. I've got to speak with Eloise about meeting her husband."

"Why not go directly to Kurtis?"

"One thing that I learned from my father is that a man's wife can persuade him into doing almost anything."

Eloise pursed her lips and shook her head. "I'm not sure what you're talking about. You want me to ask my husband to give you more time to work? I didn't know your research had a deadline."

Roland blushed. "Well, it's hard to explain but I really need more time. You see, I've fallen a bit behind in my work—according to the schedule we originally discussed." He chuckled and cleared his throat. "He listens to you."

"I'll ask, but that doesn't mean he'll say yes." Eloise spun a gold bracelet around her wrist. "You disappeared not long after I mentioned Laurie."

Roland's eyes widened. He looked away from her. "I went to check on some things in the kitchen."

"I apologize for bringing him up like that, but I thought since Rose was becoming a young woman that I should give her something special. Something she wouldn't forget."

Roland sighed. "I understand."

"She's so beautiful. I hope you tell her that. Once a woman knows her true beauty, she's unstoppable."

"Unstoppable?" Roland winced, rubbing the back of his neck. "Rose is already a strong force as it is. It's been difficult trying to raise her in Lawrence's place...I mean, she's my niece. I used to spoil her...now I'm trying to parent her, and she wants no part of it. She called me boring the other day. I used to be her favourite person..."

"She's at that age. She'll grow out of it." Eloise gazed over at him and smiled warmly. "You were like that once."

"I was not!" Roland swallowed hard as the redness returned to his face. "Not like her, that is..."

Thompson Hood peered over at Rose and blushed. He was taken aback by the way her round eyes sparkled. Thompson reached for her hand and held it gently between his fingers as he leaned toward her. "Tell me, how is that friend of yours?"

Rose glanced toward the stairs. "My friend?" She laughed. "Oh, you mean Nicholas. He's..." Her smile faded.

Thompson eyed her. "Has the fever not left him?"

"Not yet," Rose said softly, slipping her hand away from his. "But he'll be better in no time."

"I hope so."

Rose gave him a weary grin. "He's an orphan. I'm hoping that he'll be able to stay here."

"Your uncle's already looking after the three of you. He doesn't even have a job."

Rose simply smiled.

"I don't expect you to understand these things. You're still young after all."

"I'm only three years younger than you are. And if Nicholas stays here, he'll probably have to find work. My uncle doesn't need a job right now and—"

"People won't hire him." He pressed his lips together as she slid away.

"Who? Nicholas or my uncle."

"Your uncle," Thompson whispered. "He's built up a nasty reputation, and I heard he used to be very sickly."

Rose pouted. "Tom."

Thompson froze at the grim expression on her face. "I shouldn't have said that." He reached for her hand again.

Rose clenched her fists tightly and drove one into his shoulder.

Thompson yelped and glared at her. "How *very* mature of you."

Rose stood up and made her way past all her guests and up the stairs. Thompson quickly stumbled up after her.

"Rose, I'm sorry."

Rose shushed him and tiptoed toward the nursery; the striped ribbons in her hair floated gently behind her. She knocked then propped the door open.

Thompson raised his brow. "What on earth are you doing?" he asked.

"Nicholas, it's me." She gestured for Thompson to follow her.

He did.

Nicholas lay on his back with his head hanging off the edge of the bed. He sniffled and stared at the girl with a blank expression on his face.

Rose shivered. "Is that window open?"

"It's hot," Nicholas whined, turning over onto his stomach. "And you're not supposed to be in here. Miss Warren told me."

"Rose, let's go. He looks absolutely dreadful...and I'd rather not catch anything," Thompson said firmly.

"Don't worry," Rose giggled. She knelt down and gave Nicholas a gentle smile. "I just wanted to see how you were."

"I'm all right." Nicholas looked away from her.

Thompson grabbed Rose by the arm and pulled her to her feet. "Stay away from him. He's contagious. You nearly died two months ago!"

Rose lowered her head.

Thompson pecked her on the cheek and smiled. "I can't imagine this world without you." *I can't watch her go through that again.*

Nicholas shut his eyes and yawned, brushing his hair over his ears as he turned from them.

Rose's shoulders tensed up. The kiss tickled her cheek as if an ant crawled on her face. She cleared her throat. "We should go. I just wanted to check on him."

Thompson nodded and glared at Nicholas. He stopped and shook his head. *Of course, she's worried about him. She knows what he's going through.* His expression softened, and he looked at the boy with pity. He took Rose by the arm and led her out of the room. He held her hand. "Your friend will be fine. I'm sure once his fever goes down, he'll be back on his feet."

Rose nodded and squeezed his hand, tears sliding down her cheeks.

Thompson squeezed back gently.

15

The damp cement floor chilled Zana. She sat curled up in the far corner away from the other women who sneered at her—called her beast, dog, and animal. There were nights when the women whimpered in the cells beside her, begging to be let out.

The officers who came in and out scared her, especially the one called Gray. He had an effect on the other men. They drank his words as if they were the purest water.

Officer Vincent Gray kicked the bars of the cell. Zana jumped. He gave her a smile with his lips, but his eyes stayed cold.

"I'm thinking I'll hang your brother." He laughed.

Zana turned from him, digging her nails into her skin.

"Hanging is a little more humane than burning. Don't you think?" He paced back and forth in front of the cell. He stopped, glanced down at her, and smirked. "I have friends of mine out looking for young Mr. Slayden. Whoever finds his diseased corpse gets a prize."

"Why do you hate us so much?" Zana pulled herself to her feet.

"Because you're disgusting."

"Oh, really?" Zana sneered at him. "I disgust you so much that you feel the need to come here every day just to let me know? Why I'm flattered."

As he approached the cell door, Zana's legs shook. She held her breath, wishing she'd kept her mouth shut. The women in the neighbouring cells cheered.

"Beat the little brute!"

"Why not just burn her and the brother both, eh?"

Vincent's eyes grew wide as he opened the cell door.

Zana stared at him. His hand rose from his side. She grabbed his arm before he could hit her, but another officer hurried into the cell, striking her with his club. Vincent pulled away from her and spat in her face.

"P-please stop," one of the other officers begged. "She's had enough."

Vincent turned to him and smiled. "She tried to attack me."

"We keep beating her and beating her...and she doesn't cry," the young officer said, looking down at his hands. "She's not a murderess. What crimes did she commit?"

The other officer glared at him. "You pity this ugly mutt?"

"Oh, Paisley, young, naïve Paisley." Vincent walked toward him. "It isn't what she's done. It's what *they've* done."

"That's right! This is for all the innocent people they killed during the war!" the other officer screamed, slamming his club into Zana's back.

She looked up at the young officer, Paisley. Terror lit his eyes as Vincent put an arm around him.

"You see, Paisley, the reason she doesn't cry is because she knows she's done wrong."

Paisley trembled.

"Perhaps you should head back up to your desk. There's no need for you to be hanging around down here with the prisoners."

He nodded, dragging his feet down the hall.

So, there are good people left in this world.

Vincent jammed his boot into her head. She floated, disconnected from her body as blood spilled from her nose. The images surrounding her faded away, but she could hear him: little Nicholas—calling her name in the middle of the night after waking from a scary dream. She used to cradle him in her arms, like a mother would, and shush him until he fell asleep. He was tiny then, and she'd promised to always protect him. But now, she saw him screaming and screaming because the monsters in his dream were still there, chasing after him.

Dianna clutched her purse in the backseat as they crossed over the bridge to Riversburg. Roland and Peter were behind schedule with their promise to Mayor Hood and didn't have time to accompany her. Peter attempted to protest after Rose's party, but Roland assured him that with Mr. Leon driving her, Dianna would be perfectly fine. She knew Riversburg better than either of them.

The last time she'd been there, her uncle had been cross with her. Glancing at the grey-haired man in the front seat, Dianna prayed she wouldn't have to see him. He hadn't said a word to her since she got into the car. She knew Mr. Leon and Mrs. Gibson were both indifferent toward her. Dianna couldn't blame them. She, too, was disgusted with the way she broke off her relationship with Roland. Though she still felt guilty, she couldn't bring herself to apologize. Pain like that was hard to forget.

As they entered the town, Mr. Leon drove much slower. She brushed out the wrinkles in her dress and bit her lip. "Is there something wrong?"

"Aye, madam, there is."

Dianna peered out the window of the car and gawked at the smoke in the distance. "I hope no one's hurt."

Leon nodded. "Where's this pharmacy?"

"It's a little farther in town." Dianna watched the smoke.

Nicholas came to mind, and she trembled. She couldn't bear it if the boy were ever sentenced to such a violent death.

When they finally reached their destination, Mr. Leon told her he'd wait outside. Dianna entered the pharmacy and was greeted by a bald man with a large, friendly grin.

"Good afternoon, Miss. Is there anything I can do for you?"

Dianna drew in a deep breath and returned a smile. "I need something for that dreadful fever that's been going around. For my sister's son."

The pharmacist's smile faded. "How old is the boy?"

"Fourteen. Can you help him?"

"I have some medication in stock...but it's not cheap." He walked behind the counter and pulled out a bottle of red liquid. "I had to import this batch from Presa and Miao. Florus was hit pretty bad, and it's been spreading 'round these parts nearly as fast."

Dianna took the medicine and nodded. She stood for a moment, examining the red liquid. As she tilted the bottle, Roland's grim but still boyish face came to mind. *He's been looking a bit pale recently... or was he always like that? No...no, he wasn't. He was vibrant. Maybe it's just me.* She looked up at the shelf behind the man. *I can't take the chance. Not after the last time.*

She pressed her lips together. "Actually, sir, I'd like to buy another bottle for myself. I'm caring for the child, and if I were to catch anything..."

"Are you sick?"

"Well, no, but like I said, if I were to—"

The pharmacist shook his head. "Supplies are low. I don't know when I'll be getting my next batch."

I can't risk waiting. She gripped the bottle tight. "I understand, but it's only one more bottle."

"This medicine is expensive, and my supply is limited."

"I can pay for both." Dianna opened her little yellow handbag. *I hope.*

"That'll be forty, Miss."

Dianna's eyes widened. "That much for only two bottles?"

The pharmacist shook his head. "For one. This stuff isn't cheap to make."

Dianna's eyes widened. "That's ridiculous. People need to eat!" She looked down at her purse, pressing her lips together. The boys had given her barely enough for one. "I...."

"I'm sorry, Miss. I can't take less than forty dollars per bottle."

It's not like I need the money for room and board. I'm staying with Roland. She rummaged around in her purse. *I've got nighty dollars in total.* She examined her reflection in the bottle. Her heart sank. *Nicholas needs this...and I'd never forgive myself if something happened to Roland.*

"*Bloka!*" a youth shouted.

The man jumped.

Dianna turned her head to look out the window. A group of teenagers playfully pushed one another on the sidewalk as they passed.

"Bloody vermin," the pharmacist sneered. "You'd best watch your purse when you leave. Those brutes could care less about what's in it." He eyed her. "You're not from around here, are you?"

She pressed her lips together, clutching her purse. "Is that a problem?"

"I can't sell to an outsider. It's hard enough trying to hide medicine from those mutts."

Dianna crossed her arms. "Listen, I have the money. I'll give you eight-five for two bottles. That's five dollars extra, in case someone decides to rob you."

The pharmacist looked her over, then snickered. "Seems fair." He held out his hand.

Dianna pulled out the money from her purse and sighed. "Is there a number that I can call if I need to order more?"

The pharmacist grabbed a pencil and scribbled the number on a piece of paper, writing the name Albert underneath. "You call this here, and I'll get you more. There'll be an additional fee for special requests."

Dianna nodded, looking at the last five dollars in her purse. *I may need to ask Peter for a loan.*

"Give this to him twice a day...oh and make sure to keep a bucket nearby. Just in case." The pharmacist handed her the two bottles. "I don't recommend walking out of here with a brown bag. Those mutts will snatch it right from you."

Dianna forced a smile, her ears hot. "Thanks for the advice."

Dianna left the pharmacy and headed back to the car. *Eighty-five dollars for watered down medicine. Unbelievable.* She tucked the bottles into her coat pockets and closed her purse as two vermin girls rushed by her, laughing as they dodged snowballs. She smiled at them as they gestured for their friends to wait for her to step between them.

Mr. Leon sat gazing out the front window. "Where to now, Miss?" he asked as she entered the vehicle.

"I'd like to pay a visit to a friend of mine," she said softly. "He lives up the road."

Adeline Crispin sat smiling at the letter she received from her son, Roland. She kissed it and pressed it to her heart. "There's music in his words. He writes so beautifully."

Roland nodded, sipping his tea. "He thinks of you often."

"I do hope he's not giving his father a hard time. Those two are always on about something." She glanced out the window. "I'm quite tired."

Roland watched her. *This visit is much better. She's having a good day.* He raised his brow as his mother went and laid down in her bed. He thought of her as a young child and wondered if perhaps she had always been this way.

Adeline smiled at him. "You look exactly like my husband."

Roland winced at the comment and placed his teacup on the table. He made his way over to the bed, sat on the edge of the mattress, and smoothed back her greying hair. "Tell the postman, my letter's taking too long. Before I know it, my baby'll be gone," he sang.

Adeline closed her eyes and hummed along. Once she was asleep, Roland placed the quilt over her and kissed her gently on the forehead. Adeline's face softened. All the creases that had formed from her long-term sorrow faded.

"I love you," Roland whispered as he got up to get his jacket. Quietly he drifted toward the door. He held the knob as he gazed at his sleeping mother. "Goodbye..." As he forced out his final words, his tongue went rough like sandpaper. "Mama."

Peter waited out front with his hands in his pockets. He waved slightly as Roland approached. "We'd better get going. The Hoods are expecting us in twenty minutes."

"I'm sorry." Roland frowned. "I had to see her. If she doesn't get visitors regularly, she...her condition worsens."

"You're looking a bit pale." Peter pointed as they got into his blue '48 Pontiac Silver Streak Torpedo—a gift from his parents. "You aren't sick, are you?"

"No," Roland snapped. "Actually, I'm feeling wonderful today."

"Well, I'm feeling nervous. I don't care how friendly you are with Kurtis' wife. He isn't someone who likes a change of plans."

Roland nodded. "I know."

It was the reason his father had chosen Kurtis to work for him at Doren Shipping. He could remember conversations at the dinner table, where Darius went on and on about Kurtis' work ethic and how he expected nothing less from Lawrence. It was no wonder Darius and Kurtis had become such good friends and why Lawrence, like Roland, started keeping secrets from their parents.

"So, how friendly *are* you with the lovely Mrs. Hood, hmm?"

Roland rolled his eyes. "She's helped me with the children...and she was a dear friend of my brother's. You know that."

"Haven't you ever noticed the way she looks at you?" Peter

pestered, leaning toward him.

Roland's eyes widened. "Why is it the only things you can think about are money and women?"

"And good wine," Peter laughed.

Roland shook his head. "She dated my brother."

"That's besides the point. So, I need three things then. Money, women and liquor."

"Oh, you don't need friends? I'm hurt."

"I suppose four, then." Peter grinned as he pulled the vehicle around the corner.

The two men laughed, though their smiles faded once they reached the manor.

"Here it goes," Peter said.

"Let's hope Mr. Hood is in a good mood today."

"A generous mood."

Roland smiled. His chest tightened. He stopped himself from rubbing the soreness. Once this was dealt with and the boy was better, he'd have less stress.

The two men were greeted by the maid at the door. She curtsied politely and asked them to wait in the living room.

Roland removed his jacket, gripping it between his fingers. His gaze tracked around the room. *It looks different every time I visit.* He skimmed the small trinkets balanced carefully along the mantel of the fireplace. A pair of miniature glass birds caught his attention. His hands trembled.

What is wrong with me? He blinked hard, inching toward the fireplace. *These look just like the ones Lawrence and Wendy had in their hutch. Wendy said they were a wedding gift from her Aunt Viola.*

Roland glanced over his shoulder at Peter. "You're awfully quiet."

Peter wrung his hands together and stared blankly at a floral painting on the wall.

Roland shrugged, turning his attention back to the glass birds. He stretched an unsteady hand toward them, brushing the head of one with the tip of his finger, something he had done as a boy with the many little knickknacks Wendy used to decorate the parlour. A familiar warmth filled him—startled him. These *were* Wendy's birds. He pulled his hand away and shook his head, clutching at his dark brown hair. "Last time I was here, I asked about these."

Peter spun toward him. "What?"

"Nevermind." Roland cocked his head, looking over the birds again. *I need to focus. If I mess this up, it could jeopardize everything.* A sharp pain zipped through his skull. He gripped the mantel for balance, guiding himself to the couch as specs of light flashed before his eyes. Roland flopped down onto the couch and buried his head in his hands. *Not now.* He pushed back his hair, leaning his head back as the patterns from the warm, blue wallpaper were swallowed up by the dark. He drew in a deep breath.

Peter sat down beside him. "How are you so relaxed? I can't feel my legs."

Roland let out a short laugh.

"I don't know how you do it." Peter rubbed his hands together. "To tell you the truth, I don't know how you do any of this."

"Any of what?"

"You know, this and the kids and your mother and Dianna. Well, I suppose Dianna is partially my fault."

Roland squeezed his eyes shut.

"Sorry. It was stupid to bring all that up."

"Yeah, it was."

"I'll shut up," Peter whispered.

"No, keep talking. Just talk about something else." Roland took a deep breath as his vision returned. He looked over at Peter, watching his friend gnaw away at the side of his thumb.

"You already have a criminal record. I don't think your family's lawyer is going to be able to help you if they find out about Nicholas."

"Peter, you're gonna end up without a thumb if you keep doing that." Roland nodded toward his friend's hand.

Peter looked over at the painting and lowered his voice. "Who's going to look after the kids if something happens to you?"

Roland leaned forward and pressed his lips together.

Peter turned a wild stare on Roland. "This was a mistake. This whole thing."

"Then why'd you go along with it?"

"I don't know. I'm an idiot. The crazier the plan, the more likely I am to join in."

"Yeah..."

Peter cracked his knuckles. "We should've brought Dianna."

Roland glared at him.

"What?"

"No. She's done quite enough."

"She's a lot smarter than you or I...or at least she thinks things through."

"She does not." Roland shook his head. "Charlotte was the one who always stopped us from getting into trouble."

"Stopped *you* from getting into trouble, you mean."

"Hey, I'm not the one who nearly drowned swimming in the lake after dark," Roland snapped.

"Let's not forget the time you showed everyone at the pub your backside."

"You weren't even there."

"Didn't have to be. Vincent and Charlotte told me everything."

"Yeah, well...I...I have nothing to say to that."

"It's probably a good thing you don't drink anymore," Peter murmured. He looked Roland over. "You know, you do look a bit off. Are you—"

Roland cleared his throat as Eloise and Kurtis entered the room. He waited for Peter to turn his attention to them before getting up.

"Roland, Peter, what a pleasant surprise!" Eloise exclaimed. She pulled Roland toward her and planted a kiss on his cheek. She might have always seemed like an older sister, but Peter was right; she was still a striking woman. No, she treated him like family. Always had.

"He's not in a good mood today," Eloise said before releasing him.

"We'll discuss this upstairs," Kurtis said coldly.

Roland's stomach turned. He nodded, pressing his lips together until all the colour faded from them.

Eloise cocked her head. "Is something wrong?"

Roland swallowed the lump in his throat. "N-no. Um...we just need—"

"To speak privately." Kurtis gestured to the staircase.

"I see. Well, let me know if you need anything, dear."

The three gentlemen made their way upstairs in silence. The constant creaking of the steps and the image of the two birds on the mantel crept back into his mind. He shivered. *I should have asked about them again.* But he hadn't. He rubbed the back of his neck, digging his nails into his spine.

The blue wallpaper seemed to swallow him the more he stared at it. *Was it always this colour?* His chest tightened as Eloise's faint humming filled his ears. *No, it was yellow. Canary.* He peered over the railing, catching a glimpse of Eloise as she made her way across the living room, her oxblood-coloured dress following her like a deep red shadow. *One of the birds had a chipped wing.* He nodded to himself. *The ones on the mantel weren't chipped, were they?* A coldness passed through him.

"The weather's been awful lately," Kurtis said, the gruffness in his voice pulling Roland from his trance.

"Pardon?"

Peter glanced at him and gave him a little nudge with his foot. "Are you sure you're okay?"

Roland nodded. Despite knowing Kurtis, since Roland was a kid, being near the man made him uneasy. Before being elected mayor, Kurtis was just someone who worked for his father—at least, before his father died.

When he was younger, Roland used to pop in to see his brother at the office after school. Their father made it very clear he hated having his youngest son running around Doren Shipping, but Kurtis, Lawrence, and Roland's godfather, Charlie, made it a fun place to go —especially when he needed a little extra spending money.

I think I still owe Kurtis twelve dollars. His throat tightened. *Maybe he forgot. He must've forgot. He wouldn't hold twelve dollars against me now. I was fifteen. I was doing him a favour. Yeah, it was payment. He wouldn't say no to us over twelve dollars.* Roland shook his head and laughed, his hands trembling. *Why can't I stay focused?*

Kurtis glanced at him briefly, giving a slight smile.

Roland steadied his hands, shoving them into his pant pockets. He managed to muster a half-grin.

"What's wrong with you?" Peter jabbed him with his elbow. "I swear you almost look green."

Roland cleared his throat. "Remember that time I went to ask my brother for money?"

Peter groaned. "Which time?"

Kurtis opened the door to a small room as the two friends whispered.

Thompson peered out into the hall from his bedroom.

"What do you mean which time?"

"Which of the seven billion times are you referring to?" Peter snapped.

"You know which one."

Peter rolled his eyes. "Is this even important right now?" He leaned back as Roland gripped his shoulders. "Stop, they're staring at us!"

Roland spun himself around and grinned, his loose curls flopping messily around his head. His cheeks burned as Kurtis, and his son eyed the two of them.

"Thompson, have you finished your homework?" Kurtis asked.

Thompson shook his head. "Is Rose here?"

"No, this isn't a social visit. When you're finished your homework, go downstairs and see if your mother needs help with anything."

Thompson nodded, giving Roland and Peter a slight wave before going back to his room.

Kurtis gestured for the men to follow him into the office, then shut the door behind them. "My wife tells me that you two need to speak with me about something. Would this by any chance be regarding your new house guest?" He gestured for Roland and Peter to take a seat.

"Yes, sir." Peter rubbed his hands together, glancing at Roland as he sat down. "You see, we're still trying to get medication for him, and he is—"

Kurtis turned to Roland and smiled. "I hope he isn't too much trouble for you."

He's smiling again. That's a good sign. Roland shook his head. *We should be more direct.* "Peter and I need more time to train him... would that be possible?"

Kurtis rubbed his chin. "I thought he wasn't any trouble for you. Why do you need more time?"

"He's too sick. He can barely make it out of bed, let alone concentrate on learning," Peter explained. "Hopefully, he'll get the medication tonight, but until he's back on his feet, we can't do more than speak to him."

Roland watched Kurtis's smile fade. His heart dropped. He held his breath, crossing his fingers behind his back.

"If I'm being honest, Dr. Gray's encounter with your beast has made me doubtful. Roland, with your condition, it doesn't seem—"

"I'm fine. You can double check with Dr. Gray if you like. I haven't had any issues. Not even a cold."

Kurtis nodded. "Funny you should say that. I did take the liberty in asking Dr. Gray about you."

"Oh?"

"He said that your health has improved greatly...but he's concerned about how much contact you have with the creature. On top of that, from what I've heard, it's quite violent. Are you really sure you want it in the same house as the children?"

"That was a one-time issue, we swear," Peter said. "Nicholas hasn't had an outburst like that since. Dr. Gray reminded him of...of someone who'd harmed him. We got that straightened out."

"You boys wouldn't lie to me, right?"

Roland and Peter nodded quickly.

Kurtis tapped his foot and hummed, giving his head a scratch. He looked Roland over, knitting his brow. "Your father would kill me if something happened to you...Eloise would too."

"My father isn't here, and Eloise doesn't need to know. Not yet, at least." His father had never cared a whit about him.

"And how exactly are you paying for this medication?"

Roland bit his lip, looking away from him. "We pooled some money together." He shrugged, glancing at Peter.

Peter scratched his nose and let out a deep breath.

"I don't want another incident like the one at the farm in Presa."

Roland's eyes widened. "Oh, of course not. I mean, there's no way Nicholas would—"

"You have no way of guaranteeing that," Kurtis said firmly. He folded his arms across his chest and leaned his head back. "I am still going to meet with him as planned."

The men's expressions darkened.

Roland's chest tightened. "Oh...okay."

Peter turned to him, a look of doubt on his face. He gripped the edge of his seat.

Roland met Kurtis's gaze. The Mayor's eyes widened as the man glanced past Roland.

Kurtis cleared his throat. "Are you sure that you can manage the *assignment*?"

"Absolutely," Roland said as Peter sank in his seat.

"Fine, I'll give you a little more time." He grinned. "If you can do what you say, I have no doubt that the research will be enlightening and beneficial to the preservation of the town."

Peter beamed. "Th-thank you so much."

Roland tilted his head. *Did he really say yes?* He relaxed his shoulders, leaning back in his chair.

Kurtis's gaze remained focused on the door. Roland turned to find Eloise standing there. He caught her eye, and she smiled at him.

"I hope you gentlemen will be staying for tea?" Eloise laughed.

The two men nodded, like kids in a candy store.

16

Dianna sat across from the large, grinning, half-vermin looking around the small kitchen. It seemed odd to her how such a tall man could manage to squeeze into such a little house. Still, the quaintness of it suited him. She folded her hands into her lap and returned the smile.

"It's been a while, hasn't it?"

"Yes, it has." He laughed. "You should have told me you were coming."

"I know, Patrick. Please forgive me."

"You don't need to ask for forgiveness. You know I can't stay mad at you."

"I have a favour to ask," Dianna whispered. "Regarding some vermin."

Patrick's eyes flickered as he inched toward her. "I'm listening."

"Micah and Suzanna Wolfe, and their grandmother Nyla. Do any of those names sound familiar to you?"

Patrick leaned back in his chair, his black hair curling around his neck. "Wolfe. As in Lord Wolfe? If they're from Dinara, then yes, I've heard of them."

"Lord Wolfe? Are you sure? I had no idea. Could you help me locate them? Their brother...he's in my care and—"

"They were in my sister's pack. Forced to migrate through Tavern. She told me where they were headed...I can't remember where. Murienne, maybe?"

"His siblings never made it that far. They were captured by an officer, Vincent Gray. I'm not sure if they're still alive," Dianna said softly.

"Well, luckily they're *Valvenok*, like myself. They won't be put to death right away...well, Micah and Suzanna won't. Their grandmother is fully vermin and doesn't carry noble status like the children. She's most likely already dead." Patrick furrowed his brow. "The children might be with their father if they're not awaiting trial."

"How can I know for sure?"

"I know a man who works at the prison here. I'll have him contact you."

"I'm currently staying at a friend's place. His name is Roland Crispin."

"I know the name." Patrick scoffed, shaking his head. "You should be careful who you keep as company, my dear."

"I'll leave you the address." *The entire Crispin family is hated in these parts for helping the Doren's ship vermin slaves out to those prisons in Presa. Why did he even bother studying vermin in the first place? Oh, right. Peter was doing it. Why else?* Dianna smiled, taking a pad and pen from Patrick. "It's in West Tavern. I'll write the number as well. Just in case."

Patrick nodded. "So...if memory serves me right, that's the boy your cousin Phoebe told me about?"

"Yeah, that's him." Dianna winced, sinking into her seat.

"She hates him."

"My entire family does...minus Peter, of course." Dianna shook her head. "He and Peter are best friends. Inseparable. Thick as thieves."

Patrick's ears twitched. "From what I heard, the two of you ran out here to Riversburg, and Phoebe ratted on you."

"She told you about that too, huh?"

Patrick nodded, ripping the paper from the notepad. "She tells me everything." He eyed her carefully. "I'm surprised you're staying with a man your entire family despises. I mean, Crispin's are all *Doksot's*...no offence. They are, though. And the rumours about that boy, Roland...they're scary."

Dianna lowered her head and shrugged. "I know he looks guilty, but Roland's just not capable of doing something like that. Besides, if it weren't for Nicholas, I'd be staying with my cousin."

"Not with your parents?"

"They...they don't know I've come back."

Patrick glared at her. "Dianna, *Bovyabik*, you need to learn to forgive yourself. Your parents know you didn't mean to hurt them. You were just—"

"I was a stupid little girl," she snapped, gripping her skirt. "I...I messed up."

"You've been running for too long. Even now, rushing in like a white knight to protect this vermin boy...it's still you running."

Dianna leaned her head back and groaned. "Patrick, why are you *always* right about everything?"

He smirked.

"I'm not using Nicholas to avoid my parents. Honestly, I just... don't know how to tell them I'm back. It's been five years, and every time I wrote to them, my mother asked if I was married and...well... you know how it is."

"My mother's still disappointed in me for being with a human girl." Patrick laughed. "Dianna, just...reach out to them. Okay? Let them know you're all right."

Dianna nodded. "I-I should get going. I need to get this medicine back to Tavern."

Patrick stood up and walked her to the door. He took her hand and kissed her on the cheek. "*Nelich Danara*," he said with a grin.

Dianna wrapped her arms around him. "Goodbye, sweet Patrick."

Patrick crouched down and breathed into her ear. "Do not let anyone know you are harbouring a vermin. People in Tavern are crazy."

Dianna chuckled. "Oh Patrick...they aren't crazy, but I know what you're saying. I'll be careful."

"I know you will. You're a smart girl."

Rose crossed her arms as the boys zipped past her and hurried into their uncle's office. Caspian stumbled forward, stopping to catch his balance. Little Julius smacked into him.

Caspian glanced behind him and rolled his eyes. "Really, Julius, watch where you're going."

"But I was watching!" Julius rubbed his nose. He sniffled. "Where's Uncle Roland?"

Rose frowned at her brothers. "We'll just have to ask about going for a sleigh ride later."

"But I want to go, now!" Julius whined. "Can't we just do it by ourselves?"

"That would be a disaster." Rose shook her head. "Someone might get hurt."

"Don't be such a baby." Caspian gave her a sly smile. "We could do it ourselves or ask Mr. Leon."

"Mr. Leon isn't here. And I'm nearly an adult. Your petty insults won't work on me."

"What's petty mean?" Julius asked.

"Well then, what are we gonna do all day?" Caspian ignored his brother.

Rose furrowed her brow. "We could pay Nicholas a visit."

The boys looked at one another.

"Uncle Roland told us not to go near him," Caspian snapped.

"Yeah, because he's really, really sick, and he's *untayjust*," Julius explained. He let out a roar of a sneeze that sent his tiny body forward, causing him to stumble into his sister.

"My goodness, Julius, you're completely soaked. Let's go change you into something dry. Then we'll eat our snacks in the library." She led Julius out of the office.

Julius wiped his face with the back of his hand and held it out. Caspian took it hesitantly and wrinkled his nose as the three went upstairs.

While Caspian helped Julius take off his shirt, Rose snuck over to the nursery. Gently, she knocked on the door. "I don't mean to be a pest or anything"—she inched her head into the room—"but I was wondering if you'd like to—" She slammed the door shut, nearly closing it on her nose. "I-I'm so sorry." Her face grew hot as the door creaked open. She looked up at the boy and gulped. "I should have waited b-before entering. I'm sorry."

Nicholas Slayden eyed her and wrinkled his brow.

"I mean...you could have at least warned me about your indecency." She glanced away from him.

"Pardon?"

"You're practically naked." Rose shielded her eyes. "And there are ladies present. You should take more pride in how you present yourself."

Nicholas looked at his silk pyjama bottoms. "I'm not sure I understand what the problem is. I have pants on."

"What would your mother say?" Rose questioned, placing her hands on her hips.

"Dunno. Don't have one."

Rose nodded, the redness returning to her cheeks. "I forgot...I'm sorry, it's just that I wasn't expecting you to be...you know...topless."

"Rose, Uncle Roland said stay away from Nicholas!" Julius hollered, charging down the hall in a large wool sweater. "He's *untayjuss!*"

"Contagious," Rose snapped. She turned to Nicholas, who

frowned at the small boy. "Nicholas, my brothers and I are going to be having our snacks in the library. Would you like to join us?"

Caspian glared at her as he made his way down the hall. "Do you want us to get the strap?"

"Uncle Roland would never hit us." Rose chuckled. "He's much too...sweet. Like chocolate cake and butter tarts."

"I love tarts. Do you like tarts?" Julius asked.

Nicholas pointed to himself. "Me? I don't know what a tart is...or a library."

The three siblings stared at him, their eyes wide as saucers.

"Okay, fine. I'll go get the snacks, and you two take him to the library and explain to him what a tart is." Caspian groaned. "It's like you've been living under a rock all your life."

Nicholas laughed. "Actually, my house was under a large birch."

Caspian shook his head. "I think this illness has infected his brain."

Rose glanced into the nursery and spotted a red robe lying on the floor. "Nicholas, could you put that on." She pointed.

Nicholas nodded. Once he was decent, he followed them to the other side of the hall, into a small, dark, closet-sized landing.

Rose tripped as the door slammed shut behind them, catching herself against the wall.

"Be careful, Rosie!" Julius cried, bumping into Nicholas. The youngest looked up at him, large round eyes wide as saucers. "Wow. Look at the blue fireflies."

Quickly, Nicholas turned his head, covering his face. The faint blue glow fading beneath his bangs.

"I can't see a thing. I'll get a lamp," Rose whispered, clutching her shoulders as she inched away from the wall.

Nicholas furrowed his brow. "I can see just fine. What are you looking for?"

"There's a set of stairs somewhere around here. I-I can't see them...and I...I don't like how dark it is."

"I can see them. Take my hand."

"I can't see it...." Rose trembled, lowering her head. She flinched as Nicholas took her hand in his. It was warm.

"Julius, can you take her hand?"

"I'm holding her dress," he squeaked.

Nicholas led them up the stairs, where they met another door. "Is it here?"

"Yes. Be careful when turning the knob. It's a bit loose," Rose said.

Nicholas opened the door and squinted as the bright, warm light flooded into his eyes. He let go of Rose's hand, shielded his face, and gazed around the large room. "This place is enormous!"

"There's my lamp." Rose sighed, making her way over to the small coffee table.

"This is our secret place. No one else comes in here except for our uncle," Julius said. "Rosie reads us books, and we have yummy snacks. Oh, and this big chair"—he pointed to a large red sofa—"is mine!"

Nicholas smiled and sat down on a pile of pillows on the floor. "I've never seen so many books."

"My father read a lot...and I read a lot. Most of these books are his."

"This is my bear." Julius held up a large, fluffy teddy. "His name is Harry."

Nicholas nodded. "He has a very nice green sweater."

"Tabitha made it for him. I think it makes him look handsome." Julius hugged the bear.

"Harry is the best dressed bear in all of Tavern." Rose giggled, dancing about the room.

"If you don't mind, I need a lamp to be able to see where I'm going," Caspian shouted from below.

Rose grabbed her lamp and fled down the stairs.

Nicholas watched Julius stare at him. The little boy seemed fixated on his eyes. After a moment, Julius shrugged and sat down next to him. "Do you have any toys?"

"No, I'm too old for toys."

Julius puffed up his cheeks, pursed his lips, and blew out.

Rose glared at him. "Stop that. It's rude."

"It sounds like a trumpet." Julius grinned.

"No, it sounds like a fly." Caspian placed the snacks down on the table and gestured for everyone to come over. He handed a round, cup-shaped pastry to Nicholas. "This is a tart. You eat it."

Nicholas nodded and took a small bite. He blushed. The Crispin children stared at him. He took another bite, allowing the filling to melt against his tongue and turned away from them. "It's delicious," he purred.

"What's your favourite snack?" Julius asked.

"Bread and honey," Nicholas said.

"I love drinking honey in my tea." Rose smiled. "Oh, Nicholas, do you want to pick the story for today?"

Nicholas winced and glanced at her over his shoulder. *Deisso. I can't read...how am I supposed to pick something.* He shook his head quickly. "M-maybe another time."

"Okay then, Caspian, you can choose one."

"Don't pick anything scary! I hate scary stories," Julius cried.

Caspian rolled his eyes. "I was going to choose an adventure this time."

Julius sat down on the couch with Harry, placing a couple of tarts onto his lap.

"*The Treasure of Shark Tooth Peak* or *The Floating Gown?*"

"*The Floating Gown* is way too mature for us," Rose said firmly.

Caspian smirked. "It's not even scary."

"I didn't say scary, I said mature. You're ten. *The Floating Gown* is for old people, like Uncle Roland."

"Okay then, *The Treasure of Shark Tooth Peak!*" Caspian handed her the book. "Read away."

Rose opened up the novel and held it securely in her hands. She read aloud as if she were an actress on stage. She was the sailor, the ghost, the young maiden.

Nicholas watched in awe as the girl whispered, hollered, and even produced tears. His heart raced as the story progressed and though his head drooped, he remained captivated by the performance.

The Crispin children laughed and even began to add their own scenes to the book. The brothers chased one another with invisible swords.

Nicholas found himself smiling, forgetting his fangs for a brief moment. He covered his mouth with his hand as Rose glanced over.

Julius latched onto Rose as he darted away from his older brother. Caspian lunged at him, knocking his sister flat on her bottom as she tried to get out of their way.

Nicholas' eyes widened. He got to his feet and held out his hand to her. "Are you all right?"

Rose laughed and nodded, accepting his hand. She brushed off her dress and shot her brothers a threatening glance. "They always get like this when they have sweets."

Nicholas pulled a couple strands of his long dark hair behind his ear. Clumps of it stuck to his neck. He gave Rose a gentle smile, then lowered his eyes. "I really like the way you tell stories."

Rose grinned back as her eyes wandered to an object dangling from the boy's ear. He followed her gaze, his fingers brushing against the feather he usually hid beneath his hair. She studied it briefly until Nicholas covered it up. He shot her a look as she gestured to it. His eyes cold.

She shut her mouth and held the book close to her chest. "Y-you should hurry back to the nursery before anyone realizes you're missing." She turned to her brothers. "We should get started on our assignments before Uncle Roland comes home."

"My teacher didn't give me anything to do today." Julius grinned.

"Then go play with Lisa's daughter," Rose instructed. "I'm sure she'd love some company."

"Miss Opal has a daughter?" Nicholas cocked his head to the side. "Actually...I think she may have mentioned that. What's her name?"

"Alicia," Caspian smirked. "Julius wants to marry her."

Julius smacked his older brother and puffed up his chest. "No, I don't!"

"Boys, go do whatever it is you need to do." Rose placed a hand on her hip and pointed to the stairs.

Caspian laughed and snatched the lamp, grabbing Julius by the arm. "Run before the ghost gets us!"

Rose chased after them. "How many times do I have to tell you not to run with the lamp!"

Nicholas dragged his feet as he followed far behind them.

Thud!

Nicholas' ears perked up. He cautiously made his way down the steps as he listened to the two brothers giggling in the hallway and the shuffling of feet nearby. His eyes flickered as he spotted Rose attempting to pull herself up off the stairs.

"Are you okay?" he asked.

Rose didn't answer. She continued to struggle.

Nicholas stood beside her. "Did you fall?"

Rose nodded.

He frowned and watched her press herself up against the wall. He could hear her sniffling. He leaned toward her. "Are you hurt?"

"Th-they know I don't like the dark." She looked at him, trying to stop the tears spilling from her eyes. "I tripped. I'm all right."

Nicholas cocked his head. "It's not that dark."

"It is. At least for me. I can't see anything." Rose trembled.

Nicholas took her by the hand and led her the rest of the way. "I really shouldn't be this close to you," he said when they reached the door.

"Where is he?" Mr. Rissing barked from down the hall.

Nicholas squeezed Rose's hand.

"Ouch," she snapped, pulling away from him. "That hurt."

"Go on without me." He stepped away from her. "I'm going to hide until he goes away."

Rose raised her brow. "Okay."

Nicholas tucked himself into the corner by the door and listened to the pounding feet and booming voice of Peter Rissing. His stomach turned. *Why are human's so fragile?* He held his hand up to his face. *I guess I should be more careful with her...her hands are pretty small.* He looked toward the door and gulped.

"Would you just try and relax? He's probably downstairs getting something to eat," Lisa said.

"You were supposed to keep an eye on him. Now he's loose," Roland snapped.

"Tabitha needed me in the kitchen. She's cooking for three extra people."

"Damn it, Lisa!"

Nicholas held his breath.

"Would you relax, he couldn't have gone far." Lisa huffed.

"R-relax...you want me to relax when that...." Roland glanced at his niece as she tiptoed into her room. "Lisa, I don't think you realize how serious this is."

"I'll look for him around the house, all right?" Lisa tossed her hands up, but the crack Nicholas spied out from didn't reveal the two men.

"You'd better hope he's still here, or so help me..."

"Master Crispin, you don't look so good," Lisa said softly. "Why don't you go lie down? I'll see to the boy and let you know when he's back in the nursery."

"I'm fine. I'll be in my office."

Peter shifted closer to Lisa. He glanced past her then smiled at her, shaking his head. "I'll go see if he's out at the guest house."

"Okay..." Roland headed down the stairs.

When Nicholas was sure the two men had gone, he tiptoed out of his hiding place. He made his way toward Lisa and placed a hand on her shoulder. "Um...Miss Opal."

Lisa spun around and glared at him. "Where were you? You were supposed to stay in the nursery."

"I know...I'm sorry." Nicholas looked toward the staircase. "Where is Mr. Crispin's office?" he asked.

"It's the door right next to the stairs..." Lisa said softly. "Why?"

Nicholas made his way downstairs.

Lisa's jaw dropped. "W-wait, where are you going? Please don't bother Master Crispin." She hurried after him.

Nicholas stopped in front of the door, held his breath, and knocked.

"Come in."

He entered.

Roland looked up at the vermin, his gaze cold. He gestured for Nicholas to take a seat in front of the desk.

Lisa stood in the doorway, her face pale.

"Shut the door. And leave us."

She nodded, shutting the door gently behind her.

Nicholas hesitated to meet the man's eyes. When he did, he recoiled at the mental slap.

"Where were you?" Roland folded his hands on his desk.

"Hiding."

"Why weren't you in the nursery?"

"I needed fresh air," Nicholas lied, looking away from the man.

Roland slammed his hands on the desk. "You aren't to leave the nursery!"

"I know sir...I-I came to get the punishment I deserve. I disobeyed you."

Roland wrinkled his brow. "Punishment?"

"You know...when you don't follow the rules, you're supposed to get punished," Nicholas said. "So...what's my punishment?"

Roland sighed. "I didn't expect this from you."

Nicholas frowned.

Roland stood up and glared at the creature. "Miss Warren should be back with your medication soon. If I were to beat you, she'd lose it on me..." The man's expression darkened as his voice trailed off.

Nicholas cocked his head, eyeing Roland's distant gaze.

Roland blinked and shot Nicholas a stern look. "You'll be meeting with the mayor soon. If he doesn't..." Roland rubbed his temples. "Well, I'm sure you can infer. Yours will not be the only neck on the line if we can't impress him."

Nicholas' ears perked up. "Rose is yelling at her brothers again. I think they're—"

"Miss Crispin. You will address her as that from now on," Roland snapped.

Nicholas nodded.

"Just...go," Roland muttered. "I want to be alone."

"Y-you're not gonna punish me?"

"Do you want to be punished?" Roland asked, raising his brow.

"No...not really."

"Then get out."

The vermin backed away from the desk hesitantly. His dark gaze fixed on the man who glowered at him. Nicholas held his breath as he turned toward the door. Roland muttered to himself. He seemed to do that often.

Roland peered over at Nicholas and glowered. His stomach turned. *Should I beat the brute?* The animal's shoulders tensed up. He shook the thought from his head.

"What are you still doing here?"

Nicholas turned to him. "I just...I don't know."

Roland stood up.

Nicholas lowered his head. He stood still, waiting.

Roland knew that stance. He knew that look. His throat tightened.

The creature was waiting to be hit.

Roland's eyes swelled with tears. "Look, just go, okay? I'm not in the mood." Actually, the animal impressed him. One lesson, and he was willing to present himself for an error in judgment. Roland turned away from him. "Just stay in the nursery. Next time you disobey Mr. Rissing or I, there will be consequences." Roland watched the vermin's lids grow heavy. "Nicholas...are you all right?"

Nicholas nodded and gulped, stumbling into the door behind him.

Confusion swirled across the animal's face as Roland opened the door and escorted him to the staircase. "I've got him!" he shouted.

Lisa and Tabitha came hurrying into the hall.

Tabitha folded her arms across her chest. "Nasty brute."

Nicholas winced.

Roland pointed up the stairs. "Nicholas is not to leave that room until he is well."

Lisa looked away from him and nodded.

Nicholas staggered up the staircase.

"Lisa, I'm sorry...I'm not myself," Roland whispered. The look on her face, her downcast eyes, and submissive shoulders spoke volumes of his own poor behaviour.

"That damn animal and that reckless girl are putting too much pressure on you." Tabitha glowered. "You should have kept them both in the guest house."

Lisa crossed her arms. "That place is falling apart. Nicholas would've died out there."

"You're sticking up for the boy?" A hint of surprise betrayed him.

Lisa didn't answer.

Roland lowered his head, taking a seat at the bottom of the stairs. "Lisa, I'm sorry I didn't mean to—"

"You shouldn't let your fears cloud your judgment, Master Crispin," she said coldly.

Tabitha raised her brow, inching toward him. She knelt down and stretched out her hand, running it along his forehead. "Roland, I've said this more in the past few weeks than I have in the last three years —are you all right?"

Roland raised his head and nodded, forcing a smile. "I just feel...a bit under the weather is all." He turned his attention to Lisa. "Take the rest of the day off. Peter and I will keep an eye on Nicholas until Miss Warren returns."

Lisa and Tabitha glanced at one another.

"Are you sure? What about the other children? Won't they need looking after?" Lisa asked.

"We'll manage." Roland turned to Tabitha. "I'll come help you in the kitchen."

"There's no need for that. I'm being paid to do this job, am I not?"

Roland took her by the hand. "I've overworked both of you without giving either of you so much as a thank you. Please, just let me show you my gratitude?"

Tabitha patted him on the head. "You haven't cooked since you were little. You'll only be in the way." She shook her head and chuckled. "Don't look at me with those sad blue eyes."

Roland got up onto his feet and sighed. "If you won't let me help, then I'll let you leave early tonight."

Tabitha nodded. "All right, love."

As the two women left, Roland gazed up the staircase and spotted the vermin peering through the railing. There wasn't a point in lecturing the creature again. He'd shown improvement in his manners today, and Roland wanted to stay positive, especially after the meeting he and Peter had with Kurtis earlier that day. Instead, he sat at the piano and played a gentle tune that he'd once heard a maid singing while hanging the clothes one summer in his youth.

"M-Mr. Crispin, does this song have words to it?" Nicholas asked meekly.

"Mhmm...but I can't remember them." Roland stopped and looked at him. "Shouldn't you be in the nursery?"

Nicholas backed away from the railing and sat in the frame of the nursery door. He swayed to the song as Roland played.

Peter returned to the house and eyed Roland curiously. "Did you find him?"

"Yes, he came to my office. The two of us had a chat."

"I hope you gave him a good smack. Little brat."

"I didn't."

Peter leaned over his friend's shoulder. "You're joking, right?"

Roland ignored him and continued to play.

"You're too damn soft, Roland. He won't give you an ounce of respect now."

"Dianna should be here in time for dinner, right?"

Peter glared at him and nodded.

Roland played a harsh note and cringed as a sharp pain shot through his head. He rose from his seat and hurried up the stairs.

"Are you all right?" Peter called after him, furrowing his brow.

Roland was getting sick of everyone asking him that. There was nothing wrong with him. He was just stressed. "Keep an eye on the boy. Lisa..." He gulped, rubbing his temples. "I gave Lisa the rest of the day off."

Peter leaned his head back and moaned. "Damn it, Roland..."

Roland's hands shook as he entered his bedroom. He opened the top drawer on the dresser and grabbed a silver tin filled with little round tablets. He popped one in his mouth and pulled out the cork from the green decanter on the dresser, and took a swig. His eyes burned from the smell. He placed the tin back into the drawer and sat at the edge of the bed by the window, yanking the curtain shut. A throbbing pain jolted through his head. He shivered.

"I've worked myself too hard," he said softly. He scanned the room. It still had traces of his mother and father. The long emerald drapes that kept the sun from shining in, a few of his mother's sketches hanging on the wall by the bathroom, the mint green wallpaper that's floral patterns made his head spin and the dark mahogany furniture that matched the office. He hated green. It reminded him of his father, but he couldn't bring himself to change it. The only safe place in the house was the nursery. It wasn't full of ghosts. Not like here. His head bobbed down to his chest as he shut his eyes.

"You're fine. It's just another bad headache."

17

Dianna opened the front door to the Crispin estate and brushed the snow from her long grey coat. She took the medicine bottles from her pocket, gently placing them on the small end table by the door. The silence was unusual. She hung up her coat and grabbed the bottles, clutching them to her chest as she made her way into the parlour. Her green eyes panned across the room, falling on the dusty gramophone by the fireplace. She glanced over her shoulder, then knelt down, looking at the Alana Token album resting there.

"When was the last time you were played?"

A tap on the shoulder startled her. Tabitha looked Dianna up and down, a scowl on her face. "Where's Mr. Leon?"

"He said he was going to head home for the evening." Dianna hopped to her feet, her cream-coloured taffeta skirt catching against the fireplace. She cleared her throat, stepping off to the side. "It's awfully quiet."

Tabitha glowered. "Go fetch the boys for dinner. The children are already washing up."

Dianna forced a smile, taking the medicine upstairs with her to the nursery.

Caspian passed her on the stairs, turned and pointed to the bottles. "Is that for Nicholas?"

Dianna nodded. "I'm hoping he'll start to recover after taking this."

"It helped Rose a lot." Caspian kicked at the wooden railing. "How much was it?"

Dianna eyed him.

"We had to sell my father's horse to get it for Rose," he whispered.

They sold Dusty? Dianna gripped the bottles of medicine. "It's all right. I had some money put away."

Caspian nodded.

Dianna noted the pained expression on the little boy's face.

"It's my turn to set the table." Caspian shoved his hands into his pocket. "I'd better hurry before Tabitha yells at me."

Dianna watched the boy stomp downstairs. *I can't believe Roland would sell that horse.* She shook her head, straightened her back, and waltzed into the nursery. The paltry sum Roland and Peter had scrounged for the medicine had barely covered the first bottle. How much more expensive was it two months ago?

"Where's Roland?" Dianna asked her cousin.

"His bedroom. He left me alone to take care of this bloody creature."

Nicholas glowered.

"This vermin is a lost cause." Peter dragged his hands down his face.

Dianna dangled one of the bottles above his head. "He is to take this twice a day." She placed it on the nightstand and gave Nicholas a smile. "Hopefully, you'll feel better after taking this for a few days."

"You actually got it?" Peter's jaw dropped. He hugged her tight and kissed her on the forehead. "Oh, you're absolutely brilliant."

Dianna smirked. "It wasn't cheap."

"I'll pay you back."

"Tabitha asked me to come get you for dinner. Make sure you give this to Nicholas first, all right?"

Peter turned to Nicholas and scowled. "If you don't behave yourself, you aren't getting any supper."

"Peter, leave him be. I'm going to get Roland."

Dianna kept the second medicine bottle tight to her chest as she walked down the hall. She gently knocked on the bedroom door. It had been a long time since she'd been in his room. *Knowing him, it probably looks the exact same as it did five years ago.* She smirked at the thought but was surprised when Rose opened the door.

"I'm sorry for being late, but I had to finish the page I was on."

"Actually, I was looking for your uncle...did he move rooms?"

"Yes. I got too big for the nursery, and he didn't want me sharing with my brothers, so he let me have this room, and he started sleeping in the room down the hall."

"The one with the double doors?"

Rose nodded, skipping out into the hallway.

Dianna cautiously made her way to the grand room. She knocked three times and waited, cocked her head and knocked again.

"Roland, are you in there?" Dianna opened the door and found the man sleeping, his head resting on his hand. Her face softened. The last time she'd seen him like that was when they stayed at the hotel in Riversburg. She laughed to herself, remembering how shy he was lying next to her in the bed. He'd refused to lay under the covers and even put a pillow between them.

"I just want to do this the right way," he told her.

"It's not like we're doing anything. We're just going to sleep," she argued.

"It doesn't matter. I...I want to marry you first. We'll have the rest of forever to sleep beside each other."

Dianna had spent the night running her hand through his brown hair while he slept. At the time, all that mattered was that they were together. Roland had never left home before, and she knew it was hard for him to leave without saying goodbye to his brother. It was especially hard for both of them to lie to Peter and Charlotte, who were probably worried sick after waiting for them back in Tavern. Still, all she'd thought of was the faint smile on Roland's lips as he slept and the soft tickling of his hair between her fingers.

Dianna glanced around the room. The curtains were pulled shut. She shivered, looking at the wedding photo of Darius and Adeline hanging above the bed. *He looks so much like his father now.* She inched toward him, reached out her hand to pat his head, then pulled back, pressing her lips together. *What am I doing?* Gently Dianna shook his shoulder.

"Roland," she whispered.

He rubbed and opened his eyes.

Dianna handed him the bottle.

Roland held it firmly.

Dianna glanced away.

Roland drew in a deep breath and nodded, holding it out to her.

"I already gave Peter the one for Nicholas."

He eyed her.

"I got one for you. Just in case."

"Why would you do something stupid like that?" he snapped, setting the bottle next to the lamp on the nightstand.

Dianna winced, her voice catching in her throat. "You know why. Nevermind. Dinner's ready." She turned toward the door.

"I'm not hungry."

She looked back at him, watching as he stared at the medicine sitting on the nightstand. She followed his eyes as they wandered toward her reflection in the mirror at the far end of the room. *Roland never turns down food.* She stepped toward the edge of the bed.

Roland swallowed hard. "You can go."

"Are you sure you don't want anything? It smells wonderful."

Roland sniffed the air. "Tabitha made tarts." Roland made an effort to sit up.

Dianna giggled.

"What?" Roland snapped, getting to his feet and following his nose to the door.

"Oh, it's nothing." She grinned. "I just forgot how much you love sweets."

Roland pressed his lips together and walked into the hall.

Dianna looked over at the open drawer on the dresser and leaned to peek inside. She spied a small round tin left open. A few little white tablets filled the bottom. She ran her hands along the sleeves of her black sweater and glanced toward the door.

Roland stood in the hall watching her.

She slammed the drawer shut and hurried out of the room, trailing behind him toward the stairs.

Dinner was quiet, which was unusual for the Crispin's. Roland watched his niece and nephews exchange looks with one another, then with him. He glanced up at the two cousins, Peter and Dianna, who awkwardly gazed at one another, then went back to eating.

Julius tapped his spoon on the edge of his bowl and pouted. He let out a moan that caused both his siblings and uncle to direct their attention to him. Julius looked up at them and scowled. "What?"

"Stop that. It's rude," Roland said.

Julius sulked and slumped down into his seat. "May I be excused?"

Roland rubbed his temples. "No, Julius, you may not." He found himself staring at Dianna as she spooned a bit of stew into her mouth. His eyes examined her face with care, noting the differences in her appearance. He couldn't get himself to imagine the girl he'd courted so long ago. Roland lowered his head slightly, still keeping his eyes on her.

How could she have changed so much? When they first met, he'd found her annoying. He and Peter would hide from her before school started and would take off on her when she tried to tag along with them into town. Roland had even made it a ritual to pull her pigtails and toss them about. He wasn't sure why, but one day he thought of her as rather pretty, and soon his heart would pound hard in his chest when she came near, and his face would grow hot when she addressed him.

Tabitha and Adeline noticed a change in his appetite, and Roland's teachers claimed that he was constantly lost in thought.

When Lawrence arrived from his home in East Tavern for his scheduled visit, his mother pulled him aside and told him of her concerns.

Roland sank into the memory, reliving it. Lawrence had found his younger brother lying on the bench by the pond.

"Roland!" Lawrence cried, ducking behind the bench.

Roland shot up and toppled over onto the grass, his heart racing. He turned his head from side to side, gasping for air.

Lawrence reached underneath the bench and tugged on his brother's heel.

Roland yelped and scrambled on his hands and knees away from the bench. He gawked in terror as his brother climbed over the top of the bench and pounced on him, pulling him in tight for a hug.

"Get off me!" Roland pushed Lawrence's face away from him. "I said, get off!"

"Awe, didn't you miss me?" Lawrence pouted, lying down in the grass next to his brother.

Roland glared at him. "You're a grown man. Pulling pranks like that is...it's—"

"I couldn't help myself. You were too relaxed." Lawrence laughed. He looked at his brother's eyes and sat up. "You look exhausted."

"I am," Roland admitted. He pulled at the grass by his feet. "I haven't been sleeping."

"Is something bothering you?" Lawrence pestered, smoothing back his hair.

Roland shook his head. "Tabby is going to have a fit when she sees my clothes."

"She's making a cake."

"Who?"

"Tabitha." Lawrence chuckled. "I've missed her cooking."

Roland smiled.

"So, I hear you've gotten yourself into trouble at school," Lawrence smirked. "What's that about?"

"I wasn't paying attention."

"What were you paying attention to?"

Roland's face flushed pink. "I've just been too tired to listen to those boring old crows yak on and on about the importance of trade."

"Trade is important." Lawrence teased. "Without it, I wouldn't have been able to buy Wendy that lovely silk scarf."

"You're such a pain."

"Yes, I know."

Roland found himself laughing aloud, gazing off into space past Peter's head at the painting of the tree by the pond.

Tabitha smacked his wrist. "Elbows off the table."

Roland blinked and folded his hands into his lap. He gave Tabitha an apologetic look.

"You've barely touched your food."

"I'm sorry. My mind was—"

"Some place else. Yes, I know."

Peter smirked. "A little too much wine, maybe?"

Roland grimaced. "You know I don't drink."

"You poured yourself a glass," Dianna pointed.

Roland cocked his head and eyed his wine glass. "I don't recall doing so."

"You did," Caspian muttered. "And you made eyes at Miss— ouch!" His sister pinched him. He glared at her. "Why'd you do that?"

Rose shot him a threatening glance. "You should remember to think before you speak."

Caspian stuck out his tongue.

Roland pushed the wine away and frowned at his meal. "Tabitha, have you brought anything to Nicholas yet?"

"Not yet." She tucked another serviette into Julius' shirt.

Roland grabbed his bowl and a piece of bread and headed toward the stairs.

"Aren't you going to eat anything?" Tabitha knitted her brow.

"I'm not hungry." He shrugged off his unease and headed for the second floor.

Roland opened the nursery door and found the vermin flipping through a book. "I brought you something to eat."

"Okay."

"What are you reading?" Roland placed the food on the nightstand.

Nicholas' eyes grew wide. He shrugged. "Just something Rose gave me." A blush filled his cheeks. "I mean, Miss Crispin."

Roland slid the book away from him gently. "Midnight Garden. How do you like the book so far?"

"It um...it's all right. I haven't read very much."

Roland nodded. "Which part are you at?"

Nicholas hung his head. "They entered the garden."

"That's fairly early on in the novel." Roland pointed. He opened up to the first page and traced his fingers along his brother's faded signature. He smiled. "Promise me that you'll be careful with this?"

Nicholas nodded.

"I'll be back later to give you your medication."

Nicholas raised his head. "I already took some."

"You did?"

"Mr. Rissing gave it to me before he left for dinner."

Roland nodded. He looked toward his brother's old bed, at the opposite end of the room. "Okay. Try and eat as much as you can."

His gaze fell on the book. "I've got some other books that you can read. There's a library upstairs. What kind of stories do you like?"

Nicholas averted his eyes. "I can't...um, I can't really read."

Roland turned to him and pressed his lips together. "Can you recognize letters or symbols? Do you know what your name looks like?"

Nicholas shrugged. "My brother and sister can write. They went to school."

"Why can't you?"

"I didn't go to school. I wasn't allowed."

Roland frowned. "Eat your supper."

"Okay." Nicholas sat at the table beneath the window and woofed down the stew. He gave Roland a broad, toothy grin. "Ish 'ood," he said with his mouth full. He swallowed hard and tore at the bread with his teeth. "Danks Mitter Ispin."

"Please don't talk with food in your mouth. You're spitting it all over the place...and you could choke." Roland marched over to the table and took a seat across from him.

Nicholas' eyes flickered as Roland spooned up the stew and waved it in front of his face.

"It's important to take the time to enjoy your food. You should take small bites. In this case, try not to slurp." He handed Nicholas the spoon.

Nicholas nodded. He opened his mouth and bit down on the spoon.

Roland's eyes widened, watching the vermin's fangs tear away at the beef. *Those are sharp.* He cleared his throat, scratching his head. "Could you try not to chew with your mouth open?"

Nicholas glowered, smacking his lips together.

Is he trying to test me? Roland craned his neck. "Nicholas, could you please chew with your mouth closed?"

Nicholas swallowed and grabbed another mouthful of stew. "*Ha.*" He popped the spoon into his mouth, pulled it out and wrinkled his nose as he chewed quietly.

"Next time, try and keep your elbows off the table. Okay?"

Nicholas nodded.

Roland stood up and smiled. "I'll see you later then."

"'Kay." Nicholas waved to him. "*Danara.*"

"No vermin words, remember?" Roland shut the door. He shook his head and forced himself to return downstairs to the dining room.

18

The following morning, Nicholas tossed back and forth in the bed and groaned. He turned onto his side and looked at the other bed near the door. Both beds had the same red sheets and white pillows. They would've matched perfectly if not for the paintings on the frames. Nicholas slid onto his belly and looked at the headboard of his own bed.

The painting there was of a bear playing the drums. *Why would a bear ever play music? Humans are so Bloka.* His eyes lit up as he glanced at the corner of the headboard. Something was carved into the bed—symbols like the ones in Rose's books. He stretched out his hand and ran a finger along it. *It's been here a long time.*

The boy crawled out of bed and scanned the room. He'd spent so much time lying in bed that he'd never actually looked around. Nicholas wandered over to the closet and turned the knob. Clothes hung there, as they should. The boy glanced down by his feet at a frayed stuffed bear and picked it up. *These humans really like bears.* He picked up the teddy bear, ran his hand along the sewn smile. The bear's button eye didn't match its other at all, and the thread of its mouth unravelled a bit. It was definitely a lot older than Harry,

Julius' bear. Nicholas brought the bear over to the bed, sat down, and smiled.

"*Hallet* bear." He frowned, shaking the bear's hand. "*Matya Na Elde* Nicholas. *Naska Daknov Na?*"

Nicholas had the bear tilt its head and lowered his voice into a growl. "Hey, you can't use those words Mr. Slayden, you *Bloka!*" He smacked himself in the head with the bear and leaned back.

"*Doksot!*"

"Watch your mouth!" the bear grumbled. "If your grandmother heard you talking like that, she'd smack your behind with a stick!"

Nicholas smirked. "I must be really bored...huh bear?"

"We should get outta this place," the bear growled. "They'll skin you alive and eat you for dinner. They're fattening you up, Nicholas. That's why the kids are always giving you snacks. Humans eat animals. That's what they did to me! Skinned me and stuffed me."

Nicholas scrunched up his face. *I do feel a bit better. If I'm quiet, maybe I can sneak downstairs and out the front door.* His heart stopped. "I...but I don't know where to go...and Rose and Miss Warren—"

"Are humans. Or did you forget?" the bear snapped.

Nicholas rubbed his head. "Why the heck am I talking to myself like a damn *Verjik?*" He looked at the bear and scrunched up his face. "You have sharp teeth, and humans make toys of you and paint you on their furniture...I have sharp teeth, and they beat me and spit on me...tell me I can't be myself. Study me...domesticate...whatever that even means. I'm not *Bloka,* and I'm not some little kid either. But I... I'm more scared of leaving than I am of staying. If I go, I won't have any more medicine, and something bad might happen to them."

He pressed the bear to his chest.

"Human's get killed all the time for helping vermin...I don't want anyone to hurt Miss Warren or Rose...or even those *Verjik* kids...." His ears twitched at the clip of footsteps on the stairs. *Too late to run now.* He sat up as the footsteps made their way to the door. *Only one person.* As the knob turned, he pulled his legs up onto the bed.

ARDIN PATTERSON

"Were you...talking to someone?" Roland asked, glancing around the room.

"Just myself," Nicholas mumbled. "Since no one else is home anyways...not that they're allowed in here."

Roland pressed his hand against Nicholas' forehead. "Your temperature seems to have gone down." He eyed the teddy bear then shot his head in the direction of the closet. "Why do you have that?"

Nicholas shrugged. "I just found it."

Roland snatched it from him, glaring at the boy. "I...it's old. I..."

"Is it yours?"

Roland sat down next to him and nodded.

"You look a bit too old for toys, Mr. Crispin."

"So, do you. Besides, I haven't seen him in years. I...here." He handed the bear back to Nicholas and frowned.

"Hey, how old are you, anyhow? You don't look much bigger than my brother." Nicholas eyed him.

"How old is your brother?"

"Eighteen."

"Hmm...I was eighteen six years ago," Roland smirked. "Can you do math?"

Nicholas wrinkled his nose. "Just because I can't read doesn't mean I can't count."

"Okay then, what's eighteen plus six."

"Is this a part of my domestication? Because sometimes it seems like I'm just doing a bunch of pointless stuff."

Roland sighed. "It is, and it isn't. I'd have you doing more, but I really don't think you're up to it yet."

"Up to what?"

Roland shook his head. "Maybe if you prove to me that you can do math, I'll let you do something else."

Nicholas tapped his chin. "Eighteen is...*Vochin. Vochin, Ata, Schek, Elde...*"

"Um, you're speaking in—"

148

Nicholas held up his fingers. *"Vasat In, Vasat Va, Vasat Tra, Vasat Schrei*...Oh! You're *Vasat*...I mean twenty-four."

Roland furrowed his brow. "You can count in your language and ours?"

Nicholas nodded. "It's faster to count in Valdin Zungta."

Roland scratched his head. "You do know you're not allowed to use those words, anymore right? At least...not in front of people."

"Iya Nasei."

Roland glared at him.

"I...I mean, I know. I know. It's just, I'm always worried about my ears and my teeth, and I have to be gentle, and I have to wear shirts all the time, even when I'm sweating buckets."

"Who said you had to wear a shirt all the time?" Roland asked.

"Rose–Miss Crispin."

Roland snorted.

"Because it's not decent or something? My sister never got mad at me for it when we were at home or when we went swimming. I don't see what the big deal is." Nicholas turned to the headboard of the bed. "By the way, what does that carving say down there?" He pointed.

Roland leaned back and squinted.

"Well?"

"Roland."

Nicholas nodded. "So, this is your bed?"

"It used to be. You've definitely been in this room too long if you're starting to get into everything."

"Whose bed is that one then?"

"M-my older brother's."

"The one that died?"

Roland nodded.

"I'm sorry."

Roland shrugged. "It happened five years ago."

"When you were *Kyevin*...nineteen."

"Yeah."

"Julius is five...so he was just a baby then?"

"Yep." Roland lowered his head. "Nicholas um...listen, don't mention it around my niece and nephews, all right? It was...it was scary for them. I just—we don't talk about it."

"I actually thought you were their father when you first brought me here. But then, you didn't look very old so..."

Roland massaged his knuckles. "Yeah, it was Rose's birthday when we found you."

"It was? I thought her birthday was when she had that big party with all the loud people downstairs?"

Roland shook his head. "That was just the day of the party."

"Humans are such...well, you know, you just do stuff that's well...*Verjik*." Nicholas muttered, rubbing the back of his neck.

"I don't know what that means, but I'm going to assume it was insulting."

"It's not...that bad." Nicholas shrugged. "It's like...it's sort of like saying someone is strange, I guess."

Roland raised his brow. "Your type tried to burn down West Tavern during the war and went around painting themselves in human blood, and you call us strange?"

"*Deisso*. Why would anyone want to cover themselves in someone else's blood?"

"I don't know. I just...well, that's what we learned in school."

"We paint ourselves, yes, but with paint...like makeup. And we do it during harvest season."

Roland raised his brow.

"When I first came here, I actually thought you were all trying to poison me," Nicholas said softly. "I heard humans were masters at poison."

Roland laughed. "We didn't even realize what you were at first. Not until I heard there'd been an...incident nearby."

Nicholas shrugged. "I knew what you all were right away. Human's smell really bad."

"We...what?"

"I mean...it's not bad necessarily, it's just strong. Like in Dinara, the humans we traded with always dumped oils and things on themselves. It made my nose itch."

"It's called soap."

"We use soap too."

"Okay, cologne and perfume then."

Nicholas raised his eyebrows.

"It comes in these bottles, and you spray yourself or pat it on to smell nice."

"Yeah, I don't think so."

Roland laughed.

Nicholas lowered his head. "Y-you aren't really...that scary, actually, Mr. Crispin."

Roland eyed him. "I'm not?"

"No. I mean, I figured if the kids liked you, then you probably weren't a bad person. Mr. Rissing scares me, though. He's always yelling at me whenever I do something—right or wrong. Sometimes... it's just, I don't know what you two are talking about." Nicholas fiddled with the bear and sighed. "Even Miss Warren told me you aren't actually a jerk all the time."

"Peter's not a bad guy. He's just worried we won't be able to domesticate you in time. We tried to get an extension but..." He eyed Nicholas. "How strong are you usually?"

"I'm stronger and faster than my brother Micah. He's only a half-vermin. I'm a full-blood *Valdinok*."

"What's a *Valdinok*?"

"Me. A vermin. It's what we call ourselves in our language. Humans are *Hiloven*. Half-vermin's we call them *Valvenok*."

Roland nodded. "So, you're stronger than your older brother?"

"And faster."

"And faster." Roland scanned the boy. "But you're not very big."

Nicholas groaned. "I'm still growing, okay? Everyone's always calling me little. I'm not that small."

"I didn't mean to offend you."

"Yeah, well, my sister still acts like I'm a baby all the time. So, does everyone in our pack. I always get left out of everything because I'm the youngest." Nicholas's stomach gurgled.

Roland nodded. "Why don't you come downstairs to the kitchen. Lisa and Tabby went out anyway, and I'd like to go over your table manners with you again. See what you remember."

Nicholas groaned loudly, leaning his head back.

"You hungry or not?"

Nicholas glared at him. "Yeah."

"Leave Pippi here." Roland pointed to the bear.

"Hey, what's with you humans and bears anyway?" Nicholas followed him down to the kitchen.

"What do you mean?"

"You know, you got them painted on things and made into toys and have them playing the drums. It's just creepy."

"Creepy?"

"Bears don't play drums."

Roland shrugged.

"Well, what's with the bear thing?"

"I don't really get it. They're cute, I guess. See, my brother got the bear as a gift for..."

"You?"

"No. My parents had a hard time having children."

Nicholas nodded.

"Laurie liked bears a lot, so when my mother was pregnant, she painted them on some of the furniture in the nursery. If you look at the nightstands, they have little flowers painted on them. Those were from the twins." Roland mumbled, opening the pantry. "My mother talks about them sometimes. My brother kind of told me about Darian. It's complicated...I guess burying four children broke her heart."

"Your family has a lot of, well, dead people."

"All families have dead people. Just some are already dead before we come along, and some die while we're still here. Death is just a natural part of life."

Nicholas nodded. "I...still it's, well, I've never had anyone I care about die before."

Roland frowned. "Yeah, well, I should've died years ago."

"W-what?"

Roland pressed his lips together. "Did you want a sandwich?"

Nicholas nodded. "Uh, Mr. Crispin, you say really, um, strange things."

Roland turned to him. "Do I?"

"Yeah." Nicholas sat down at the table and eyed him. "Like before, when I was in that other house, you said something about dying too."

Roland recoiled, rubbing the back of his neck.

"Are you sick, Mr. Crispin?"

"I'm better now."

"You don't look better. Did you have the fever?"

Roland narrowed his eyes then shook his head. "They didn't know what was wrong with me. I was just sick."

Nicholas nodded slowly.

"Sandwich, yes or no?"

"Okay."

"Yes or no."

"Yes, please."

Roland tossed the bread onto the counter and opened the fridge. "We have leftover beef."

"I love beef...my teeth just want to rip it to pieces."

Roland smirked. "You're a very messy eater."

"You people keep forgetting to feed me. I mean, I'm up there all day starving, and then one of you *Bloka* remembers I need food. If it weren't for the kids bringing me stuff, I probably would've died of starvation."

Roland blushed. "I'm sorry, it's just...when Tabby isn't here, I usually forget."

"You forget that you need food to live?"

"Yes, actually. I only seem to remember when I'm hungry."

Nicholas nodded. "Hey, is it strange if...if I like talking to you?"

Roland shrugged. "Peter might say it's bad for me to be so casual with you, but I'm tired, and I honestly don't like yelling at you all the time. This is far more manageable. Maybe Dianna is right."

"Talking to you kind of reminds me of talking to my brother," Nicholas said quietly. "Micah's always been really smart and stuff. He went to school with some human kids in Dinara...until they kicked him out."

"He got kicked out?"

"For fighting. Zana left after that, too. Nyla was really upset. Micah was going to go to college someplace over here, I think."

"Riversburg?"

"Maybe, I don't really know," Nicholas muttered. "Is school fun?"

Roland handed him a sandwich and scratched his head. "Well, I didn't really go to school for long. Peter made it fun, but my teachers were really annoying. Then college...college was all right, I guess. I mean, I didn't really want to do vermin studies, but...well...."

"What's vermin studies?"

"We study you and your kind. But I'm realizing my professors were extremely misinformed. Nothing in those stupid textbooks was even remotely accurate. I mean...the teeth thing, yes, but your language doesn't sound like...well, they described it as rough and vile. It sounds more musical to me."

Nicholas attempted to take a small bite of his sandwich.

"Remember, don't chew with your mouth open."

Nicholas nodded.

"And you remember what Tabitha said about the elbows on the table?"

Nicholas pulled his elbows back.

"Try to eat over the plate." Roland pointed. "And you didn't put the napkin in your lap."

Nicholas put the sandwich down and glared at him. "Why do I need a napkin for a sandwich?"

"To keep your clothes clean," Roland said firmly.

"Humans must hate doing laundry."

"We do, actually. Especially when we have little girls around who own over a hundred different dresses."

Nicholas smirked. "Rose does have a lot of dresses."

"I can't understand it. I mean, I won't deny that I used to buy her a lot of clothes when she was younger. I just, I don't know. It was kind of fun taking her out and watching her get all excited. Now it's just work. I can see why my brother was always telling me to stop buying her things."

Nicholas laughed. "My sister doesn't have a single dress. She just wears pants."

"Pants are more practical if you ask me. I don't think I've ever seen Rose in a pair of pants, not even while she's doing her chores. The girls I knew growing up wore pants on the weekends or after school. Even Rose's mother preferred them when she was working in the garden...Rose is very particular about her clothes."

Nicholas blushed. "I can't really picture her in pants. Rose is very...gentle."

"Gentle?" Roland chuckled. "My niece is not gentle. She used to...well, she's rough when she wants to be."

"Humans are not rough. When I held her hand, she said it hurt."

"You what?"

"When I was holding her hand before, she said that it hurt. Humans are really soft. I always have to be extra careful. I mean, her hands are also really small, so I guess maybe I should've expected that."

Roland sat down at the table and eyed him. "Why were you holding her hand?"

Nicholas's ears twitched. He straightened his back and bit his lip. "I was scared...and I just kinda grabbed it."

Roland leaned toward him. "Mhmm."

"I didn't mean to hurt her, honest. I just kinda forgot how little she was."

"You're only a year older than her."

"I meant her size. She's small."

"You're small."

Nicholas glared at him. "Are you making fun of me?"

Roland grinned. "I might be."

"Well, stop." Nicholas groaned.

"What are you gonna do about it, huh?"

Nicholas raised his brow.

Roland leaned back and laughed. "I'm sorry. I'll stop. You're funny to watch, that's all."

"Funny how?"

Roland shrugged. "Eh, maybe I'm just easily amused."

Nicholas turned his head, listening. He smiled. "Miss Warren's back."

Roland raised his brow.

"Hello?" Dianna called.

"In the kitchen!" Nicholas shouted, sitting up straight. He pulled the napkin onto his lap, brushing it out neatly, then adjusted himself, beef sandwich in hand, sure to open his mouth only enough to take a nibble.

Roland's eyes widened. "W-what you...you—"

Dianna strolled into the room and removed her gloves. "You're downstairs?"

Nicholas gave her a big grin. "Mr. Crispin said I could have my lunch here today."

Roland's eye twitched as he stared at the vermin.

Nicholas tried his best not to laugh. *I told them they didn't need to teach me how to eat. Even vermin know the difference between good and bad table manners.* He smiled at Roland and turned back to Dianna. "Where did you go this morning?"

"Originally, I was going to go see someone, but um..." Dianna rubbed her hands together, a gloom washing over her. "While I was in town, I overheard someone say that the police are looking for you."

Nicholas put his sandwich down. "I–w-why?"

"Well, Vincent Gray apparently has them all out searching," Dianna said softly. "You don't think Dr. Gray told him anything, do you?"

Roland pressed his lips together. "He's good at keeping secrets."

"Are you sure?"

"I've known the man my whole life," Roland said firmly. "I trust him."

Nicholas' hands shook. "T-they're going to kill me."

"I won't let them hurt you." Dianna hurried to his side. "I promise. Nicholas, look at me." She turned his head toward her. "I'll keep you safe."

"We both will," Roland reassured him. "And Peter too. You just, you have to do your best to cooperate. I'll try not to yell as much anymore, and you try to control your emotions. Unfortunately, there's not much I can do about Peter."

"Like you've ever controlled your emotions," Dianna snapped.

"Not the time," Roland muttered.

Dianna blushed. "Right. You're right. I'm sorry."

Nicholas looked at the two of them and nodded. "I won't let them hurt you either."

"You don't need to worry about us." Dianna took his hand. "We'll be all right."

"Humans who harbour or protect vermin illegally within non-vermin zones shall be hung by the neck until dead," Nicholas quoted. "First thing you learn growing up with half-vermins. Humans are *Verjik*. They just kill and kill and kill, and they don't stop."

Dianna took his hands and squeezed them gently. "No one is going to be killing anyone." She turned to Roland. "We'll keep you up in the nursery and just explain to the other children that they shouldn't be mentioning you to anyone."

Roland nodded slowly. "If anyone asks about you, we'll say that you were a boy who was injured during the vermin attacks on the farms."

Nicholas frowned. "But that would send them after my pack."

"We still don't even know if your pack was responsible for that."

Nicholas shrugged. "There's been talk of merging from all over the country. I wouldn't be surprised if another group came through here around the same time. I'm just..."

"You're scared," Dianna said. "And it's okay. So are we." She brushed his hair back out of his face and smiled at him. "But the mayor promised that you'd be safe with us."

Nicholas smiled back at her.

"Now, I did notice when I came in how neatly you were eating," she said, laughing. "A little too neat, perhaps."

"I was trying to show off," Nicholas admitted.

Roland furrowed his brow. "You really are like a dog...you bark when people are at the door, and you're constantly trying to get praise from her."

Nicholas glared at him. "I'm not a dog."

"I...I didn't mean it like that. It's just that you're sort of...you're like a puppy."

"A puppy is a baby dog," Nicholas growled.

"Maybe just...don't compare him to animals." Dianna shook her head.

Roland nodded, shoving his sandwich into his mouth.

Nicholas' jaw dropped. "How come you can eat like that, and I can't?"

Roland swallowed his food and sulked. "I eat like this when I'm upset."

Dianna giggled.

"I eat like that when I'm happy, but I get in trouble for not taking small bites and for chewing too loud!" Nicholas groaned. "You make me hate eating."

Roland leaned his head back. "I'm not sure if I want to hit something or just hide from everyone."

"Or, you know, you could just sigh, like you always do," Dianna smirked.

"I don't always sigh."

"You do."

Roland sighed and glared at her. "Leave me alone."

Dianna sat down in the chair next to Nicholas and took off her coat. "You'd better hope your niece doesn't hear anything about Nicholas in town."

Roland nodded. "She's...well, she always thinks she needs to know everything about everything."

"Especially now, it is best she doesn't find out."

Nicholas tugged on the sleeve of his shirt. "They...um...humans, they don't punish children when their parents do bad things, do they?"

Dianna shook her head. "Not usually."

Nicholas drew in a deep breath. "Okay. Just making sure."

19

Rose tiptoed out of her room, careful to close the door as quietly as possible. She held her breath, listening to it squeak shut. *Stop door! Please stop. Pretty please.*

"Going somewhere?" Roland asked.

Rose jolted away from the door, eyes wide. "W-where did you come from?"

Roland raised his brow, shaking his head. "Listen, I really need to talk to you."

"I...um...well, I was..."

"Going to the nursery?"

"Well...yes but—"

Roland shoved his hands into his pocket and nodded to the library door. "Come along."

Rose nodded, rubbing her hands together as she sheepishly followed her uncle. She shivered in the dark on the steps. "Uncle Roland...I...I can't see so, so could we maybe—"

Roland stopped on the steps and turned to her. "The dark won't hurt you."

"I know, but..." she pressed her hand to her chest and gulped.

Her throat tightening as the darkness swam around them. It distorted the look on her uncle's face. She tried to draw in a breath, but her lungs refused.

Roland came toward her and took her hand. "You like the library, right?"

Rose nodded, squeezing him tight.

"Don't worry, I've got you," he said gently. "We're almost there."

Rose forced in a deep breath as he opened the door to the library. Through the window, the moon hovered above. She stared at it while Roland turned on the light.

"I'm sorry, I should've had someone come and fix the light in the staircase."

"It's okay," Rose whispered.

Roland ran a hand along the row of shelves. "I haven't been up here in a long time."

Rose sat down on the couch and let out a sigh. "So, what did you want to talk about?"

"Nicholas." Roland turned to her. "I want to talk to you about Nicholas."

"What about him?"

"Well, he um...have you told anyone about him staying here?"

Rose scanned his face. "Was I not supposed to?"

Roland sighed. "No, I mean...I didn't think about it at the time."

"Think about what?"

"Nicholas was in a bad situation before he came to us." Roland sat down beside her. "He was running away from some pretty mean folks. I just—well, we all need to do our best to protect him until he gets better."

Rose gripped her nightgown and bit her lip. "Why didn't he say anything?"

"He told me. I just didn't think about it until Miss Warren mentioned it this morning." Roland interlaced his fingers and stretched them back. "So, just to keep you and your brothers safe... and Nicholas too...could you not say anything about him to anyone?"

Rose nodded quickly. "Of course!" She lowered her head. "What sort of people was he running away from?"

Roland glanced away from her. "I'm not really sure. A rough crowd. Really bad. That's all I know."

"Were they the ones that hurt him? Gave him those bruises and that cut on his leg?"

"Yes, I think so."

Rose clasped her hands together. "So, why are we talking about this up in the library? You could've told me downstairs."

"I also wanted to speak to you about sneaking into the nursery at night. That needs to stop. It's inappropriate. And Nicholas mentioned he grabbed your hand or something. He hasn't tried anything, has he?"

"What do you mean?"

"I don't know..." Roland muttered. "Whatever it is, boys try to do."

"You're a boy. You should know."

"I do know. That's *why* I don't want you going in there at night." He puffed up his cheeks and groaned loudly. "It's not that I don't trust you or him, but I was a teenager once and, well, I just don't want you to get hurt, okay?"

"Nicholas wouldn't hurt me." Rose shook her head. "And you're such a hypocrite. Tom has been in my room before, and you've never said anything about it."

"I knew he was there. It's different. No one was sneaking around, no one was ill or in their PJs, and I've known him since he was born. We just met Nicholas. It's, well, different."

"No, it isn't. Both of them are teenage boys."

"I...you...why are you like this?" Roland smirked.

"Like what?"

"Like your father."

"I...I don't know."

Roland scratched his head. "We, um...we haven't spoken about them in a while."

Rose shifted in her seat and nodded, scrunching her toes.

Roland eyed her. "I just…"

"We don't have to," Rose said quickly.

Roland leaned his head back. "I know I haven't been the best role model. I really messed things up. I mean, you wouldn't be so scared of the dark if—"

"Uncle Roland."

He frowned.

Rose nudged him with her foot and smiled gently. "You're doing fine with Caspian and Julius. They love you. We don't have to talk about any of it if you don't want to."

"It's not that I don't want…I just can't."

"I get it."

"I'm sorry."

"It's okay." Rose wrapped her arms around him.

Roland nodded and got up off the couch. "I wanted to give you something. Your grandmother painted it." He went behind the couch and pulled out a painting of a horse. "She…well, she said it was for me but, she doesn't even know who I am."

"Dusty!"

"Yeah." Roland laughed. "I thought back about that book you got for your birthday, the one with the horse on it. I realized that the horse sort of looks like him."

Rose nodded.

"So, I thought, maybe we could put this up in here or in your room somewhere."

"When is Grandmother coming home?"

Roland shrugged, leaning up against the couch. "I don't know, sweetheart. When she's better."

"Will she get better? Can I see her?"

Roland scratched his head and shook it.

"Also, why did you and Miss Warren break up? I've heard some crazy stories about you two recently."

Roland gritted his teeth. "That's not something I want to talk about either."

Rose rolled her eyes. "I wasn't that little, you know. I do remember seeing her at the house when I was visiting."

"You do?"

She nodded. "It wasn't until recently that I realized she was the same girl. I mean, I haven't really seen you around any girls since Grandmother left."

"You're so nosy."

"I just want you to be happy."

"I'm plenty happy."

"Uncle Roland, I'm serious."

"So am I." Roland laughed. "You and your brothers make me very happy. I don't need anything or anyone else."

"What about Tabitha and Mr. Leon or Lisa?"

"Well, Tabby is different. She raised me."

Rose put down the painting and turned to him. "Well, I don't think you should be so mean to Miss Warren. Just because you two aren't in love anymore doesn't mean you can't be friends."

"Oh, I definitely can't be friends with her," Roland snapped.

"Ugh, you're acting like a child."

"No, I'm not. You don't even know what happened. You were seven."

"Well, from what I've heard, it was some tragic forbidden love story. One that would make your heartache and then burst." Rose threw herself onto the couch, placing a hand over her forehead. "And one fateful day, the two of you, locked in an embrace were—"

Roland shook his head, laughing.

"Look, Uncle Roland, you're very handsome and very...um...well, you're not that interesting, you're mostly boring, but maybe that's why you two were destined to be together?" Rose sat up. "I mean, Miss Warren is so amazing, and she's travelled places, and she knows so much."

Roland furrowed his brow. "I wasn't always boring."

"Yeah, you used to be fun, but then you started acting like every other adult."

"Well, I have to be an adult."

"I know, but we used to go out and buy sweets and play at the park, and you used to make up silly songs for us," Rose said quietly. "You don't do that anymore."

Roland pulled himself up over the couch and sat down. "You're right. I'm not much fun to be around." He crossed his legs, giving her a gentle nudge with his elbow. "But like I said, I have to be an adult. I can't be doing what I used to do. I wasn't exactly a model person, Rose."

She slid away and looked out the window. "You used to come home really late all the time, get into fights with Grandmother and Tabby. You'd disappear for days but, I mean before that, before we all came to live here, you were my friend. Now, you're just my uncle."

Roland pressed his lips together. "Well, you're growing up too, and I think we needed the boundaries. I liked having fun with you and Cas' but, well, you two don't listen then."

"Lisa has fun with us, and she's Alicia's mom."

"I know. I just I don't know how to be like that anymore."

Rose frowned.

"Tell you what, how about tomorrow we all do something?"

"Can I invite Miss Warren?"

"I...sure. *Fine*, I guess."

Rose beamed. "What are we going to do?"

"I don't know. What would you like to do?"

"Well, Julius and Caspian wanted to go sledding."

"Sledding?"

She nodded.

"I guess we could find a good hill somewhere."

Rose hugged him tightly and kissed his cheek.

"Now, I think you need to get back to bed."

"Um...could I actually sleep in here?"

"Last time I let you do that, you were up-all-night reading."

"But the moon is so pretty, and the stairs are extra dark, and I just like it here."

Roland nodded. "All right, but if I come back up here later tonight and you're still awake, you're going right back to your room, young lady."

Rose winked at him and stuck out her tongue. He laughed and set out an extra blanket for his niece.

The next afternoon, Roland groaned, dragging the sled up the hill. Julius hopped behind him in the deep snow, following in his boot prints.

"Uncle Roland, you know, did you know what happened at school before?" Julius asked.

Roland glanced back. "What?"

"Mrs. Hansen said I was a really good speller."

"Oh?" Roland grinned. "I'm glad to hear it."

"And Joey Carpenter threw up, so he had to go see Dr. Gray."

Roland bit his lip. "That's not good."

"Yeah, he's *contanus*."

"Pardon?"

"Con-tay-nus!" Julius shouted. "Don't you know what *contanus* means?"

"Contagious!" Rose cried. "For the millionth time!"

Julius glared at her.

"Oh!" Roland laughed. "Joey is contagious?"

Julius nodded. "He got the fever, so he can't come to school."

Roland frowned. "I see. Well, you just remember what Dr. Gray told you when Rose was sick."

"Wash my hands and don't share snacks?"

Roland nodded. He glanced back at Dianna and Rose as they started to laugh. He sighed and placed the sled at the top of the hill. He turned to Caspian and smiled. "You okay, Cas'?"

"Yep!" Caspian grunted, dragging another sled behind him.

"Are you sure you don't need any help?" Dianna looked back at the boy.

"I got this, ma'am. I'm pretty strong."

"Oh, well, all right." Dianna grinned.

Rose shook her head, plopping her sled next to Roland's at the top of the hill. "This is a really good spot, Uncle Roland."

"It's so high up!" Julius said, jumping up and down. "We can even see Thompson's hotel from up here and the library. Oh, and the docks!"

Roland reached into his coat pocket and pulled out a tissue. Snot dribbled down Julius' nose. He shook his head and knelt to wipe it.

"My boogers are running away!" Julius laughed.

Rose scrunched up her face and pretended to gag.

Roland shot her a threatening glare. "He's little."

"I *know,* but both of them are so gross."

"I'm not gross, Rosie." Julius frowned. "I never even pick my nose."

Roland held up Julius' mitten covered hand and waved it in front of his face. "But you still bite your nails."

"So does she!" Julius snapped, crossing his arms. "Everyone does bad habits, you know."

"That's true." Roland turned back to Caspian as he threw the sled against the others. "All good there?"

Caspian nodded, trying to catch his breath. "You're old. How come you got up here first?"

"How old do you think I am?" Roland laughed.

"Older than me," Caspian grumbled. "Aren't old people supposed to be slow?"

"Uncle Roland's a papa, not a grandpa," Julius said firmly. "Papa's are really strong."

Roland flinched and turned toward Dianna. "When was the last time you went sledding?"

She shrugged. "I honestly can't remember."

"Last time I went, I fell off the sled, and snow got into my coat, and I was really cold." Julius pouted. "But then I got some hot chocolate, so I was all warmed up!"

"I miss the warm weather already." Roland shivered, rubbing his shoulders.

"What?" Caspian cried. "But what about the Frost Pageant or the Snowflake Ball or all the presents?"

"I don't get any presents. I'm the one who buys them," Roland said.

"Y-you do?" Julius whispered, eyeing him. "But I thought the little Snow Fairies brought them?"

Dianna's eyes widened.

"T-they do! I mean the ones that *I* give you, not those ones."

"Those are magic presents," Rose said, giving Julius a smile. "That's why the Snow Fairies wrap them in gold."

"Oh...okay." Julius sat on the sled. "Who wants to ride with me?"

Rose and Caspian glanced at one another.

Caspian slammed his finger onto his nose and stuck out his tongue. "Not it!"

Roland groaned.

"I'll ride with you." Dianna climbed in behind him.

Julius smirked. "Ha, ha! I get Miss Warren!"

Caspian and Rose glared at him.

"You can take Uncle Roland. I wanna go extra fast so—"

"Well, so do I." Rose snapped. "And I'm the oldest, so I should get to go by myself."

"Yeah, well, you're only three years older, smarty pants."

Roland marched over and grabbed the other two sleds. "Julius' sled can sit three people."

"Great, you ride with them then!" Caspian grinned. "Rose and I can go by ourselves."

Roland furrowed his brow. "But I'm the oldest."

"But, Uncle Roland, I always have to go with Julius!" Caspian moaned. "And I've never been on a hill this big before." Caspian stared up at him and batted his lashes. "Can I please go by myself?"

Roland sighed. "Yeah, fine, have fun."

Rose's jaw dropped. "What about me?"

"Here," he grumbled, shoving the other at her. "But you're both carrying them back up here."

Rose smiled. "Thanks, Uncle Roland!"

Roland shook his head and wandered over to Julius and Dianna.

"And then I just rolled it up into a little ball and put that on top, so my snowman was super big!" Julius said.

"Oh wow!" Dianna laughed. "That's crazy!"

"It was so super crazy." Julius nodded. "But he got broked because Caspian's friends accidentally broked him."

"Oh no."

"They said sorry."

"Well, maybe you can make another one?"

"Yeah, but I'm going to do one hundred million snowballs for his body!"

Roland smirked. "One hundred million?"

Julius nodded. "And it'll be as big as our house!"

"Whoa, that's big." He laughed.

"Are you gonna come ride with us?" Julius asked.

"I guess so. Your brother and sister apparently think I'm too old and boring to go with them."

"That's mean. I'm going to kick their butts!"

"Julius."

"I mean, bums."

Dianna burst out laughing. "Why don't we race them?"

"Yeah! Let's race those booger babies!"

"Julius." Roland snapped.

"Yes?"

"Let's kick their butts," Roland smirked, crossing his arms. He spun toward them and grinned. "Hey losers, we're racing!"

Rose and Caspian turned to them.

"You can't beat us; you've got three people." Caspian snorted.

"Loser has to run around in their long johns," Roland smirked. "Outside."

"What?"

"You in, or are you chicken?"

"Roland, seriously?" Dianna laughed.

Roland pulled the sled toward the edge of the hill. "Hope you wore an extra pair like I told you to."

"But I don't want anyone to see my underwear," Julius whined.

"It'll be fine." Roland pushed the sled. "You two ready or what?"

"Oh, I'm ready," Caspian snapped. "Ready to make you eat my dust!"

"This is so dumb." Rose groaned, climbing onto her sled.

Roland eyed them carefully. "Ready...set...."

His niece and nephew glared at him.

"Go!"

Roland pushed the sled forward and hopped into the back behind Dianna, hugging her close. His heart rate accelerated, and he wasn't sure if it was from the running start or being so close to her after all this time.

All three sleds shot down the hill, snow blowing up in their faces. Julius squealed, covering his eyes as Dianna latched onto him.

"Hey, no fair!" Caspian shouted. "You guys got a running start!"

Running start. Extra weight. Roland grinned. *They never stood a chance.*

As the other sleds neared the bottom of the hill, Roland brushed off his pants. Rose and Caspian glared at him.

"You cheated!" Caspian snapped, hopping off his sled.

"We went so fast!" Julius giggled.

Dianna laughed. "You have snow all over your face."

Caspian stormed up to Roland, placing his hands on his hips.

Rose shook her head. "I am *not* walking around in my underwear."

"Technically, Caspian lost," Roland smirked.

"But you cheated, so that means I didn't lose because it wasn't fair."

Roland laughed. "I didn't cheat."

"Race me again by yourself, and we'll see!"

"I'm bigger than you. So, I'll go faster, regardless."

"What?"

Rose smacked her forehead and groaned.

"You can't make them walk around in their underwear, Roland. That's cruel," Dianna said gently. "They'll freeze."

Roland grinned. "Not my problem."

"But then their noses will get all cold, and they'll sneeze all over!" Julius cried. "And then their toes will fall off because they're frozen!"

Caspian's face went red. "I...I didn't lose, so...you...you're a cheater!"

"You can't get mad every time you don't win," Rose grumbled.

"I don't!"

"Yes, you do." Rose rolled her eyes.

"Sometimes, when I lose, I cry," Julius told Dianna.

"So, does your uncle," she whispered.

"I heard that." Roland turned. "Name one time."

"When I beat you up in front of all the boys in eighth grade."

Roland blushed.

"You beat up Uncle Roland?" Caspian laughed. "But you're a girl!"

"I beat you up all the time," Rose snapped.

"Yeah, but you're my sister. That's different."

"How?"

"You're bigger than me."

Rose shrugged. "True."

"Why did you beat up Uncle Roland?" Julius asked, wagging a mitten covered finger at her. "That's not nice."

"Because he pulled my hair every day and called me names."

"You bullied Miss Warren?" Caspian cried.

"I...it was...." Roland stuttered, his cheeks burning. "I just did it because Peter did."

"Peter's my cousin. We're allowed to tease each other. We knew each other's limits. You, you were just being a jerk."

"Ooh," Caspian smirked deviously.

"Well, you didn't have to kick me in the stomach," Roland muttered. "I got the wind knocked out of me."

"I felt bad afterward."

"No, you didn't. You literally stood over me, laughed, and then left with Charlotte."

Caspian eyed them. "Charlotte?"

"Our friend."

"You guys are friends?" Caspian said, scratching his head. "I thought you hated each other?"

Roland held his breath. "We don't. Not really."

"You don't really hate me?" Dianna asked.

"I do."

She raised his brow.

"Do I seriously have to run around in my long johns because I'm wearing my red ones, and I don't want anyone to see," Caspian grumbled.

"No. I don't want you getting sick."

Caspian grinned.

"Wait, so do you hate me or not?" Dianna asked, hiding something behind her back.

Roland scanned her as he cautiously backed away. "What happens if I say yes?"

She smiled.

"Dianna, don't even think about it. I will literally fight you."

"You're going to fight her?" Julius cried. "No! Don't do that!"

Dianna lunged toward him. "Well, do you?"

"I don't know," Roland laughed. "I swear if you—"

Dianna chucked the snowball at him and burst out laughing as it smacked him in the chest.

Roland's eyes went wide. "Are you serious?"

"Julius, save me!" Dianna cried, hiding behind him.

Julius screamed as Roland balled up a large chunk of snow and aimed it at them.

Smack.

Smack.

He turned to Rose and Caspian. "Oh, so that's how it is!"

"You cheated in the race!" Caspian shouted, throwing another.

Roland threw a snowball at his nephew and ran.

"Get back here, cheater!" Caspian cried as he and Rose chased after him.

"If you stop attacking me, I'll buy you hot chocolate in town!" Roland hollered at them.

Caspian jumped on his uncle's back and laughed. "You're going down!"

Roland slipped and fell face first into the snow.

"Roland, are you okay?" Dianna asked, racing over.

Roland turned to her and smiled.

She smirked.

"I hate you." He grinned.

She shook her head and laughed.

Caspian piled snow onto Roland's back. "Cheater, cheater, snowman eater."

Rose groaned. "It's pumpkin."

"Stop being mean to Uncle Roland." Julius stomped his feet.

"Okay fine." Caspian chuckled, getting up.

"Why doesn't bribery ever work with you?" Roland asked, sitting up.

"Because I'm not Rose," Caspian said as Julius brushed off Roland's back.

"A fairy pooped on your back. A fairy pooped on your back," Julius sang. "A fairy pooped on your back, and now you have to see a purple birdy in the tree."

Roland turned to him. "What?"

Julius giggled.

"How about we get some hot chocolate? I think your Uncle's had enough." Dianna chuckled, helping Roland to his feet.

The children nodded and grabbed the sleds.

"Uncle Roland, can you please carry mine because it's really kind of heavy for me," Julius asked.

"All right, give it here." Roland took the rope.

Julius chased after Rose and Caspian as they made their way toward the main street.

⸻

"You know, you suck." Dianna's arch nemesis said. She never wanted to be at odds with Roland, but in this instance, she'd side with Rose.

Dianna laughed as they strolled down the street, the kids skipping ahead and looking in the shop windows. She shrugged. "Who saved you from getting completely covered in fairy poop?"

He laughed. She hadn't heard the joy in his voice for so long.

Roland nudged her shoulder with his. "You started it."

"I wasn't the one that told them they had to run around in their underwear."

"I wasn't actually going to make them do it. I'm not a monster."

She shook her head. "You're such a child."

"Have you seen these children? I'm not anything like that."

Dianna reached for his scarf, fixing it gently. They stopped a moment as the children danced ahead in the snow. "You have snow stuck to...all of you."

"Do I?"

She gazed into his eyes, searching their blue depth for the boy she knew not so long ago. "Even your eyebrows."

Roland brushed his face with his hand. He tucked his scarf back beneath the collar of his coat and turned to catch up with the kids.

"Oh, Dianna Warren!" a high-pitched voice called out.

The pair turned toward the café and a black-haired woman in a knee-length, grey jacket.

"Constance?" Dianna gleamed. "I barely recognized you!"

Roland waved slightly and leaned the sled up against the wall.

"Well, I heard you'd come back from your uncle—I work for him at the bank—but my goodness, you got so pretty while you were away." Constance wrapped her arms around Dianna. She turned her attention to Roland. "Your silly little friend, Peter, was supposed to call me, by the way."

"Was he?"

"Yes."

"We've been busy."

"Doing what exactly? Going to parties?"

"Working. You know he probably just forgot, Connie."

Dianna turned to him and raised her brow. "You both have been *so* busy. My cousin's working right now, actually."

Constance tossed a black curl behind her shoulder and folded her arms across her chest. "Tell him not to bother. I'm seeing Edwin Pye this evening, anyway."

Roland's eye twitched. "Edwin?"

"He works at your father's company." Constance said, propping her hand beneath her chin. "Tall, gorgeous smile. Not as big of a flirt as Peter. More of a—"

"Uncle Roland, can we please pet Mrs. Willow's new puppy?" Julius begged, tugging on Roland's coat.

Roland turned to him and nodded. Dianna winked at the youngest Crispin.

"Oh, am I keeping you two from something?" Constance asked.

"Not really. We were just taking the children for hot chocolate."

"They're so cute!" Constance squealed. "I can't wait to have my own. You're so lucky. I mean, that you—I um..."

Roland smiled at her. "I know what you mean."

"Are you two planning on having any of your own?"

Dianna cleared her throat. "What?"

"Well, aren't you engaged? That's what I heard."

Dianna's insides fluttered.

Roland winced, forcing a smile. "No, we aren't."

"We aren't together. We're just working together." Dianna took a deep breath, lowered her head, and brushed the snow from her pants. *Does he always have to be so blunt?*

"Oh..." Constance said, lowering her eyes. "Well, this is awkward, isn't it?"

"No." Roland laughed. "No, it's okay, Connie, really."

"I'm so sorry. I should probably go. I have some things...you know things, and, okay, nice seeing you, Dianna!"

Dianna and Roland watched as Constance hurried away, sliding along the ice in her tiny blue heels.

"How does she walk in those?" Roland asked.

"Lots of practice," Dianna said.

"That was awkward."

"Engaged?" She gave a nervous laugh.

"I know."

There was an unusual gruffness to his voice. It turned her stomach. *He'll never forgive me.* She swallowed her uneasiness, mirroring his irritated expression. "Like you're the only reason I came back here." Dianna groaned.

Roland rubbed his neck. "People around here like to gossip, you know that."

Dianna lowered her head. "I have a feeling those three are going to ask you for a puppy next."

"Oh, I know." Roland moaned. "But after Rose's party, I don't think we need to be making any big commitments. I mean, where am I supposed to get the money from?"

Dianna eyed him. "Are you—are you all doing okay?"

"Those three?" Roland smirked. "They've got their mother's fortune and my father's company, and the estate, and their mother's aunt's home in Presa. They're perfectly fine."

"Your parents really didn't leave you anything?" She scanned his face. Despite his grin and playful tone, Dianna caught the cold flicker in his eyes as he stared at the children. Her heart sank deep into her chest.

"It's just stuff. I don't need it."

"What in the world?" Dianna grabbed onto his arm. "How could he do that to you? You're his son!"

Roland looked away from her. "No, I'm not."

"Whatever happened to, 'This pub belongs to Darius Crispin. I'm Roland Darius Crispin, so I can do anything I want because I'm a spoiled little prick?'" Dianna asked mockingly.

A young man in a flat cap stopped, gazed over at the pair, and cocked his head, peering at them through his fogged glasses. Dianna turned Roland toward her, glancing at the man. She noted the redness in Roland's cheeks. "What, were you too drunk at the time to remember what a brat you were? Let's see if this jogs your memory. You climbed up on the counter and—"

"I didn't say it like that." Roland blushed. "And, my father never once addressed me as his son. Most people didn't know he had two sons until I started school."

"When you were thirteen?" Dianna shook her head. "I'm sorry, but your parents were really..."

Roland shrugged. "They had their reasons."

"Yeah, well, not even the piano? I mean, it's your piano."

Roland pulled away from her. "I don't want to talk about this right now."

"You never want to talk about anything. What about your mother? Can't you at least ask her for it?"

"It doesn't matter. I've been teaching Rose here and there. I don't really use it anymore."

Dianna crossed her arms. *There's no way he'd quit playing.* She recalled the neglected gramophone in the parlour. *Then again, the house gets eerily quiet without the children around. I don't think I've even heard him hum to himself.*

The young man across the street pushed his glasses up over his round nose and shoved his hands into his coat pockets, his dark eyes fixed on Dianna. She looped her arm with Roland's and turned him away, briefly making eye contact with the young gentleman.

"My father didn't expect me to be around this long, you know that."

"But he should've at least left you something. I mean, no wonder people think you—"

Roland glared at her. "People say a lot of things about me. I'm used to it."

Dianna drew in a deep breath. "I haven't had hot chocolate here in so long." She glanced away from him.

The young man waved at her.

Roland nodded, making his way over to his niece and nephews. "I might get a coffee."

"You drink coffee?" Dianna laughed, tracking the man. "I thought you hated coffee?"

"I do," he mumbled, glaring at her.

Dianna pressed her lips together. The young man stumbled into her, slipping a hand into her pocket. She met his fleeting gaze.

"Patrick," he mouthed before hurrying off.

"Uncle Roland, isn't she *so* cute!" Rose squealed, pulling his hand toward the puppy.

"I—we aren't getting one," Roland said firmly.

"Aww! But they're so adorable." Julius pouted, batting his lashes.

"No. No! We're not getting a dog. We already have an extra mouth to feed."

The three Crispin children beamed up at him.

"Pretty, pretty please with a cherry on top?" they chimed.

Dianna tried her best to muffle her laughter as Roland dragged them away from the puppy and into the café. She reached into her pocket and pulled out a crumpled slip of paper.

"Trust me, the last thing we need right now is a dog," Roland grumbled.

20

Vincent marched down the hall with two young officers following closely. The human captives rose up and ran toward the bars of their cells, waiting to see who would be judged this time.

Vincent stopped in front of the male vermin's cell and smiled, peering in at the caged animal. "Beautiful day, isn't it, mutt."

The creature gazed up at him. Its tired brown eyes barely focusing.

"Your request to see the judge has been approved. On your feet, brute." Vincent kicked the bars. The two officers opened the cell door and inched toward the monster, ropes and cuffs ready.

The vermin didn't struggle. It hung its head as it should while they bound it and forced it out into the hall. The vermin squinted as light flooded into its eyes. It stepped beyond the jailhouse into the snow and shivered violently. Its body swayed as it slumped over. The animal hadn't eaten in some time. Vincent made sure of that. They behaved better when they couldn't think straight. The vermin dragged its feet as the three men pulled the creature to the courthouse.

The creature's head bobbed up and down. Vincent smirked. If the beast was not sentenced to death, he hoped death would somehow find him. They all deserved to rot for destroying his family. Sixteen years ago, when a small group of vermin snuck into Tavern and broke into the house, Vincent had been playing downstairs while his mother tidied the kitchen. They didn't even hear the beasts enter through the back door. One snapped his mother's neck before his eyes. She didn't even have a chance to beg for her life. The youngest of the creatures dragged him out into the alley and pierced its sharp teeth into his small shoulder. Vincent hit it in the face with his toy train, and it let him go. He learned early on that vermin were willing to kill the innocent and defenceless. There was no point in showing them any mercy.

The courtroom was packed. The bailiff stepped forward as the doors opened. "All rise. The West Tavern court is now in session. Judge Marston, now presiding."

The judge walked with the weight of his title toward the podium and took his seat. The doors reopened, and Vincent Gray led the vermin to the front of the room.

Well-dressed men and women gawked at the miserable creature and chatted amongst themselves.

The judge slammed his hammer. He glared at the vermin and shook his head. "Mr. Micah Wolfe, you were caught stealing medication from Dr. Martin Gray earlier this month. However, you and your sister are descended from a very wealthy, renowned family, or so you say. I will, because of your claim, allow you to speak on your own behalf." He gestured toward the officer at the side door.

The bedraggled animal looked up at the judge from under greasy bangs. "Our younger brother was sick. We had nowhere to live, and the longer we remained outdoors, the worse he got." The beast caught its breath. "For all we know he might be...be he...he might be—"

From the side doors, an officer shoved the young vermin girl and dragged her by her hair to the front of the room.

"Suzanna." The vermin met the other beast's eyes and reached out.

"Hold him tighter," Vincent ordered, turning to Nev, his most trusted officer. Nev would keep the vermin in line.

The vixen's eyes filled with fake tears. "They told me you were dead."

Vincent glowered. *Do they honestly think we'll fall for their theatrics?*

The male held its breath, ready to unleash its fury upon the crowd, but it turned back to the judge. "Please, sir, my sister did nothing wrong. Let her contact our father and go home. I'll accept whatever my punishment may be. I'm the one who stole from Dr. Gray. Zana shouldn't be punished for something I did."

Vincent grabbed the female by the jaw and grinned. "Your dear sister assaulted an officer."

The male lurched toward him. "Take your filthy hands off her!"

Its sister pulled her face away. Vincent slapped the beast. The sow yelped and cried, "Nyla! Nyla!"

The crowd and jury watched in seething silence. Every last person in that room knew the filth of the blood that ran through the creature's veins, even if they were only half-breeds.

Dianna gripped onto her purse and shivered in the stark courtroom. Yesterday, Patrick's friend had given her a note about the hearing. A heavy weight grew in her chest as she watched the Wolfe siblings struggle toward one another, screaming. Nicholas would be safe, for now, but how much longer until word got out that he was at the Crispin's estate?

"The vermin, she's very beautiful," a man in front of Dianna whispered.

The two men to either side of him nodded.

"Shall we buy her?" he asked, and again they nodded.

Dianna gritted her teeth. "Disgusting," she muttered. The Wolfe siblings were torn apart. Vincent Gray smiled. *It's like he's laughing at them. He is. He's enjoying this.*

The judge slammed down his hammer again, glaring at the officers. "This is a courtroom, not a torture chamber!"

Zana bit her lip and turned to him. "Please, let us see our father," she sobbed. "If we don't get a hold of him soon, we might not find our brother in time!"

"The more of your kind that's removed, the better!" Vincent shouted, riling the crowd.

"Mr. Gray, please contain yourself," the judge said, shooting him a look.

Zana eyed Vincent carefully, her hands trembling. "Why do you hate us so much?"

The young Mr. Gray met her eyes and puffed up his chest. "Don't speak to me unless first addressed, you brute!"

"What have I ever done to you?"

Vincent slapped her again. "Silence!"

Zana glared at him, keeping her head held high. Defiant. Proud. Unafraid.

Vincent's face turned a violent scarlet. He raised his hand to strike her again.

"Mr. Gray, I will have to ask you to leave," the judge said firmly.

The young man sneered at the official. "As you wish."

Dianna met his gaze, but glanced away from her old classmate as he strode out of chambers. She turned her attention to the front as Zana got down on her knees and whimpered softly. Dianna's heart dropped, watching Micah stretch out toward her.

Nev yanked him back.

Micah shut his eyes.

Dianna clutched at her skirt as Zana turned to the judge. "Please, your honour, allow us to contact our father for the sake of our brother. He's innocent, and he's very sick. Don't let him suffer because of us. Our father would be heartbroken if he lost all three of his children."

Dianna's eyes burned as she watched the tears fall from the girl's face.

"Your father committed a crime by engaging with a vermin. You are living examples of sin." The judge sighed. He looked down at the young girl.

Dianna dabbed her eyes quickly and eyed Judge Marston as he sat for a moment in silence, looking back and forth between the two accused. His eyes finally rested back on Zana. He bit his lip and tapped his finger on the podium.

"However, as you are the by-product of a crime you could not control, I cannot hold you responsible for the actions of your kin. You have my permission to try and reach your father. We will meet again, with Dr. Gray present, within a week's time."

The siblings tentatively smiled at one another as they were led from the room.

Dianna hugged herself, keeping her focus on the men in front of her. The one fiddled with a gold watch on his wrist then adjusted his silk cravat. She didn't have the money to outbid him for the girl. She considered begging Roland or Peter, but the thought of anyone paying to own the young woman made her stomach turn. *If I don't think of something soon, that child will become someone's prize.*

21

———

"**L**ovely day, isn't it?" Thompson grinned, taking a seat next to Rose on the school's front steps. He sat rubbing his hands together as he waited for her to address him. *She's off in her own world again.* Most days, that's where he found her, alone on the steps with a book on her lap.

Two girls from his class, Sofia and Kiyomi, stepped past them, looking down at Rose. The hard glare Sofia shot was no pricklier than her tongue. "Careful Thompson, if her uncle catches you getting too close, he might stab you."

"Can it," Thompson shot back, causing the girls to twist around to face them.

Rose kept her eyes on her book, tugging briefly on the ribbon in her hair.

"Oh, that's right, you're not scared of the Crispin's, are you," Sofia smirked, tapping a gloved finger to her cheek.

Kiyomi rolled her eyes. "Come on, Sofia, the bell's gonna ring any minute."

"I just can't understand why you're so keen on hanging around her. My mother wouldn't even let me go to the party. I heard her uncle was sizing up his next victim the entire time."

Kiyomi pressed her lips together, glancing at Rose.

Thompson crossed his arms and shook his head. "I can't understand why you always feel the need to—"

"It's all right, Tom. My uncle never stabbed anyone." Rose turned the page. She lifted her head slightly and grinned. "He shot them."

The girls took a step back.

"Let's go find Wayde." Kiyomi pulled Sofia by the arm. "See you in class Thompson."

Thompson scratched his head, watching the girls run off. "Huh, you handled that pretty well. I'd say you'll do just fine once I'm off at college."

Rose remained in her exact spot, unshaken, as always.

He licked his lips, clearing his throat as he slid closer to her. *Will she really be okay on her own?* No hint of wariness lingered on her face.

Thompson leaned toward her and peered at the book she read. "Is it any good?"

"It's magnificent," she answered, still engaged in the pages of the novel.

"Looks like you're really enjoying it."

Rose glanced at him. "Tom."

"Yes?"

"It's a little difficult trying to read while you're hovering over me."

Thompson nodded and leaned back. "I was wondering about that boy." He eyed her carefully. "The one staying with you. Has his health improved?"

Rose frowned. "I'm not sure. My uncle refuses to let me anywhere near him."

"I see. Well, it's for the best. It'd be terrible if you were to get sick again." Thompson slid the end of her ribbon between his fingers. Heart pounding heavily, his eyes remained fixed on Rose. *If that boy gets her sick, I swear I'll...* He blinked the thought away.

She knitted her brow and tightly pressed her lips together.

"You seemed excited about the gift my mother gave you."

Rose looked at him. "I am."

"That's great."

"Was there something you needed, Tom?" She closed her book.

"Oh, no. Just wanted some company."

Rose swallowed hard and pressed her book against her chest. The bell rang out, signalling the end of their break. "Well, I'll see you later," she said softly.

Thompson nodded, offering her his hand.

Rose took it, and he pulled her up from the step.

"Would it be all right if I took you skating tomorrow?" Thompson looked away from her as the other students rushed past and into the school. He squeezed her hand—all he'd dare while the teachers were watching.

Rose's face flushed bright red, matching her gloves. "I-I suppose."

Thompson's eyes lit up. "Wonderful! I'll come and get you around noon."

Rose nodded, letting go of his hand.

Roland sat down on his desk and raised his brow. He turned to Peter as he shut the office door.

Dianna pressed her head against the brown cushion and bemoaned, "What should I do?" It was the fifth time she'd repeated the phrase, and still, neither of the men knew what she was talking about. Dianna shot up and looked at them. "If I were to do something drastic, would you—"

"Get yourself into trouble, and we'll domesticate that creature anyway we see fit," Peter teased.

"I just don't know what to do." She sank back down into her seat, running a hand through her strawberry-coloured hair.

Roland glared at her. "Peter and I have a lot of work to do, so if you don't mind, we'll just leave you to your...whatever it is you're doing."

"Roland, is it possible for Leon to take me out of town again?" Dianna gazed up at him.

"Yes, but can I ask where and why?"

"Well, I need to see Theodore Wolfe."

"*Thee* Theodore Wolfe?" Peter exclaimed. "As in one of the richest men in the country?"

She nodded.

Roland eyed her, crossing his arms. "Now, what business do you have with Mr. Wolfe?"

"He..." Dianna bit her lip. "A friend of mine, she...she's unable to see him herself and—"

"A friend of yours knows Theodore Wolfe?"

"I don't need to explain myself to you. If Mr. Leon is unable to take me, then I'll find some other way." She shot Roland a fierce look.

He sighed then shook his head. *Here we go again.*

Dianna grabbed hold of his hand and gripped it firmly.

Roland's eyes widened at the warmth of her palm, then he winced. *Any tighter, and I'll lose all the feeling in my fingers.* He eyed her.

"If I must, I will take a horse and go. If you deny me that, I shall walk. No matter what, I am going to see Theodore Wolfe."

"He doesn't have a horse for you to gallop off with." Peter turned to Roland. "And I don't see the point in inconveniencing all of Tavern just so you can run off on one of your little adventures."

Roland glanced down at her small, freckle covered hand and pulled away from her. "Why bother asking? We both know your mind is already made up."

"Ro-Roland..." Dianna gazed into his eyes.

He turned from her; his chest ached. Roland hated when she looked at him like that. It brought back too many memories. He never stood a chance against her over-bright, pleading gaze. "If you can't make any other arrangements, then I'll ask Leon if he's willing to take you to see Mr. Wolfe. I have no idea how this ties into whatever drastic thing it is you have in mind, but if you'll excuse us, Peter and I must get back to work. We're on a tight schedule."

Dianna nodded. "Thank you. Both of you. Thank you so much."

Roland narrowed his eyes at her as Peter followed him out of the room.

"That cousin of mine has to be the strangest person I've ever met." Peter laughed, brushing his curls to the side of his face. "Taking a horse? She can barely ride."

Roland balled his hand into a fist. He could still feel the warmth from Dianna's touch, lingering on him. "Let's focus on getting Nicholas trained, so we don't end up getting hung."

The two men made their way to the nursery.

Peter handed his notes to Roland.

Roland examined them as they walked down the hall. *Why in the world would she need to see Theodore Wolfe? And how would that lead to her doing something drastic...perhaps that is what's drastic?*

"So, you really think teaching him with images will work better?" Peter glanced over his shoulder. "Roland?"

Roland blinked and hurried to catch up. "What's that now?"

"I asked if you think it will work." He waved the sketch pad up in the air.

Roland nodded. "Uh...yes, I think so. Or I hope so."

Peter rolled his eyes. "At this point, I'm willing to try just about anything."

Roland opened the door.

Nicholas sat, perched on the windowsill. His brown eyes flickered as the two men entered. It turned Roland's stomach.

"We've come prepared today." Peter flipped the sketch pad open. "So, you had better be on your best behaviour."

The vermin turned to him and nodded.

The two men sat around the table and laid out their notes while Nicholas watched with a scowl on his face.

"Come sit," Roland snapped. He was in no mood for the boy's antics.

Nicholas climbed down from his seat by the window and joined the two men. He held his head down but peered up at them through his long dark brown bangs.

"Since you aren't able to comprehend written language, Peter has brought you something to draw with."

"We figured even an uneducated brute could draw a simple picture," Peter taunted, tossing the sketch pad at the boy.

Nicholas caught it with ease and snapped it down onto the table.

"Quick reflexes." Peter jotted in his notebook.

Roland shook his head as Nicholas glared at them. "Your frustration will only make this more difficult."

Nicholas winced. He opened up the sketch pad and flipped to a clean page. "What do you want me to draw?"

"Draw us a picture of anything you like." Roland gave him a smile. "Today, we will give you that freedom."

Peter gave the vermin a pencil.

Nicholas took it in his hand and drew. At first, the two men believed their effort had been wasted, but soon the smooth strokes the vermin made on the page took shape. There were, what appeared to be, men hiding in the bushes, stalking a small fox.

Peter grabbed Nicholas by the wrist and pulled the boy's hand away from the sketch. "Roland, look at the detail."

Roland stared at the drawing, his eyes growing wider and wider. *This is amazing.*

"I wasn't expecting this from a brute," Peter whispered, still clinging to the boy's wrist.

"Where did you learn to draw like this?" Roland examined the hundreds of strokes in the fox's fur.

Nicolas jerked his arm free. "Nyla."

Peter laughed. "I think we'll continue to use this technique."

Roland nodded. "Definitely."

Nicholas's ears twitched. He slid his chair toward the window and looked out at the pond.

Roland knew who was out there and scowled.

22

Rose's cheeks burned as Thompson took her by the hand and lead her around the frozen pond. She watched her footing while she squeezed his hand.

He gave her a warm smile. "You have nothing to fear."

She swallowed the lump in her throat. The two of them glided across the ice. Thompson grinning from ear to ear, Rose holding on to him for dear life.

Rose stumbled forward on a turn. "Not so fast!" she cried, clutching onto his arm.

"Sorry. I'll slow down." He pulled her close. "You're doing really well." He readjusted her fuzzy black beret and kissed her cheek.

Her face went red. She shoved him away, tumbling backward onto the ice.

He rushed to her side and knelt down. "Are you okay?"

She covered her cheeks with her mittens and glared at him.

Thompson lowered his head. "Rose, I really—"

She held out her hand. "I'm an awful skater, aren't I?"

He grinned, helping her back onto her feet. "Awful isn't the word I'd use."

I shouldn't have pushed him, but he shouldn't have startled me. Rose dusted herself off. Her feet began to slide out from under her.

Thompson held onto her elbow. "You just need to work on your balance. You know, this would be easier if you were wearing a pair of pants. A dress isn't exactly practical for skating."

"Oh, hush!" She puffed up her cheeks and stuck out her tongue. "I'll have you know that I am perfectly poised in this dress."

Thompson gave her a smile. "It was merely a suggestion. I just don't want you getting hurt."

"Can we go around again?" She glanced away from him.

"Sure." He nodded, leading her toward the middle of the pond. "Don't panic. Just trust me." He gripped her hands tightly. Thompson let out a laugh and spun around with her. With each spin, Rose's eyes grew wider. Her heart leaped when he smiled at her. He led her off the pond and removed his skates. "We should do this again. Maybe next time, you'll feel a little more confident."

Rose nodded. "I haven't been skating in years."

"Did you have fun?"

Rose gazed at him. She squeezed her hands together. "Yes...I did."

Rose spotted Nicholas peering over the railing as she entered the house. She removed her coat and gloves before giving him a smile. He smiled back.

"Have you seen my uncle?" she asked.

Nicholas nodded. "He and Mr. Rissing went into his office." He pointed toward the office door.

Rose glanced at the door and then turned her attention back to Nicholas. "You're looking much better."

"Well, I feel better." He lowered his head, eyeing her from behind his bangs. "It looked like you were having fun outside."

She nodded. "Maybe you can come next time."

"*Nei*. No, I wouldn't want to have your friend pulling me around by my arms like that."

"You two could have a race. Thompson's really fast!" Rose pulled up her warm black socks over her stockings. She looked up sharply and eyed him. "Wait, you were watching us?" Her eyes widened as his face went red. "Whatever you do, don't say anything to my uncle," she whispered, inching toward the bottom of the stairs. "He's been acting strange lately. I don't want him to overreact."

Nicholas tilted his head in the direction of the office. Peter and Roland came out into the hallway.

Roland glanced at Nicholas and then turned to Rose. "Did you have a good time with Tom?"

"Yes, I did." Rose removed her hat, glancing back at Nicholas. "I forgot how much I enjoyed skating."

"It looks fun, I suppose."

"Haven't you been skating before?" she asked her uncle.

"I'm afraid not."

"Well, you should. It's like dancing, only I think I'm much more graceful when I'm practicing the waltz than on a pair of ice skates." She laughed.

"What are you doing out of your room?" Peter snapped, catching sight of Nicholas.

Nicholas backed away from the railing.

Roland sighed. "He's probably restless."

Peter glared at Nicholas. "That boy shouldn't leave his room. He knows that. He could make someone sick."

Rose frowned and made her way toward the staircase. "Perhaps he's just looking for a bit of company?"

"Which will be provided during his lessons," Roland said firmly, placing a gentle hand on her shoulder.

Rose rolled her eyes and turned from him. "You're so fearful of this fever that you're mistreating our guest."

"I don't want to hear another word from you. Do you understand?"

Rose drew in a deep breath and shut her eyes. "I understand perfectly." She marched up the steps and shot her uncle a firm glance.

Nicholas let out a sigh.

"I apologize for the way you're being treated."

"I don't want to get you into trouble," Nicholas mumbled, turning away from her.

Rose shook her head and went to her bedroom, cautiously watching the boy as she opened the door. The strange feather earring that dangled just above Nicholas's shoulder caught her attention.

Nicholas met her gaze. He carefully covered the earring with his long dark hair. His eyes flickered as he turned from her.

Rose gripped the knob, her heart racing. She shut the door and pressed her back against it, listening to Nicholas' footsteps out in the hall and pressed her hand to her cheek. Thompson's kiss still rested there. *Maybe if he'd asked to kiss me, I wouldn't have pushed him like that.* She wrapped the black ribbon tied to the end of her pigtails around her finger. Her face grew hot as her stomach knotted. With each twist, she saw the flicker in Nicholas' eyes. *If he kissed me, would I have—*she yanked the ribbon from her hair and shook her head.

"If that happened, Uncle Roland would lose it."

23

Dianna held her breath as the Chevrolet Luxury Deluxe rolled up to the gate. *Don't blow it. This may be the only chance you get.*

"State your name and business," the gatekeeper ordered.

"My name is Dianna Warren. I'm here to speak with Mr. Wolfe. I have important news regarding his children."

The gate-keeper laughed. "Oh, really? Lord Wolfe doesn't have children."

"Well, then, I have news of two youths posing as his children," Dianna snapped. "Please, sir, this is of great importance."

"If Lord Wolfe wishes to speak to you, then you're welcome inside. Otherwise, get out of here."

Dianna stepped out of the car and glared at him. "He *will* see me."

The gatekeeper backed away and turned to the young boy beside him. "Send word to Lord Wolfe. Say there's a young lady here to see him. Wants to talk about his children."

The boy nodded and scurried down the dirt path toward the mansion.

Dianna folded her hands together and turned to look at Mr. Leon. He turned on the radio and rolled down the window.

"Nice weather we're having." The gatekeeper gave him a nod.

"It's snowing," Mr. Leon said.

"That it is."

What is taking so long? Dianna wrung her hands and held her breath. She looked up at the gatekeeper and forced a smile, clearing her throat as she fiddled around with the clutch on her yellow bag. The gatekeeper looked over his shoulder.

The little boy raced back down the path toward them. Wheezing, he wiped his forehead and pointed to Dianna. "He says he'll see her."

The gatekeeper glared at Dianna, reluctantly opening the gate.

Dianna smiled grimly, climbed back into the car, and watched from the window as Mr. Leon drove up along the property.

Large white pillars held up the mansion's front entrance. Her eyes widened as she spotted a group of small houses near the back of the property. It almost looked like a miniature village. The fountain near the entrance had swans carved into the bottom and a woman standing at the top, playing the harp. It entranced her.

She thought back to the first time she had been invited to the Crispin estate all those years ago. Compared to her family's farm and her uncle's manor, the Crispin's home was like something out of a fairy tale. The beautiful lush garden, the gazebo near the pond. Less grand than the Wolfe estate, but more welcoming.

The first time Roland kissed her cheek, they'd been walking in the garden after Peter went off with their friend Charlotte. Roland had looked over his shoulder and pecked her cheek so fast, he nearly missed her face. The kiss had spread from her cheek to the rest of her body as though he'd planted a little kiss on her heart.

Dianna lowered her hand and placed it in her lap. *How did things turn out this way?* She shook her head. *Focus! This isn't the time to be daydreaming.*

Mr. Leon got out of the car and opened the door for her. He held out his hand and raised his brow. "Are you all right?"

Dianna pressed her lips together. "I've got butterflies."

"Perhaps I should accompany you?"

Dianna squeezed his hand as she stepped out of the car. "Would you?"

Leon winced. "If that is..." He pulled his hand away and rubbed it gently. "What you wish, Miss."

"Sorry."

Leon sighed. "After you."

Dianna walked up the staircase. The porter opened the grand door to let her in. As Dianna thanked him and entered, she paled at the grandeur of the interior. A golden chandelier dangled above her head, the jewels hanging from it, like little glass tears. Her jaw dropped as she looked down at minutely detailed trim that ran along the edge of the wall. The large windows of the house filled the hall with light that bounced off the eggshell hue of the walls. The drapes that hugged them were the fairest shade of blue. She loved blue; that shade reminded her of the hydrangeas in Roland's garden.

The chandelier drew her gaze upward again; the ceiling was decorated with floral carvings that ran straight down the long hallway bringing warmth to it all, opposite to the intimidating exterior. It was completely unlike the interior of the Crispin estate. That house had a gloom to it that lingered like its unchanging décor. The Wolfe's mansion, however, in its grandness nearly stole her breath away. "It's absolutely lovely."

Leon nodded. "Yes, it is."

"You must be the young lady who's come to speak with me." A tall man with dark hair waltzed into the hall, giving her a gentle smile. He held out his hand to her, his grin shifting his neatly trimmed moustache. "I am Theodore Wolfe."

Dianna nodded, eyeing the perfect fit of his tailored suit and silk tie. "It's a pleasure to meet you, sir. My name is Dianna Warren. I, um, have something very important to discuss with you."

"Regarding my children." Lord Wolfe gestured for her to follow him.

"Yes, sir."

Theodore Wolfe entered a small sitting room and shut the door behind them. "Tell me, what do you know of my children?"

Leon stood by the door and watched Dianna cautiously.

"They're in grave danger. I, well, actually, my cousin and his friend came across a boy named Nicholas Slayden. He's been in my care, and he's got that dreadful fever. Um...well, he told me about getting separated from his brother and sister, and they're on trial, and you're their only hope, and I'm worried that your daughter might be—"

"Please, slow down." Lord Wolfe gently cupped his hands together. "I can't possibly keep up."

Dianna nodded and glanced at Mr. Leon for support. The driver's kind eyes helped remind her she was among friends. Her pulse slowed. "Micah and Suzanna Wolfe are in serious trouble."

"And Nyla?"

"Nyla?"

"Their grandmother. What has become of her?"

Dianna eyed him. "I don't know, but I attended the trial, and I do know that unless you step in, your children will be harmed."

Lord Wolfe sat down and looked at her. "Why are they on trial?"

"For stealing medicine for Nicholas. Someone must've realized they were of *Valdinok* blood."

"And Nicholas?"

"He's safe—for now. He's getting better. He's very worried about his brother and sister. I didn't tell him about this."

"I don't know if I can do anything for him. He's not my child," Lord Wolfe whispered.

Dianna gripped her purse tightly, pressing her lips together. "I'm only asking that you stop them from persecuting your children. Nicholas is in a better position."

"Where do you live?"

"Tavern. I'm staying at the Crispin manor. That's where Nicholas is."

"Tavern?"

Dianna's heartbeat raced at the gentleman's tone. She watched him as he adjusted his tie. She looked down at her hands, her eyes boring into her yellow purse. "If we don't do something, they'll hurt your daughter. I know it."

"I've made up my mind." He stood up and went to open the door. "Clarissa, Seraphina, pack my bags. I'm leaving for Tavern in an hour! Harold, please get my car ready."

Dianna sat up straight, eyeing the handful of servants outside the door. *Where did they all come from? How long were they listening to us?* She shook off her confusion, turned to Leon and beamed, clapping her hands together as her eyes filled with tears. "Oh, Mr. Leon, isn't this wonderful?"

Leon shook his head and smiled. "You always have a way of getting exactly what you want, Miss Warren."

Roland sat on the edge of his bed, fiddling with the lid on the medicine bottle. His ears rang loudly, still picking up the children running about the house. *Good. If they're in the library, they're not near the vermin.*

He raised his eyes up as little feet pounded against the ceiling. *Those three couldn't keep quiet to save their lives.* He winced, meeting the empty eyes of the photograph of his mother and father on the dresser. Roland shook the image of muddy shoe prints on the stairs from his head. He drew in a deep breath. His eyes burned from exhaustion.

Mud. The broken window. Charlotte. Blood under Roland's fingernails. The cigar box in his father's office. Lawrence's warm, crooked smile. Little red polka dots splattered across Rose's white dress. Dianna's freckles. His heart crumbled in his chest.

He exhaled and sprawled out on the bed; his blue eyes fixated on the liquid swirling about in the bottle he held above his head. *Did she buy one for Peter, too?* His eyes shot open as the bottle slipped from his fingers. Roland grunted, catching it between his chin and his collar bone, then slid it out and squeezed his eyes shut. *She's always running off somewhere. School. Rich men's estates. Riversburg.*

He opened his eyes as the door swung wide.

Tabitha waltzed into the room with a basket and kissed her teeth. "Do you ever clean up after yourself?"

He rolled onto his side and watched her. "It depends on my mood."

"If everything depended on that mood of yours, nothing would ever get done." She picked the dirty clothes up off the floor. In the bathroom, Tabitha gave a loud huff as she threw the yellow woven basket to the floor. "You'd think an animal lived here."

"An animal does live here, remember?"

Tabitha turned to him.

Roland grinned.

"What am I going to do with you?" She set the towels in the basket.

He laughed, pushing past the painful memories, and sat up, placing the bottle in his lap.

Tabitha eyed it and cocked her head. "What's that you got there?"

"Medicine."

Tabitha inched toward him. "It'd better be."

"It is. Dianna bought it for me." Roland handed her the bottle and scratched his head.

"Did she, now? Well, that was surprisingly thoughtful."

"You can have it."

Tabitha bit her lip and gave it back to him. "I couldn't do that. If you got sick, I wouldn't be able to forgive myself."

Roland shrugged. "It's not like I've never been sick before, Tabby."

"Before, you didn't have three children to look after. Four if you count that horrible creature." She brushed the hair from his face.

He wrinkled his nose and swatted her hand. "Would you quit that?"

"You could at least comb it out. It looks like a bird decided to make a nest on your head! I'm not letting you leave the house looking like this."

He glared at her as she smoothed down the untidy brown curls that jutted out around his head.

"You need to take better care of yourself. You spend so much time looking after those three that you forget to take your medication. You're not fooling anyone with those bags under your eyes. How bad have the migraines been this time?" She raced toward the dresser and pulled open the drawer.

Roland's cheeks burned as she pulled the tin out at waved it at him. *Damn it.*

"Roland Darius Crispin, I ought to give you a smack!"

"I...well, I haven't exactly—"

Tabitha glanced into the hall and shut the bedroom door. "This is why she went and got you that medicine. You can't keep doing this to yourself. Did you even reschedule your appointment with Dr. Gray?"

He looked away from her.

"Well, it's a good thing I gave him a call then."

"Tabby!"

She crossed her arms. "Don't Tabby me. You should've seen him at the start of the month like you were supposed to."

"Things happened. I'm perfectly all right."

"Are you sure? Because last time I checked, you had a vermin come stay with us." She slammed the tin down onto the dresser.

"That's exactly why I didn't reschedule. Nicholas might try to kill him again."

"Then go to his office."

Roland shook his head.

Tabitha drew in a deep breath and sat down across from him. "Why are you torturing yourself like this?"

"I'm fine."

"You look tired."

"I'm always tired."

Tabitha pressed her lips together and nodded. "Well, then, if you refuse to take care of yourself, then perhaps I shouldn't bother doing your laundry."

Roland eyed her.

Tabitha stood up, grabbed the basket and dumped the clothes on his bed. "You can do your own wash."

"But I've never—"

"Unless, of course, you make an appointment to see Dr. Gray."

"I'm not even sick," he snapped.

"Oh, and the children will be needing their things washed as well." Tabitha headed toward the door.

Roland leaned his head back and groaned.

"Are you going to make the appointment?"

He glared at her. "Absolutely not."

Tabitha spun toward him. He jerked back and cleared his throat. "Why are you so stubborn?"

"I'm not stubborn."

"Just go to the doctor."

Roland shook his head.

"Are you sulking?" Tabitha looked him over critically, then opened the door and went out into the hall. "This is ridiculous."

Roland sat for a moment and eyed the tin, crossing his arms. He glanced at the photo of his parents and swallowed hard. *You're the reason I'm trapped here in this bloody city.* Roland got to his feet and chased after Tabitha. He raced toward the stairs as she headed into the parlour, mumbling to herself.

The doorbell chimed.

Roland stumbled down the stairs, nearly missing the last step as he crashed into the door. He groaned, gazed heavenward, and straightened his back, tucking in his shirt before unlocking the door.

"May I come in?"

He shot his head in the direction of the parlour. *How could she?* He smiled at Vincent Gray and nodded.

"My father asked me to come check on you."

"Really?" Roland spotted Tabitha's small eyes peering from behind the arch.

"He seemed concerned. Say, how's your niece?" Vincent asked, brushing the snow from his jacket. "I heard Connie ran into all of you the other day."

"Rose is fine. The children are upstairs playing. Did you want coffee or tea or—"

"If she doesn't mind, I'd love one of Mrs. Gibson's hot chocolates."

Tabitha darted into the hall and pulled Vincent down by his scarf, pinching his already red cheeks. "Awe. Of course, Officer." She smiled and gave him a little wink.

Roland glanced toward the stairs. *You haven't come to visit since October. Why are you suddenly showing up like this?* He blinked as Tabitha lead Vincent into the parlour.

"Roland, why don't you ask Peter if he'd like to join you. I'm sure he's tired from all that reading." She looked back at him.

Roland nodded and raced upstairs to the nursery. *Why is Vincent here? Why?* He opened the door and slammed it behind him, pointing at Nicholas, who sat with Peter at the table. "He needs to hide. Now." Nicholas cocked his head, his ears twitching.

"Who were you talking to downstairs?" the boy asked.

"It doesn't matter. You just need to hide. Stay in the bathroom or something. Just do not leave this room." Roland tried to catch his breath. He latched onto Peter's arm and pulled him up out of the chair.

Peter tried to pull away. "I'd appreciate it if you didn't ruin my new shirt."

Roland shot his head back and dragged him out of the room. "Tabitha's making hot chocolate."

Peter eyed him.

Roland shut the door and gestured for him to head downstairs. "We have a guest."

As the two of them made their way into the kitchen, Roland sighed at Tabitha's melodic cooing.

"Have a cookie, dear. Oh, I wish you'd have worn your uniform. It makes you look so grown up."

Roland wrinkled his forehead.

"Can I have a cookie, Mrs. Gibson?" Peter asked, taking a seat next to Vincent at the table.

"Can you?" Tabitha scoffed, shaking her head.

Roland smirked and sat across from them.

Tabitha placed a plate full on the table. "All that's missing is Miles."

Roland winced.

Vincent laughed. "My cousin's been fairly busy."

"Oh, I'm sure. It's been so long since I've had you boys here for a visit. You've all grown so much."

"I'd rather not deal with Miles," Roland grumbled, stuffing a cookie into his mouth. He paused. *Can Nicholas hear us from the kitchen? He did say vermin have exceptional—*

Vincent grinned. "Same here." His smile grew as Tabitha placed the decorative cups onto the table. He turned to Roland and leaned forward. "To tell you the truth, my father's been begging me to stop by and check on you."

Roland glanced at Peter. "He has?"

Vincent nodded. "I know you avoid reading the paper, but there's been an incident. It didn't happen too far from here. I won't lie, you came to mind, but I've been..." He let out a sigh and shook his head.

"What incident?" Peter asked.

"Vermin."

"Vermin?" Peter echoed.

Roland met Peter's eyes briefly.

"They're getting too bold." Vincent gripped the cup between his fingers.

Tabitha cleared her throat as she brought over the pot and poured the hot chocolate into their mugs. "Is there any other reason your father may have wanted you to stop by? Perhaps a certain someone missing his usual appointment?"

Vincent nodded quickly and grinned. "Yes, he also wanted me to ask how you were doing."

Peter leaned forward. "Appointment?"

Roland glared at Tabitha as she poured the beverage into his favourite cup. Since he was four, he had insisted on using it. He liked its yellow colour and the flowers painted on it. His father found it ridiculous that Roland would want to use a moustache cup since he had no hair above his lip at the time, but Roland's persistence and the odd tantrum caused him to cave. No one else could use the yellow moustache cup except for Lawrence, of course. Roland always made an exception for Lawrence.

"Rolly?" Peter waved his hand over his face.

Roland blinked and turned to him.

"Thought we lost you there for a moment." Vincent laughed.

Roland nodded and looked down at his cup. "Just thinking."

"About Dianna?" Vincent asked.

Peter choked on his drink and turned to him.

"Connie said—"

"Never listen to a word Constance says." Peter rubbed his throat.

Tabitha shook her head. "There's no sense in thinking about that girl anyway."

Roland lowered his head. "I wasn't."

"After what she did."

Peter sank in his seat and frowned. "We were only kids."

"Only kids." Tabitha scoffed, pointing at Roland. "Turned this one into a felon."

Vincent drank down his hot chocolate and laughed. "Peter's got a point. We were, what, nineteen?"

"Sixteen. Dianna was fifteen," Roland mumbled.

"Exactly. It was a spur of the moment thing."

Roland gave Vincent a smile. *No, it wasn't.*

Vincent looked down at his watch. "I hate to eat and leave, but I promised to meet up with Nev and Cato at the pub, and I still have some errands to run for my father."

"You're leaving already?" Tabitha frowned.

He stood up and gave her a hug. "It was nice seeing you, too. I'll be sure to come by again once things have calmed down a bit at work."

Roland and Peter nodded.

"Oh, before I forget." He placed a silver tin on the table in front of Roland.

Roland slapped his hand over it. Peter craned his neck as Roland slid the tin down onto his lap. "Thank you."

Vincent nodded and pat him on the shoulder. "Don't worry about the bill. Okay?"

Roland spun around in his chair as Vincent headed out of the kitchen.

Tabitha cleared Vincent's cup and looked over her shoulder.

"You did call Dr. Gray, didn't you," Roland whispered, shooting her a look. He hurried to the door.

Vincent looked up at him as he put on his shoes. "Tell the children I say hello."

"Wait, I can't take this." Roland held out the tin.

"It's fine."

"At least let me pay for it."

Vincent's eyes fell on the piano. He opened the door and gave Roland a smile. "It's already been paid for."

"But I didn't—"

"I told him you did."

Roland eyed him.

"Sad you don't play anymore," Vincent said.

Roland gripped onto the tin.

"I'll see you around." Vincent tipped his hat and headed out into the blustery cold. Roland locked the door behind him as Tabitha and Peter emerged from the parlour.

"I always liked that boy." Tabitha pressed a hand to her cheek.

"Did you pay for this?" Roland asked, holding up the tin.

She shook her head.

Peter cocked his head. "I thought you said you weren't—"

"I'm fine." Roland turned from them. He looked at the piano and shook his head.

24

Dianna was surprised when Theodore Wolfe decided it would be best to ride in the car alongside her. He wanted to keep his visit a secret from the public until he could figure out what to do about his children.

Curiosity swelled as the time passed. Dianna had so many things that she wanted to ask the man. Things about his life, how he felt knowing his only children were in danger, why he decided to go back to Tavern with them. Still, she remained silent and watched the gentleman stare out the window at the open fields. It was not her place to intrude on his thoughts.

Theodore brought along his messenger boy in case he needed to have a letter sent to his servants at home. The scrawny boy had large eyes that gawked at everything. His thick, blond, curly hair glowed whenever the sun peeked into the car.

Theodore lowered the blind. "You're probably wondering why I decided to be so secretive." He glanced up at Dianna.

The car rocked back and forth as they pulled off the main street onto the forest road.

"I haven't been outside of this area in years. Others might find it odd that I suddenly decided to go away."

"Actually, to be quite honest, I'm more curious about Micah and Suzanna," Dianna admitted.

Theodore nodded and lowered his head. "Would you like to hear a story, Arthur?"

The messenger boy nodded. "Yes, please!"

Dianna tilted her head.

"Back when I was a boy, of about ten, my father decided to purchase some servants. Slaves."

Dianna furrowed her brow while young Arthur's eyes grew wide with excitement.

"My father allowed me to choose a slave for myself. I picked a little seven-year-old girl. That girl, from that day forth, followed me like a lamb, and I didn't mind. She was my dearest friend." Theodore's eyes glossed over. "I loved her more than anything. After my parents passed away, I married her. I knew they wouldn't accept the fact that I was in love with the help. People were very cruel to her. Very cruel. We had children, but she sent them away when they were about seven years old. Then, one day, she just left. She didn't even say goodbye. I suppose she felt forced to love me, but my heart wants to believe she felt the same."

Little Arthur pouted. "Did she ever come back?"

"I'm afraid not. After she took the children, she disappeared. I haven't seen her in years." Theodore clenched his fists.

Dianna's jaw dropped. "You poor soul..." she whispered. "Alone in that big house."

"Lord Wolfe ain't alone. He gots me an' the others tah keep 'em company," Arthur protested.

Dianna smiled at him.

"And for that, I am truly grateful." Theodore turned his attention to Dianna. "Does Tavern follow the laws regarding half-vermin?"

She pressed her lips together. "In this case, they are. If they weren't your children, Micah and Zana probably would've been executed."

"I knew I should've sent for them when their mother left, but I was worried about what might happen to their grandmother."

Dianna watched him as he fiddled with his hat.

"My name and title can only protect them so much. My wife and I realized that when they started school. This whole vermin versus human nonsense is ridiculous. The war ended forty-four years ago."

"Do you think it would have been best if everywhere else was like Tavern or Verglas?" Dianna asked.

Theodore scoffed. "What? With their no vermin laws? Absolutely not. Both sides were at fault. To this day, I believe the entire thing was merely about survival. We never should've separated in the first place."

"But according to stories, at least the ones I grew up within Tavern, we were never meant to be together in the first place." Dianna cleared her throat as Theodore eyed her. She tucked a strand of hair behind her ear.

"What do you believe?" he asked. "How do you, as a human from Tavern, feel about vermin?"

"I believe both vermin and humans should be treated with respect. The way they were treating your children made me sick to my stomach."

Theodore lowered his head. "Let's hope the people of Tavern make an exception for them. I already lost them once. I can't imagine losing them again."

"How are you feeling this morning?" Roland asked, pulling a chair up beside the bed.

His mother's face lit up. "Do you have any letters from my little boy?"

Roland nodded and pulled them out of his coat. "He's been busy lately."

Adeline took the letters and pressed them to her chest. "His letters always brighten my day. I worry about him a lot. Roland's been very ill since he was a baby."

"His health has been pretty good recently."

"Oh? That's wonderful to hear!" She tucked the letters underneath her pillow. "What is Darius up to these days?"

Roland bit his lip. His stomach churned violently whenever he had to deceive her. It was as though someone repeatedly punched him in the gut. "Your husband has been working with Mr. Hood on a new project. I don't know all of the details, but I know it's just a bit of an experiment right now."

Adeline smiled. "You really do look just like him. The same blue eyes, dark hair. Even your voice. It's comforting. It's very comforting."

Roland stared at her. "I'm not Darius."

"I know that, dear."

"Don't confuse me with that man."

"How could I?" Adeline asked, looking him over. "He's my husband. No one else could pose as him. I know him better than the back of my hand."

Roland nodded. "You love him a lot."

"Love him? I adore him. I would do anything for him."

"I wish I felt that way about another human being." Roland sighed. *I did once.* He swallowed a lump in his throat. *But she turned on me, just like the rest of them. Dianna, Charlotte...the whole damn lot of them.* He clenched his fists and turned from her.

Adeline took his hand in hers and drew him toward her. "No... you don't have his eyes," she whispered, peering into him.

Roland pulled away from her and stood up, his legs shaking. "I'd better go. I have to...I have—"

Adeline stared at him. "I know those eyes."

Roland nodded. "I visit often. Y-you should recognize me by now."

Adeline shivered. "Those eyes. Sad eyes. I-I remembered he...you—"

"I'll have your nurse come and check on you, ma'am." Roland inched toward the door.

"Those aren't Darius' eyes," she mumbled, hugging her knees. "He...he killed him. He killed Darius."

Roland hurried out of the room and held his breath. "Damn it!" He stormed down the hall, tears flooding his eyes.

———

Roland held tightly onto his hat as he entered the house.

"The wind's awful today!" Tabitha exclaimed, forcing the door closed behind him. She shivered and turned to him as he pulled his boots off.

Roland brushed the snow from his coat before giving it a good shake.

"You're making a mess," she snapped. "Here, give me your socks and mitts so I can hang them by the fire. And go change out of those clothes. You'll catch a cold."

Roland dropped his gloves into her hand and peeled off his socks.

"Thank you," Tabitha said, gathering his things. "After you change, come down for some tea." She peered at him with her knowing eyes.

Roland glanced up the stairs and spotted the vermin boy peeking through the bars of the railing. He shook his head and dragged himself up the steps, his frozen feet sticking to the wood as he walked.

Nicholas scurried back to the nursery and crawled into bed.

Roland entered the room and pulled the sheets off the boy's head. "Why must you insist on disobeying me?"

Nicholas gave him a sheepish grin.

Roland shook his head, eyeing the boy's fangs and let go of the sheets. He turned to the door, rolling his eyes as Nicholas crawled back out of bed.

"Mr. Crispin, sir," he called, following Roland at his heels. "Your face is all red. Is it cold outside? I miss the snow. I was watching it from the window see, and I thought soon I might not know what snow feels like. That is since I'm only allowed to be in this big room. And sir, I'm also becoming very bored. If I don't die from this fever, I might just die from growing too—"

"Could you please be quiet?" Roland hollered, nostrils flaring.

Nicholas backed away and nodded.

"I have things to do. Go back to the nursey and don't disturb me!" Roland slammed the door and lowered himself to the floor. He pressed the back of his head up against the door and drew in a deep breath. *I can't do this anymore.* He shut his eyes and listened to the hail beat against the windows.

Two brisk knocks rapped the bedroom door.

"Roland, are you there?" Tabitha turned to look at the curious vermin, sticking its head out the door.

She banged harder.

"Roland, I brought you your tea."

She rattled the hinges. "Roland?"

"Still no answer?" Lisa said, coming up the stairs, cradling her daughter in her arms.

"He was really upset with me," Nicholas confessed, coming out into the hall.

"Get back to your room! You could get someone sick!" Tabitha hollered.

Nicholas groaned and leaned against the wall. "Why not just open the door?"

"Mr. Crispin likes his privacy," Lisa said. Tabitha knocked again.

"So, do I, but everyone's always coming and going out of my room without asking."

"It's not your room, you mongrel. Personally, I think you should sleep in a cage."

"Tabitha!" Lisa snapped as her four-year-old clung to her neck.

"Move out of the way, you old *Beidma*," Nicholas muttered, shoving between the women.

"What did you call me?" Tabitha snapped, trying to keep her tray balanced. "You know, you could have knocked over the good pot."

Nicholas shrugged and opened the door. "Mr. Crispin, I left my room and came to disturb you even though you said not to!" he shouted. He let go of the knob when the door smacked into something. He stepped back and scanned the dark room. "He's not here."

Roland held his head and pushed the door out of his way. "Mr. Slayden."

"Oh, look, he's um...there on the ground," Nicholas squeaked.

Lisa and Tabitha glared at the creature.

Roland got to his feet and rubbed his head. "Perhaps, I just wanted to be left alone?"

"You know, it's your own fault. Should've answered the ladies when they were calling you. Explained you wanted to be left alone," Nicholas argued.

Roland grabbed the vermin by the collar and smirked. "You're a pain in the—"

"Language, gentlemen." Lisa barked. "Roland, he's right, and Nicholas, stop pestering Master Crispin."

"For goodness sake, Roland, you're acting like a child." Tabitha shook her head. "What's got you in such a sour mood?"

Roland let go of Nicholas and took the tea tray from her. "Just a bit tired is all." He forced a smile. "Let's go have tea downstairs, shall we?"

Tabitha eyed him and nodded.

"Can I *please* come?" Nicholas begged.

Roland sighed. "All right. Lisa, could you gather the children?"

"Of course, sir."

Nicholas followed behind Roland and Tabitha as they went down the stairs. Roland's legs wobbled as he walked. He gripped onto the railing.

"Roland, you're unusually quiet this evening." Tabitha placed a hand on his back.

Roland drew in a deep breath. "I'm fine, Tabby."

Nicholas sniffled and wandered toward the piano.

Roland gazed at him, raising a brow. "What are you doing now?"

Nicholas backed away from the piano and bit his lip. "Oh, nothing."

"Nasty little vermin," Tabitha muttered.

Nicholas shot her a threatening glare.

Once they were seated by the fireplace, it wasn't long until they were joined by the others.

Julius pulled himself up onto his uncle's lap and reached for the tea tray. "Why is Nicholas downstairs?" he asked, grabbing a tart.

"I was going mad in that room." Nicholas grinned. "If I'd stayed any longer, I'd have started growling, and my eyes would've rolled back like this!"

Rose kicked the boy and glared.

"If you're mad, you'll have to go to the hospital." Julius pouted. "And then we won't get to play with my new soldiers. I'm having a battle today."

"A battle, eh?" Roland ruffled his nephew's hair and glanced over at Nicholas. "Did you have any toys when you were younger?"

"No, but we made a skipping rope once. My brother was good at skipping. I usually got tangled."

"We have skipping ropes!" Julius exclaimed.

"You had no toys then?" Caspian said, wrinkling his brow.

"Not everyone can afford such luxuries." Tabitha stretched up her hand toward a loose curl on Roland's head. He ducked underneath, and she shook her head. "You children should be very grateful for what you have. There are children running loose about the streets covered in filth."

"Do they play in the mud?" Julius asked.

"No, they just don't bathe." Caspian snorted.

"I hate baths," Julius muttered.

"They smell like a horse's behind." Caspian laughed.

Nicholas rubbed the back of his neck and looked at Caspian. "I'm guessing you folks haven't been around poor people before."

"Oh, yes, we have!" Julius nearly dropped his tart onto his uncle's lap. "There's a boy that goes up there"—he pointed to the chimney—"and when he comes down, he looks like a raccoon with these big black circles around his eyes."

"That boy makes a mess of the rug," Tabitha snapped.

"His name is Doc, and he's five, just like me!"

"If Nicholas were smaller, he'd probably be more suited for the job," Roland said, glancing at the fireplace.

"Doc says he has ten brothers and a sister. Isn't that strange?"

"I've got six siblings," Lisa said gently. "My brothers and I would clean chimneys, and our sisters Linnie and Edythe made lovely hats and dresses. You have to work if you want to eat."

"Speaking of work, Nicholas should begin earning his keep now that his health has improved a bit." Tabitha looked over at the vermin. She eyed him as he smiled at Rose and passed her the sugar. "Nicholas, do you have any previous work experience?"

"Pardon?"

"Have you worked before? You've got workers' hands."

Nicholas' face flushed pink. "I've been working most of my life."

"You've probably had very little education or none at all."

Rose shook her head. "Nicholas reads quite well."

Nicholas lowered his head and ran his fingers along the patterns on the rug.

"Really?" Tabitha glared at him.

"Nicholas, I've found you a job. You'll be meeting your employer soon." Roland said, brushing crumbs off of his pants. "What did you do at your last job?"

"I helped sell things."

"What sort of things did you sell?"

"Vegetables, jams, crafts. Sometimes we sold tonics."

"Did you sell mushrooms and onions?" Julius asked.

"Yes?"

"Yuck!"

"I thought you liked mushrooms." Roland set his nephew down beside him.

"No way, they come from mud!" Julius cried.

"Most vegetables do," Nicholas said, wrinkling his nose. "Haven't you ever gardened?"

"No?"

"It seems as though you're all belittling Nicholas," Rose said bitterly.

Nicholas smiled at her and glanced away, taking a drink from his teacup.

"Having such a character in our home is...it's—"

"It's what, Tabitha?" Lisa picked up the empty tray. "My upbringing was no different than this boy's."

"True, but you're still higher than this mongrel."

Nicholas flinched.

"Tabitha, a word, please." Roland glared at Nicholas as they made their way into the kitchen.

"That little beast could ruin her," Tabitha snapped. "He should be kept away from the other children."

"Don't use those terms so loosely," Roland whispered harshly.

"That's what he is. A diseased creature."

"The children aren't to know."

"Well, they should know! Forbid she returns those gentle gazes."

"Gentle gazes?"

Tabitha wrung her hands together and bit her lip. "A young heart is so easily swayed."

"Yes, I know." Roland sighed.

"Haven't you noticed?"

"Noticed what?"

"The way he looks at her."

Roland crossed his arms. "How Nicholas looks at who?"

"Rose. It's plain as day. That girl is nearly a woman, and if she is anything like your brother she'll continue to love blindly like a child. If we don't tell her what that monster really is, she might return his affections."

"That won't happen." Roland laughed. "Nicholas isn't a fool."

"Young love can make one very foolish. You, of all people, should know that. I'll do what I can to keep them from being alone together. I suggest that you encourage her suitors to step up their game."

"Aren't you being a little paranoid, Tabby?"

Tabitha shook her head and opened the kitchen door. "Believe whatever you like, but I know that gaze Roland. It's the same way you look at Miss Warren."

"I no longer have any feelings toward her."

"Your lack of honesty will get you into trouble."

Roland stood in the kitchen and sighed. *I suppose having Thompson around more often wouldn't hurt.* He leaned against the door. *But Rose might get annoyed and ask me not to. Once Nicholas starts working, he'll have less time to spend around the house.*

"That'll fix things." Roland moved away from the door and headed back to the children. He spotted his niece and the vermin boy sitting side by side, immersed in a conversation. His skin crawled as Rose took the boy's hand and lead him to the piano.

"My uncle taught me how to play it for the pageant." Rose scooted over to make room for the boy on the bench. "It would be fun if next time you could accompany me."

"But I don't know how to read music, Miss Crispin."

"Rose," she snapped.

"Rose, Nicholas." Roland peered at them. *How do I look at Dianna?* He watched his niece and the vermin boy smile at each other. *If he smiles any wider, she'll see those fangs of his.* He held his breath.

The two glanced over at him.

"Nicholas is a musician, and he knows the song I performed for the Frost Pageant!" Rose said excitedly.

"A musician?"

Nicholas looked away and nodded.

"Why is it that you're suddenly at a loss for words? You couldn't stop chatting earlier."

"Roland, I'm trying to perform." Rose held her hands over the keys.

Roland cringed, taking a step back. "You know you should really be more respectful. I'm your uncle, after all."

"I am very respectful. In fact, you're welcome to critique my playing."

"I'd love to." Roland laughed.

"Catching snowflakes on our tongues in the winter cold," Rose sang, playing the gentle melody.

Roland spotted Lisa and Tabitha whispering to each other, eyeing the pair at the piano.

"And we're skating across a frozen pond, hand in hand."

"Round and round we go," Nicholas chimed. "Like a ballerina on a music box."

Rose blushed and placed her hands onto her lap.

"W-why did you stop playing?" Nicholas asked.

"Your voice is. I didn't expect that."

"I'm sorry. I won't sing anymore."

"No! Please do." Rose covered her mouth and laughed. "You sounded quite lovely."

Nicholas' eyes flickered. He turned from her and smiled. "O-oh."

Tabitha shot Roland a glance as she headed upstairs.

Roland pressed his lips together. "Nicholas, you should probably get some rest."

"Could I stay and listen for a while longer? I'm not even the least bit tired, and I—"

"Do as you're told," Tabitha commanded from the rotunda.

Roland winced and turned to the boy. "You were only invited for tea. Tea is done, so back to bed you go."

Nicholas glared at him and stood up. "Yes, sir," he hissed haughtily.

Rose spun around to face her uncle. "Tabitha's being awfully rude to Nicholas. He doesn't need that. He's been through enough already."

"There's method to her behaviour."

"She's never been this way toward anyone else."

"Yeah, not even Doc," Caspian pointed out. "What is it about Nicholas that makes you all act so strange?"

Roland stretched his lips into a tight grin and shrugged. "I'm not sure what you mean by acting strange, but please know that Tabitha has her reasons."

Rose and Caspian eyed one another.

"If you say so," they said.

25

"Tell me about yourself," Theodore said, giving Dianna a gentle grin.

"Oh, there isn't much to tell."

"Well, that isn't fair. I've told you about myself. The least you could do is share something. Are you married?"

Dianna chuckled. "Me, married? That would make my mother happy. She wants grandchildren. I just haven't found the right man."

"My mother and father would have enjoyed having grandchildren."

Dianna clasped her hands together. "I never thought that my life would be so, so...well, you know how when you're young you make all these plans for your future, and every year you find yourself growing farther away from that goal? Things just haven't gone the way I expected. I suppose I expected too much."

"I can relate to that." Theodore lamented.

Little Arthur wrinkled his brow and shrugged. "Being all grown up seems a bit of a pain t'me."

"It can be." Dianna laughed. "I remember when I was a little girl,

I wanted to be married with five children and live in a beautiful blue house by the water. I wanted to watch the boats sailing by."

"And your wish didn't come true, eh?" Theodore frowned, a look of melancholy washing over him.

"No, but things changed. I went and travelled after I realized there was so much more I wanted to do with my life. I guess I have an adventurous spirit, or perhaps I'm simply curious, and I don't know how to sit still or stop talking for that matter." Her face grew hot. "I apologize for that."

"We don't mind, Miss," Arthur said, hopping up onto his knees to see out the window. "You ever been to see the other side of the ocean?"

Dianna shook her head. "Only as far as Presa. I enjoy visiting little towns here and there. Mainly, I just like meeting new people."

"My pa went to the other side of the ocean, way out there." He pointed. "See, when he gets back, my mama says I'll be all grown, and I can maybe go there with him."

Dianna sat quietly for a moment. "It must be beautiful, the other side of the world."

"I can only imagine it. But I sure hope whoever is over there is nice to my pa."

"Me too." Theodore smiled. "I find it hard to believe that a woman like yourself wouldn't have any suitors."

"Yeah, you're real nice," Arthur said.

Dianna blushed. "I've had some, but I just haven't felt the right way."

"How do you know if it's the right way?" Arthur asked.

"Because I've felt it before."

"So, then why not go marry that fella?"

"Because, Arthur, we aren't very fond of one another anymore. We've grown up."

"Just because you're grow'd up don't mean you have ta' change how ya' feel in yer heart or what ya' dream about." Arthur firmly plopped down into his seat.

"You're right. I know you are. Sadly, nothing can change the things that have already happened."

"But there's lots of things that ain't even happened yet."

"He has a point." Theodore patted the boy on the head.

Dianna nodded and drew in a deep breath. *What if? Why?* These questions played inside of her head constantly.

What if she'd never found out about Roland's secret? Why didn't she attend his father's funeral? What if she had? Would it have made a difference? Why didn't she stop herself from doing something so foolish?

She'd replayed that moment in her mind for years. When Roland was struck by her father and the look of horror on her mother's face when their parents finally found the two of them at a hotel in Riversburg...She could remember Mrs. Crispin crying and begging to know, *why, why, why?* And Roland stumbling through his words, only to say that he was sorry over and over again. His father had approached him before her parent's dragged her from the room...

Dianna swallowed the lump in her throat and turned as little Arthur nodded off. She removed her scarf and wrapped it around him. To think, if their little plan to elope had actually worked, she'd be tucking her little ones into bed like this every night, in a blue house. The thought made her heart ache.

"Achoo!" Nicholas rubbed his nose vigorously as he forced back another sneeze.

His head was hot, but the rest of his body shivered from the cold sweat that drenched his clothing and clung to the hairs on the back of his neck. He rolled his eyes as the two men paced back and forth, bouncing ideas off one another. *They're wasting their time.* He wiped his nose onto the pillowcase.

Roland glared at him. "You could use a handkerchief."

"Uh wha—?"

"Like a respectable gentleman." Roland pulled a square of material from his vest.

"It's a piece of cloth." Nicholas eyed it.

"It's for your disgusting cold," Peter grumbled, crossing his arms. "Not like a vermin could ever understand proper etiquette."

Nicholas blew into the handkerchief and waved it in front of the two men. "Suppose I wanted you lads out of the picture. All I'd need to do is leave this lying around for you to use, and you'd be hit with this nasty fever."

"We've taken the proper precautions, vermin." Peter flicked the boy in the head.

Nicholas winced and laid down on his back, his gaze burning into the ceiling.

"He's got a mouth on him. He must be feeling better." Peter glanced at Roland. "Anyone who has enough energy to talk back has enough energy to work."

"That's true." Roland eyed the vermin carefully, then referred to his notes. "Your temperature has been fluctuating, but you seem to have a lot more energy now that the medication is kicking in."

"So, we put him to work," Peter smirked.

"He needs to learn first. If he doesn't have the proper tools when Kurtis arrives, we could be in serious trouble. Our necks are on the line."

"All for the sake of bloody research," Peter grumbled.

"Research that could greatly benefit all of us."

"Research?" Nicholas sat up and scanned the men's faces. "Y-you aren't gonna chop me up, are you?"

"That all depends on how well behaved you are," Peter sneered.

Roland shook his head. "It's more of an observational study. It's important for us to know our enemy if we wish to have a chance against them in combat."

"Combat? There's barely any of us left to fight. Why should I let you do your research on me if it means you're just gonna kill my friends and family?"

"'Cause, if you don't"—Peter gripped the vermin by his hair—"we ditch your hide in the woods and let the ravens eat away at your eyes while there's still some breath in you."

Nicholas clawed at the man's hand, his teeth gritting together.

"Listen to the beast growl." Peter laughed. "Think he purrs when praised?"

"Peter." Roland turned to him, eyes wide.

"Let go!" Nicholas hissed, tears spilling from his eyes.

Peter grinned and released his grip. He brushed the dark strands of hair from his hands. "Oh, my, his fur's shedding."

"That's enough," Roland snapped.

Peter stepped back and raised his hands. "I was only playing around."

"He's just a boy."

"You're starting to sound like my cousin."

"Nicholas doesn't respond well to aggression. The more we agitate him, the harder it will be to domesticate him. It's not about me being like Dianna. It's about assessing the situation and responding accordingly. Research."

"Roland, I know a thing or two about mutts. You can beat them all you want, and they still come back to you, begging for affection."

"He's not a dog."

"He's not a human either."

Although his shoulders remained tense, Roland forced out a sigh. "We'll finish this discussion privately. Let the boy get some rest."

Peter nodded. As he stepped through the door, the vermin's dark gaze pierced into him. He shivered and left.

The two men made their way out into the hall. Neither one uttered a sound as they hurried down the steps. Roland drew in a deep breath as Peter entered the office behind him. He shut the door and let out a sigh.

"I know how frustrated you are right now, but we can't be—"

"Why are you suddenly siding with my cousin? Lately, all you've done is lecture me. You act as if I've done something wrong. You didn't have any problem with my methods before, and honestly, I think your softness is what's hindering our progress."

"I'm not taking her side. I just can't bear to—"

"To see the brat squirm? To use your authority?"

"He already knows that we're the ones with the authority."

"At this rate, the entire project is a lost cause!" Peter raised his hands above his head. "He's going to meet with Mayor Hood soon, and he's still holding his head high like a cocky little brute! How do you expect him to fare at that new job you've lined up for him, huh?"

Roland groaned. "I'm just as frustrated as you are, but I'm doing my best to keep my emotions in check." He ran a hand through his hair. "Nicholas knows that in order for him to survive, he needs to please Kurtis. Honestly, I'm praying that he'll come to his senses and will do whatever it takes to impress the man when the time comes. He's not as ignorant as you imagine." Roland thought of Nicholas's behaviour at the kitchen table when Dianna came in after coming back from town. "You forget that he lived with a half-human family in Dinara for a while. We're not starting from scratch."

Peter pressed his lips together. "For a man who has put his entire family and reputation at risk, you're awfully calm about all this."

Roland shook his head. "I've been taking medication just to help me sleep at night. If I don't keep my composure in front of the boy, he'll use my fear and anxiety against me. Besides, my reputation's already gone down the drain." He shrugged and shoved his hands into his pockets.

"Fine. You may be right. I'll try and lay off a little, keep my emotions in check, but don't expect me to stop expressing my authority. We need to break his pride so that he doesn't question us." Peter met Roland's stare. "If we let him get too out of control, he'll try and shift the balance. I don't want to be dealing with a power struggle after Hood makes his decision. That is if he decides to favour us."

"The thought of him meeting Nicholas makes my stomach turn." Just because the boy acted appropriately once didn't mean he'd do it again when called on. Now Peter made Roland second-guess everything. *Damn it.*

Peter nodded. A pounding came from the front door. "Ay, there's a knock. Probably Hood, the reaper himself, come to rip us from the dirt like weeds," he jested, punching Roland in the shoulder playfully as the two went into the hall.

Roland managed a sad smile. He opened the door and gawked. Dianna entered alongside Leon, a young boy and an unfamiliar, highly sophisticated gentleman.

"Good afternoon," Dianna said, smiling at her wide-eyed cousin. "Roland, Peter, I'd like to introduce you to Lord Theodore Wolfe."

The two men struggled to find their words as the party entered the house, removing their coats and boots.

"Pleased to meet you, sir." Roland took the gentleman's coat and shook his hand.

Theodore smiled politely, glancing around. "What a lovely place you have here Mr. Crispin."

"W-why, thank you."

"Is Nicholas around?"

"Nicholas?" Roland furrowed his brow.

"Yes, I'd like to say hello. I haven't seen the boy for quite some time."

"He's..."

"Sleeping." Peter looked up the stairs. "He's had a long day. We weren't going to bother him again until dinner."

"Oh, well, in the meantime, might I borrow your telephone? I'm in town on business and need to make a few arrangements."

"Yes, of course. I have a phone in the kitchen. Um, Leon, could you show him where it is. Dianna, please tell Tabitha we have guests for dinner. I'll be right back. Peter and I were in the middle of something." Roland eyed Peter.

"Thank you." Theodore followed Mr. Leon to the parlour.

Dianna raised her brow. "Come along, Arthur, let's see if there's something yummy to eat. You must be hungry after such a long drive."

Roland and Peter raced back upstairs. They entered the nursery and found the boy lying on his back, gazing at the pages of Midnight Garden. Nicholas sat up and growled.

"Knew it was you two clomping up those stairs," he muttered.

"Do you have anything presentable to wear?" Peter asked.

"*Nei.* Should I?"

Roland inhaled near the boy. "You smell. Take a bath. Peter, watch him. I'll find something for him. I should have some old clothes lying around."

Nicholas pulled himself up onto his feet and moaned, going into the bathroom. Roland rushed down the hall and opened the closet in Rose's bedroom.

"There must be something. Where did all these dresses come from?" He shifted through the clothes, spied a box on the floor and opened it up. "Aha!"

Roland stumbled back into the nursery carrying a box of clothes and placed them on the table.

Peter glared at the vermin as he inspected his face. "You really should cut that hair of yours, or at least comb it out. It's a mess."

Roland turned toward the bathroom at the sound of water sloshing about. He popped his head in through the door and glanced up at Peter as he wiped the water from his face.

"Was that really necessary?" Peter glared at Nicholas.

Nicholas sank into the tub, his dark brown eyes peering out at the two men as water splashed onto the floor.

"Quit making such a mess!"

Roland rolled up his sleeves, yanked Nicholas up out of the tub, and handed him a towel. "I think Mr. Rissing's been tortured enough."

Nicholas pulled away from him as Roland went back out into the nursery.

He came back with the box of clothes and placed them on the counter. "All right, dry off and try these on."

Nicholas inched toward the box.

Roland and Peter hurried out into the bedroom.

"Make sure you do something about that hair," Peter snapped, popping his head back in before shutting the door.

The two men waited.

Roland's chest wrenched every time he drew in a breath. His nerves were everywhere. Not once did Dianna mention that Lord Wolfe would be coming back with her to the estate, and she never mentioned that he knew Nicholas. Roland couldn't seem to wrap his head around the situation. He wondered if it was just a ploy to put him and Peter on edge.

Nicholas opened the bathroom door and puffed up his chest. The pants were far past his ankles and dragged along the floor. The shirt was untucked, and the sleeves flapped like tiny wings below his fingertips as he crossed his arms. His hair dripped, along with the feather earring, that looked more like a jagged icicle now that it was wet. The expression on the boy's face was more than the two men could handle.

Roland was the first to let a chuckle bubble past his lips as he went to grab a towel. Then Peter burst out laughing, attempting to tuck in Nicholas' shirt.

"You look like a wet cat," Roland smirked, tossing the towel over the boy's head. He rung out Nicholas's hair and went into the bathroom for a comb.

Peter raised Nicholas' arm and began rolling up his sleeves. "Any suspenders in there?"

"Yep."

"Roll up those pants too. At least the socks fit."

"They're itchy," Nicholas mumbled. "And these are too big. Why do I gotta wear them?"

"You can't be eating dinner in your pyjamas," Roland said,

pulling at the long, wet strands of hair around Nicholas' face. "What are we gonna do with all this hair?"

"N-nothing," Nicholas whispered. "I can't cut it yet."

"I see."

"Well, there must be a way to make it look neat." Peter scratched his head.

"We could tie it back," Roland said, helping Nicholas with the suspenders.

"Don't touch it."

The two men backed away, still grinning.

"He looks like a scarecrow." Peter chuckled.

"Well, I suppose I grabbed the wrong box." Roland shook his head.

"That's enough outta you two," Nicholas barked. "Treating me like some...some—"

"His hair still looks like a wet mop," Peter snorted, slapping his hand down over his mouth.

Nicholas crossed his arms, the large shirt sliding off his shoulder. "I'm used to wearing bigger clothes. I've worn hand-me-downs all my life. Not sure why you two think it's so funny."

"Just never realized how small you were," Peter admitted. "I thought you vermin were supposed to be big, tall, brutes."

"Not scarecrows." Roland chuckled.

Nicholas narrowed his eyes.

"All right, we're finished." Roland sighed. "You are to be on your best behaviour for the rest of the evening. Do you understand? Consider this a trial run."

"Yes, sir," Nicholas muttered.

"Oh, and please do something about your hair. The mop makes it so hard for me to take that scowl on your face seriously." Peter tugged the young vermin's hair.

"Stop it," Nicholas growled.

"Scarecrow," Peter said, laughing. "A grumpy little scarecrow."

"Guests? How many?" Tabitha said, wringing out her hands at the sink. "I've barely got enough for you and Peter."

"Two more," Dianna said, handing Arthur a tart. "Don't spoil your supper now."

Arthur grinned and nodded, eyeballing the treat.

"Two more? Well, I suppose I can have someone run to the butchers for a chicken."

"I wish I could have called ahead." Dianna frowned. "I didn't mean to make more work for you."

"Tabby, I think we'll be needing some groceries." Roland waltzed into the kitchen.

"I'm aware of that."

Roland gazed at the little boy chowing down on a tart, then turned toward the two women. "Nicholas will be joining us as well."

Tabitha glared at him, placing her hands on his hips. "Is that so?"

"Y-yes."

"Well, then, how about that mutt go and get our groceries."

"Shh. You can't be calling him that. He has a visitor."

"We're feeding another animal?" Tabitha hissed, throwing her hands above her head. She paced back and forth, drawing in deep breaths.

"We'll be dining with Lord Theodore Wolfe," Dianna snapped.

Tabitha paused and spun toward Roland. "When were you going to tell me it was important company?"

"Um, when you let me." He blushed. "Just give me a list of what you need, and I'll pick it up."

"Bring Nicholas with you," Peter said, entering the room.

"You want me out alone with him?"

"He can't be wearing *that* when he meets with Hood."

"If I'm bringing him along, I expect you or Dianna to accompany us."

"Afraid of a little boy?" Dianna teased. "I'll go, but Peter, you'll need to entertain my guests."

"Hey!" Roland shot at Arthur. "Leave room for dinner."

Arthur pouted and nibbled on the tart shyly.

Dianna laughed and followed Roland out of the kitchen and up to the nursery.

"I'll let you wear my old jacket and boots," he said as he led Nicholas downstairs.

Nicholas' eyes grew wide. "You're letting me out?"

"We need to get you something proper to wear, and we have guests, so we need an extra hand with the groceries," Roland whispered. "Now, let's sneak out of here quickly and get to the Royalton."

"Why not take the other car?" Dianna questioned.

"Mr. Leon drove it all the way to Dinara. It's probably best not to push it in this weather. The Royalton is at least ten years younger." Roland tried not to take the car out if he could avoid it. His father favoured the vehicle and had bought it as an anniversary gift for his mother. Roland placed a hat on Nicholas's head and pulled it down over his ears. "Keep them hidden."

Nicholas nodded, brushing his hair out of his face.

The cold air bit as they stepped outside. The boy shivered violently at the wind and clutched himself as he followed behind the two adults toward the stable. Dianna watched him as he grinned at the crunch of snow beneath his feet.

While Roland started the car, Nicholas examined the large stable.

"Where are all the animals?" He looked at the saddle resting on the gate.

Roland sighed. "Had to sell them. Dusty was the only one left. Now we just store my father's car in here."

"Must've been lonely all by himself." Nicholas climbed up into the backseat.

Roland nodded. "We'll get you something to wear first and then pick up what we need for dinner."

"Okay." Nicholas rubbed his hands together.

The long white and blue car rolled through the snow as Roland drove out into the cold. He pulled up the collar of his jacket and shivered. "Least it's a short drive." He laughed, peering back at Nicholas.

"We should get you some good socks," Dianna said as she placed her scarf around Nicholas' neck. "And a proper hat and mitts."

Nicholas tried his best to keep his cheeks from flushing. He shrugged. "No need to spend money on me."

"I don't want you getting sick again."

"*Dar Danya,*" he mumbled.

She adjusted the scarf and patted him on the shoulder. "Remember, I won't let anything happen to you. I promise."

26

——————

"Got anything new lately, Mrs. Kipp?" Roland asked as they burst through the door of the general store with a flurry of snowflakes.

"Why, yes. This lovely pink gown came in the other day that I thought would be darling on your little Rose!" Mrs. Kipp's long skirt billowed beneath her as she adjusted her frilled apron. She rubbed her arms to stave off the chill before holding up the gown, running a hand along the embroidered puff sleeves. Although her shop was small, Mrs. Kipp had an eye for fashion, ordering only the latest styles from Presa. She could often be spotted in a bolero jacket, wearing her thin pearl choker.

"Actually, I'm looking for clothes for this young man."

The woman eyed Nicholas and grinned. "Why, I've never seen such a red nose."

Nicholas scrunched up his face. Roland and Dianna laughed.

"Miss Warren!" Mrs. Kipp gleamed. "Is that you?"

Dianna nodded. "It's been a while, hasn't it?"

"Why, you're all grown up and with Mr. Crispin. I wondered when you two kids would get together again. You were inseparable."

Roland blanched. "We aren't together," he muttered. "She's visiting Peter is all."

"Oh, my apologies. I'd just assumed. Well, little lad, why don't I measure you and see what I've got in your size."

Nicholas nodded and watched as the woman pulled measuring tape out of her apron.

"There's a pair of pants that should fit you nicely. Then the jacket. Hmm. Yes, I think I've got a decent amount. Follow me."

Dianna glared at Roland and shook her head. "You didn't have to be so blunt."

Why is she being so defensive? "I don't want people talking. It's bad enough Connie already mentioned something. You know how much they love to gossip. I've got enough of a reputation as it is."

"Um, sir, may I have this?" Nicholas asked, holding up a navy-blue jacket.

Roland looked at it and adjusted his gloves. "How much is it?"

"That one is lovely, isn't it?" Mrs. Kipp hovered around Nicholas, helping hold it against his shoulders to check the fit. "The gold pattern is quite handsome."

"How much?" Roland asked.

"It's twenty. But I'll give it to you for fifteen since you're such a loyal customer."

"That's too much," Nicholas mumbled, shaking his head. "I don't need it."

"I'll take it." Roland snatched it from the boy.

Nicholas raised his brow. "But—"

"Every gentleman needs a respectable jacket."

"I'm no gentleman."

"Well, then it's a gift."

"It isn't even my birthday," Nicholas snapped.

"I'll pay for half." Dianna groaned, pulling her wallet from her yellow bag. "You're both stubborn as mules. My goodness."

Roland watched her press her lips together as she rummaged around in her wallet. "It's fine, Dianna. I'll take care of it."

Mrs. Kipp laughed. "Do you need any boots?"

Nicholas turned to Roland, who nodded. "He needs just about everything."

"Oh, my, well then, I'll pull together a pile."

"Give me three plain shirts, three pants, a pair of boots, six pairs of socks, and two sweaters," Roland said, glancing at the shelves. *I should've asked Peter for some money before we left. I'll see if Mrs. Kipp will put these on credit. Maybe I can convince Uncle Charlie or Eloise to cover the cost and pay them back once Nicholas starts working.*

"All right. We have white, green and grey for the shirts. One of every colour?"

"Sure."

Mrs. Kipp gathered the items and placed them on the counter. "Shall I wrap these for you?"

"That would be wonderful, thank you."

Nicholas' eyes remained on the blue and gold jacket. He grinned as it was placed inside the wrapping paper.

Roland spied Nicholas' face as it lit up. He smiled to himself and watched as the boy proudly carried his new clothes out to the car. *I'll pay her with what I've got on me and get the rest to her later.* He pulled his wallet out from his jacket and handed Mrs. Kipp the money. "I'm a little short. Can I get the rest to you next week?"

Mrs. Kipp counted the money and put it into her apron. "I suppose."

Dianna gripped onto Roland's sleeve. "Are you sure you don't want me to pay for some?" she whispered.

"It's fine. I'll ask my godfather for a loan." He gestured to Nicholas, waiting outside by the car. "We'd better go. Thank you, Mrs. Kipp!"

Dianna and Roland headed outside to the car, pulling the door shut against a gust of wind.

"Now we just need to go to the butcher shop, and I suppose we should pick up some—"

"Why don't we stop by my parent's place?"

"No way. Your father hates me."

"He hates you?" Nicholas wrinkled his nose. "What did you do?"

"That's none of your business."

"True, but I'm curious."

"It will save time and money. Come along, Nicholas. I'm sure my parents would love to meet you." Dianna climbed up into the front seat of the Duesenberg Royalton.

"Oh, you're driving now?" Roland folded his arms.

"Just get in. Besides, Nicholas should change into some of these clothes before we get back."

"That's true." Roland sat beside her.

Dianna started the car and smirked, watching the snowflakes twirl.

Nicholas shivered, sank into his seat, and clutched the parcel of clothing to his chest as they passed the barn where the Crispin's had found him. Roland went to reach his hand back to comfort the boy but pulled away. They were nearing Dianna's house. His stomach turned. *She used to climb up into the tree and toss apples down to me before school.* Things were so much simpler then.

"Here we are." Dianna smiled, pulling up to an old green coloured house. "Hopefully, someone's home."

Roland caught the tentative note in her voice. He leaned toward her, resting a hand on her shoulder.

She glanced at him, loosening her grip on the wheel.

The three got out of the car and went up to the front door.

Dianna knocked and drew in a big breath. "Don't mention anything about me staying with you," she whispered.

His face flushed pink. "I wouldn't dare."

The door opened slowly, and an older gentleman peered out at the shivering trio. "Can I help you folks?"

"It's me, Dianna. I'm back in town."

The man eyed her and grinned. "Well, now, look at you all dolled up! I almost thought you were a film star with all that makeup on. So, where've you been hiding?"

"Here and there." Dianna laughed. "Peter and I are having a little party and realized we're low on food. Got anything we could buy off you?"

"Make my little girl pay?" her father smirked. "Never." He opened the door wider. "Come on inside."

Nicholas looked around the house and grinned. He glanced over at Roland, who kept his head lowered. "Sir, is something the matter?"

"Everything's fine, Nicholas," Roland muttered.

"My father says we can have a few hens and whatever vegetables we need," Dianna uttered, brushing her hair from her face.

"The hens should be enough."

Mr. Warren returned and handed Dianna a bag. "Got everything you need right there, love. Don't you be a stranger now. We've missed ya terribly. Your mother'll have a shock when she sees you. She and a few other ladies are delivering food to the Shepard's a few houses down. The fever hit most of the family. I'll let her know you came by."

"Thank you, Daddy." Dianna grinned.

Mr. Warren eyed Roland, stepping toward him cautiously. "Mr. Crispin?"

Roland gulped.

"You remember Roland," Dianna said quietly, twisting her fingers. "He and Peter are—"

"You're still hanging around this filth? I figured letting you go away and focus on your studies would help you realize his type are nothing but dirty cheats and liars. It's all blood money, Dianna. That's all it is."

Roland glowered, tipped his hat, and stormed out the door. He leaned against the railing by the door, taking in a deep breath.

"Dad," Dianna scolded with her tone, the old door barely muffling her voice.

"This boy, one of his damn nephews? You know very well that I don't want none of 'em on my property."

"Nicholas is the son of a dear friend. He's currently in my care," Dianna snapped.

Roland took off his hat, turning it around in his hands. He shook his head, listening as Mr. Warren's tone softened.

"I'm sorry, lad."

"I'll come by again soon. Please tell Mom I said hi."

"That Crispin boy is trouble. You watch yourself."

Roland met Dianna's gaze as she came outside. He started toward the car.

"Look after my little girl for me."

"I-I will, sir," Nicholas said.

"Come along, Nicholas. You'll just have to try on your new clothes later," Dianna called, turning toward the door.

Roland grit his teeth as he clutched onto the steering wheel. *That man. I should've stayed in the bloody car.*

Dianna held the bag tightly. "Roland I—"

"Don't even say it."

She pressed her lips together. "Fine."

Usually, Roland would ramble aimlessly through his frustration, but the very thought of Mr. and Mrs. Warren made his stomach turn. They were just like every other person in Tavern, they despised him for his name and nothing more. Although others managed to bite their tongues, the Warren's, along with many of the students, seemed to think it was their sole duty to ridicule, curse, and humiliate every Crispin that ever stepped onto Tavern soil. Roland understood why many weren't fans of his father, but his brother Lawrence had always been loved by everyone. All Roland had been known for before his father's death was that he was a love-sick boy who was trying desperately to gain the approval of his sweetheart's parents, as well his own.

Roland glared into the snow, hands numb from gripping the wheel, and yet the rest of him boiled with anger. His memories overtook his sense back to the day when Mr. Warren had actually struck him. Roland laughed to himself, wishing that he'd turned and knocked him off his feet today, the way he'd done years before.

I have no intention of trying to rekindle my relationship with your daughter. And blood money? Really? So, you think I did them in too. Great. Everyone seems to think I murdered my own family. I knew my father didn't plan on leaving me anything. No one expected me to live past the age of three. I know Darius cursed himself for wishing for another son. He never once blamed my mother. Sometimes I wish I'd never taken that first breath. I wish my mother had just let them bury me in the yard next to her roses. It would have spared her all the heartache.

Roland blinked hard and cleared his throat before drawing in a deep breath. "We're home. Dianna go to the kitchen with those. Nicholas, come with me, I'll help you clean up for dinner."

Dianna brushed past him, trying desperately to catch his eye. Roland met her gaze briefly, ushering Nicholas away from the stable. His heart stopped as Dianna pressed her lips together, her eyes falling toward the snow-covered garden. He rubbed the back of his neck and pushed the stable doors shut.

Nicholas followed Roland to the back of the house. "This door leads to the kitchen. I'll enter first." Roland unlocked the door. He peered inside and waved Nicholas over. Laughter came from the parlour. Roland led Nicholas toward the storage cupboard. "Go in here and change into your new clothes."

"Which ones do I wear?" Nicholas asked.

"Throw on the white shirt and a sweater. You might want to change out of those wet socks too. I'll hang up your other clothes later, so they can dry."

Nicholas nodded and shut the door.

Roland winced, listening to the sound of the boy banging around in the large cupboard. *Maybe I should have sent him to the cellar?* He held his breath as the door swung open. Roland looked Nicholas over, stroking his chin. "It all fits very nicely. Looks like you've still got a bit of room to grow as well." He stumbled back as the vermin lunged forward and wrapped his arms around him. "N-Nicholas, please."

Nicholas beamed up at him, grinning from ear to ear. "These are really mine?"

"They are."

Nicholas let go and cleared his throat. "*Dar Danya.* I mean, thanks for giving me these."

"You're welcome. Pass me the other clothes."

Nicholas nodded. "I always got my brother's old clothes. Never anything new like this from a store. And nothing with these nice colours."

Roland smiled. "Most of what I wore as a boy belonged to my older brother."

"My brother always needed new clothes since he grew so much. We thought he'd never stop growing."

Roland laughed. "Well, hopefully, you don't grow too much during the warmer seasons."

Nicholas nodded.

Peter and Dianna entered the kitchen. Peter frowned. "What happened to the scarecrow?"

"Oh, please," Dianna snapped, smacking him on the arm. "You sound like a child."

"How's dinner coming along?" Roland asked.

"Tabitha and Lisa are getting everything together. Peter just brought out some wine. Rose is performing a poem, and the boys have been on their best behaviour." Dianna walked over to Nicholas. "May I fix your hair a little? My friend Patrick wears his hair long, as well, but he ties some of it back, like this. Come have a look at yourself."

Nicholas tugged on the tail behind his head and winced, looking at his reflection on the back of a large spoon. "It looks funny."

"Really, I think you look quite handsome."

"Why'd you let her do it and not us?" Peter grumbled.

Nicholas blushed.

"Because he's sweet on her," Roland teased.

"W-What?"

"Really, Roland? Nicholas, you're officially the most mature man in this room." Dianna reclaimed the spoon.

"What about my ears," Nicholas asked, covering them with his hands.

"Your hair covers the tops of them. Don't worry." Dianna gave him a smile, leading a hand away from his ear. "No one will see."

Peter leaned over and examined the boy's head. "She's right. They're barely noticeable."

"Is that why you keep your hair so long?" Roland asked.

Nicholas shook his head.

"Well, either way, they're covered up. Wish you'd take that earring out, though," Peter grumbled. "Come on into the parlour. Our guest is waiting for you."

"Don't look at me like that. You knew we had company." Roland moaned, rolling his eyes.

"But what if...if I—"

"You'll be fine, darling. I promise," Dianna whispered, giving his shoulder a slight squeeze.

Nicholas followed the three out into the parlour. His gaze fell onto Rose, who showed such melancholy it looked as though she were broken. Her voice quivered as she spoke. She seemed far away.

"She's performing a poem we read back in school," Peter explained. "She's absolutely brilliant."

"And as the waves rolled high, they swept the men's bodies and tossed them against the cliffs. One by one, their cries were silenced. Oh, fellow fishermen wary be when the waves growl in Tavern's sea."

The small crowd applauded as Nicholas watched Rose

transform. The look of grief vanished as if a spell had been broken, and she bloomed with a gentle warmth around her. "Oh, there you are!" she exclaimed, redirecting the audience's attention.

Theodore Wolfe caught a glimpse of the vermin boy and pulled himself to his feet. "What in the world?" He dashed over and tousled the boy's hair. "You're huge!"

"You two know each other?" Rose cocked her head.

Nicholas stepped back and eyed the man cautiously.

"Last time I saw you, you must've been about here on me." Theodore grinned and motioned below his waist. "I'm glad you're well."

"Uncle Theodore?"

"Yes?"

Nicholas swallowed hard and lowered his head.

"What's the matter, Nicholas?"

Roland turned Nicholas toward him and raised the boy's chin.

"I don't know why I'm crying," Nicholas sobbed.

Roland gave him a smile. "You've had a long day."

"Lord Wolfe is your uncle?" Rose asked.

"He was raised with my children. They consider him their little brother."

"Micah and Zana, right?" Rose stepped forward, clearly distressed at seeing Nicholas' tears.

"Yes, those are their names."

"He talks about them all the time." She smiled.

Nicholas turned from them as Theodore knelt down and eyed him. "It's all my fault."

"*Elde Inrohai,*" Theodore whispered, pulling him close. He smoothed back Nicholas's hair.

Roland cleared his throat, motioning for his niece to give the two some space as Theodore continued to whisper to the boy in Valdin. He tilted his head. *I suppose he'd speak the language, having vermin children and all.*

"Everything is going to be okay. Miss Warren and I sorted it all out. You have nothing to fear."

Nicholas sniffled, mumbling something to the gentleman.

"*Ha. Elde Inrohai.*"

Roland spied Caspian inching forward and grabbed him by the wrist. Caspian looked up at him and frowned.

"What's he saying?"

"I don't know. I've never been to Dinara." Roland said gently. He prayed Theodore wouldn't expose them.

"Nicholas, why don't you dance for them?" Theodore asked, getting up onto his feet.

Nicholas shook his head, rubbing his eyes with his sleeve.

"You dance?" Rose's face lit up.

"He's a fine dancer. Quick on his feet. Quite the musician, too."

"*Nei*," Nicholas whined. "They wouldn't like *those* songs or dances."

"I like them," Theodore argued.

"Yes, but you grew up with them."

"He's still recovering from his fever. Perhaps he should take it easy?" Roland suggested.

Theodore frowned. "I forgot. They told me you'd gotten that horrible illness."

Nicholas nodded. "I would have died if they didn't stop to help me."

"Well, if you won't dance, why not sing something?"

"Uncle Theo *I-Iya Net*...um..."

Roland shot Nicholas a threatening glare. "Your uncle came all this way to see you."

"What do you want me to sing?"

"You could sing *Daisies*," Theodore suggested.

Nicholas turned to Roland.

"Go on," he said.

Nicholas nodded and bit his lip, then moved to the centre of the room by the piano. The group gathered around.

"Can you keep a secret, my lady?

I'll send ye' a basket of daisies

To prove I am true,

Pure white and wet with dew,

And to say that you'll

Keep my secret with you."

Rose let out a squeal and clasped her mouth shut.

Nicholas spun around and raised his brow. "Miss Crispin, are you all right?"

"I'm fine. You're just absolutely fantastic."

Nicholas blushed.

"Can you sing something else?" she begged, leaning up against the wall.

"Like what?"

Theodore chuckled. "Like what? Since when have you been shy?"

"I'm not shy. You just put me on the spot," Nicholas barked.

"Sorry. I've just missed seeing your performances, is all." Theodore smiled.

"We've still got time before dinner. Why not sing another one?" Roland suggested, looking him over.

"Um, okay, sure." Nicholas gulped.

"Begonia, Begonia, keep away from yah.

She lives up on the hillside.

Begonia, Begonia, when you need a favour,

She'll keep you bound for a lifetime."

Roland wandered over to the piano and hovered, listening as the boy sang.

"Why don't you play something, sir?" Nicholas said.

Roland shrugged. "I don't really play anymore."

"That's not true. You're always playing when everyone else is out."

Roland laughed. "Your uncle asked you to perform, not me."

"But I want you to play the song that sounds like this." Nicholas leaned over beside the man and tickled the ivory keys.

Roland's eyes grew wide. "How did you learn to play that without any sheet music?"

"What do you mean?" Nicholas asked, furrowing his brow.

"I told you, he's a brilliant musician." Theodore laughed. "Music runs through his veins."

Roland gestured for Nicholas to sit down and placed his hands on the keys. "I once knew a bonnie lass," he sang.

Nicholas' eyes widened.

"Whose eyes were bluer than the sky."

"She asked if I liked to dance, then asked if I wished to fly," they sang in unison.

"Now you know I'm not the type of lad to ever tell a lie," Roland smirked. "But let's just say we danced for days. We lost track of the time."

Nicholas sang the harmony above, while Roland stayed on the melody.

Roland couldn't recall ever having this much fun playing the piano. Not since his brother passed.

Tabitha and Lisa entered the room and gawked at the vermin and the man sitting side by side, singing.

"When you boys are done, dinner's on the table," Tabitha said firmly, shooting Roland a dirty look. Her face softened as he smiled back at her.

"All right, Tabby."

She shook her head. "That boy will be the end of me."

"I've never seen him like this before," Lisa said, swaying to the music. "He's absolutely—"

"Darling," Tabitha whispered. "Grinning away like a little boy. That there is *my* Roland."

Lisa giggled as Arthur and Rose danced around the room, and Theodore clapped the beat.

"I've got to agree with you, Mrs. Gibson. Roland hasn't been this giddy since the last time we went out drinking, and that was many years ago." Peter laughed.

27

"Don't you think it would've been nice to warn us ahead of time about *Lord* Theodore Wolfe coming over for a visit?" Roland asked, glaring at Dianna as she brushed her hair in the guest bedroom that evening.

"It isn't like we need to hide anything from him. He knows all about Nicholas."

Peter and Roland turned to one another, then back to her.

"How'd you know he was the boy's uncle?" Peter asked.

"A little bird told me. If you're worried about losing your precious test subject, you have nothing to fear. Theodore isn't here for Nicholas."

Peter shook his head. "How does a man like that get mixed up with those creatures?"

Dianna turned her attention to the mirror, parting her hair with her fingers before brushing out the next section. "Anyway, my job is almost done. I'll be out of your hair once everything is arranged with Mr. Hood."

"You're leaving?" Peter's jaw dropped. "But the little brute only listens to you. You can't just leave. Right, Roland?"

"Do whatever you want. You've been nothing but a pain since you arrived." Roland's stomach turned as the words left his lips. *That's not what I meant. She would've left either way*—his throat tightened as she looked at his reflection behind her in the mirror—*at least she had the courtesy to tell us.*

Dianna put down the hairbrush and glowered. "I appreciate your honesty, Mr. Crispin. Thank you."

Roland groaned. "I can't do this right now."

"Then when Roland?"

"Never."

"Never?" Dianna laughed sullenly. "Why don't you just tell me how you feel? Tell me that you hate me with every bit of breath in your body. That you regret everything we did."

"You two, um...I uh—" Peter stuttered, inching toward the bedroom door.

"Every breath in my body wouldn't be enough to express how I feel about you, Miss Warren!" Roland's hands quivered as he barked a fake laugh. "In fact, I don't think there's any way to measure how much you irritate me." His chest ached. *Why not have Peter and Charlotte lie to me for months while you avoid me, like last time? Why bother saying anything at all when you're just going to leave?*

"Perhaps, if you weren't so stuck in your ways, I wouldn't be so irritating?"

"Um, Uncle Roland, I—"

Roland shook his head, gritting his teeth. "*I'm* stuck in my ways. Really? This is coming from the most stubborn person on the face of the earth!"

Peter gazed down at Rose and gulped. "Now isn't a good time."

Rose bit her lip, stepping behind him.

"I don't see how having a conscience is stubborn. Is it so wrong to have compassion for a child?" Dianna argued.

"Oh, so now I don't have a conscience? My family is nothing but cheats and liars. We're all living on blood money, and I have no compassion whatsoever!"

"I never said any of those things!"

"Your father and half of Tavern did! You all think I'm a disgusting human being who chose to take his own father's life the very moment he told me that I wasn't allowed to go off to college."

"You know I don't think that."

"Isn't that why you ran off to Riversburg?" *Because you're scared of me?*

Dianna clenched her fists, hot tears streaming down her cheeks. "The only reason I'm still here is because of Nicholas."

"Why didn't you just stay there, huh? You'd be doing us all a favour if you left and never came back!" Roland's lip quivered. *Why did I say that?* He blinked hard, trying to swallow his guilt. *I never should've let you get involved. I keep putting you at risk.*

Dianna lowered her head and drew in a shaky breath.

"Uncle Roland."

"What is it?" he growled.

Rose stepped back and shivered. "Mrs. Hood is on the phone."

"I'll talk to her," Peter said softly. "Dianna, why don't you and I head back to my place for the night?"

Dianna sat on the bed and calmly braided her hair.

Roland stormed out of the room and stopped near the stairwell to the library. His heart dropped like lead in his chest. He drew in a deep breath and shut his eyes as Peter brushed past him.

"What is wrong with you?" he whispered.

Roland looked at him, then glanced back into the room as Peter hurried downstairs. Through the open door to the guestroom, he could see his niece inching toward Dianna.

"Miss Warren," Rose whispered, sitting beside her. "Do people really say those things about him?"

"People have never really had anything nice to say about him. Not that he gives them anything good to say. I know he's not a murderer. He's just broken."

Rose tucked her knees into her chest. "He seemed happy before. Everyone was happy."

"Roland's happiness comes and goes. It can be blown out as easily as a candle."

"Don't leave, Miss Warren. My uncle can't do everything by himself."

His heart dropped in his chest.

Dianna patted her on the head and pulled her close. "I know. I know. But I can't stay forever."

"Eloise, it isn't like you to call so late," Roland said. "Peter said it was urgent." He'd found Roland in the library and pulled him down to the kitchen phone.

"My husband wants to meet with Nicholas before he goes out of town on business."

"When is he scheduled to leave?"

"Next Thursday."

Roland covered the receiver and swore under his breath. "This day just keeps getting better."

"Is everything all right, dear? You sound upset."

"Everything's fine."

"Roland, don't push yourself too hard. All this stress can't be good for your health. I've delayed my husband for as long as I can, but he said he needs to meet Nicholas by Wednesday at the latest. He may just pop by during the week. I'll try and keep tabs on him so I can warn you ahead of time, but that's all I can do."

"Are you sure we can't get any more time?"

"I'm sorry, darling. There's nothing more I can do."

Roland twisted the telephone cord between his fingers.

"Why don't you and I grab lunch tomorrow? I'll come pick you up."

"I have a lot going on. Need to get ready for the visit. Maybe another time," Roland mumbled.

"I insist. You sound absolutely dreadful. I won't take no for an answer."

"All right. I'll see you tomorrow then." He sighed. "Goodnight."

"Goodnight, darling."

28

Eloise examined the young man with curiosity. She watched the way he pressed his lips together and how his gaze fell upon whoever walked past their table. It was as though he waited for someone to send a nasty remark his way. The way he sat with his shoulders tense and back straightened indicated that whatever might be said, he was ready to combat it with great force. His blue daggers would pierce anyone that dared to meet his eyes. *He got that look from his father.* Eloise smiled to herself. She continued to watch him as she drank her tea, noting the dark circles under his eyes and the frequent sighs that fled his lips.

Roland peered at her, running a hand through his hair. "The food is taking a while."

"Hmm? I hadn't noticed."

Roland's gaze fell upon an elderly couple as they walked by.

The couple saw him, whispered, and continued on.

"You're not usually this agitated." Eloise drew his attention back to her.

"I wish they'd just say it to my face. Cowards."

"Are you looking to pick a fight?"

Roland paused for a moment, then sighed. "Tavern is full of gossip."

"Oh, I know, darling, you should hear how some of the ladies go on at my garden parties. It's absolutely ridiculous." Eloise grinned, watching his expression soften. "Roland, I'm sorry that I can't buy you any more time. I really am."

"I understand. Your husband's on a schedule."

Eloise took his hand and held it gently. "I don't know what it is you and Mr. Rissing are working on, but I'm sure he'll go easy on you. I mean, our families have always been close."

Roland blushed and cleared his throat. "I just hope I can meet his standards."

"You will."

"How can you be so sure?" he said, lowering his long dark lashes.

He used to be so small. She recalled back when she and Lawrence would take turns playing hide and seek with him in the garden while their mothers had tea together. Seeing his downcast expression, she gave his hand a light squeeze. "Kurtis has great faith in you. And so, do I. I know that you work hard and are a man who stays true to his word."

Roland nodded.

The waitress came to the table and presented them with their meals. She eyed Eloise's hand on top of Roland's.

Eloise clasped her hands together and gave her a smile. "This looks wonderful."

"Enjoy," the waitress said, quickly glancing at Roland.

Roland glared at her.

She bowed her head and hurried back to the kitchen.

"Did you see that?"

Eloise cut into her meat. "See what, darling?"

"The way that girl was staring at us."

"Oh, she's probably gone off to spread some sort of nasty rumour. Ignore it."

"How can that not bother you?"

"I've learned to brush it off. If I let every pathetic person bother me, I'd lose my sanity." She chuckled. "Oh, my, this is nice and tender. I love eating here. Don't you?"

Roland nodded. "I haven't been out to a nice restaurant in years. Not since my father died."

"Too long," Eloise scolded. "You've spent too much of your life cooped up in that big old house! Enjoy the world around you. Stop letting these idiots chase you away with all of their foolish nonsense. They've got nothing better to do."

"Well, Tabby always cooks for us, so I never really thought about going out to eat."

"Oh, that woman is a wonderful cook."

Roland smiled. "Your son took Rose skating recently. She really enjoyed herself."

"He's quite fond of her. I believe he plans to marry her once she's of age, of course."

"I know my brother would have liked to see the two of them together."

Eloise frowned. "She really does remind me of Laurie."

Roland fiddled with his fork, poking away at his vegetables. "I worry about her."

"Oh?"

"She...well, Tabitha warned me not to let her make friends with the boy we have staying with us. He's a year older than she is, although it seems as though she mothers him the same way she would her brothers. I don't see her growing too—"

"Having a boy and a girl around the same age living together can be extremely problematic and can cause some pretty nasty rumours to circulate. Rose is a young lady now. Her reputation needs to be protected at all costs."

"I see, so you agree with Tabby then."

"Absolutely. It's difficult for anyone to get by with a tarnished reputation."

"That's for sure," he mumbled. "I fear part of mine will pass on to the children. You should hear some of the stories people tell about me."

"I've heard my share." Eloise laughed. "They've been a lot more frequent since Miss Warren's return."

"She'll be leaving soon."

Eloise tilted her head, lowering her knife and fork. "You two used to be so happy. I was living my love story through you, and..." she looked at him and bit her lip. "I won't talk about the past anymore." Although she learned to love her husband, Roland and Dianna did what she and Lawrence couldn't do. They'd rebelled. They ran away. *I should've followed Laurie to Presa. We could've taken Roland with us. Raised him. Kept him safe.*

"Eloise."

"It's better not to dwell on these things. Better to look toward the future."

"Eloise."

"And to...to just forgive and let go," she said, her face flushing.

Roland smiled at her. "I often wonder if you still see me as a little boy."

"Well, clearly, you're a grown man, Roland." She laughed.

"Yes, but you're always trying to protect me." He rested his chin in his hand. "You dote on me."

"Don't look at me with those big blue eyes of yours. You're a flirt, Roland Crispin. You always have been."

Roland let out a laugh. "I'm glad you forced me out of the house today. I needed this."

"Well, I enjoy your company." Eloise grinned. "Perhaps next time the children can join us for some tea?"

He nodded. "And Kurtis as well. I'll host next time."

"That would be wonderful."

The young waitress walked past the table again, glancing at the two of them.

"Perhaps, the young lady is fond of you?" Eloise teased.

"Perhaps." Roland gave the girl a smile. "That or she's heard the rumours of what I did to my father."

"Oh, hush," Eloise tsked. "You did nothing. See, you may have the appearance of a man, but you are most definitely a boy."

The house was quiet when Roland returned. He glanced about, looking to see if anyone was around. *They would never leave without telling me.* He made his way into the parlour. *Something's off. Something must've happened. I shouldn't have gone out. What if they—*

The vermin and the girl jumped up from the floor at the sight of him.

Roland glared, catching his breath. "What are you doing?"

Nicholas opened his mouth and began to stutter.

Rose giggled.

"What on earth is so funny? Where is everyone else?"

Nicholas turned to Rose.

"Nicholas can do embroidery." Rose grinned. "His flowers would please Grandmother. I was having him help me. He's quite handy. Were you out visiting Grandmother? Is she feeling well?"

"You sure talk a lot," Nicholas muttered.

"She does, doesn't she? Always, babbling nonsense." Roland smirked, crouching down to look at their needlework.

"Oh, you should see his drawings too. Aren't they wonderful? See, he did a portrait of me." Rose's face lit up.

Roland eyed the sketch. "You seem very well immersed in the arts."

"Im-immersed?" Nicholas squeaked.

"Apparently, not so much in language."

Nicholas glowered.

"Immersed basically means that you spend a lot of time on something. Like how I spend a lot of time reading," Rose told him.

"Based upon my observations, you've probably never had any education on science or business. At your age, that's very unfortunate." Roland shook his head as he stood back up.

"But art is lovely," Rose said, her voice soft as though she told a secret. "It can play the chords of your heart. Plucking every string. It's what gives life music and colour."

Roland stared at Nicholas, watching his dark eyes widen with excitement. He studied and glanced to see how close they were. The words of Eloise echoed in the back of his mind. He tried to ignore them.

The day Darius expressed his hatred toward Dianna, was the day a spark ignited within Roland. A spark that drove him to rebel against his father. He and Dianna went to Riversburg on foot. They booked a room at the hotel.

Roland gritted his teeth. He was to be a musician, and she wished to spend her days going wherever the wind took her. Now, he stood there, above a boy and girl whose dreams had yet to dance with reality. There they were, making little stitches, not worried about pricking their fingers, just plucking the flowers from within their heads and bringing them to life with their hands.

Rose stared into her uncle's face, wrinkling her brow. "Um... Uncle Roland?"

Roland blinked. "Yes?"

"Is everything all right?"

Roland pressed his lips together. "Why wouldn't it be?"

"Have you spoken with Miss Warren at all today?" she asked sheepishly.

He frowned. "I haven't."

"Well, I think you should." She returned her attention to Nicholas as he pulled his needle and closed the stitch.

"The situation between Miss Warren and I is none of your concern," Roland snapped.

"Can't talk to her now anyway. She's not here," Nicholas mumbled.

"S-she..." Roland lowered his head. "She left?"

"Yes, sir. She's with my uncle right now."

"Uncle Roland, I've never seen you so angry before...well, at least not since..." Rose said softly. "You really hurt her."

"I hurt her?" Roland grimaced, swallowing the lump in his throat. "Rose, you were much too young to know what happened between us. Let me tell you, she was the one who hurt me. I'm the one who should be getting an apology."

"Nicholas, would you like some tea? It's getting a bit cold in here." Rose chucked her embroidery hoop onto the coffee table.

Roland's jaw dropped. *The nerve of that girl!*

"I think I'll try some honey in mine." Nicholas grinned, following her into the kitchen.

Roland sighed. *Eloise is right, I am a child. A thirteen-year-old girl is telling me how I should behave. It's ridiculous.* He sat down in his father's chair and shivered. He raised his hands to his face. They were warm and wet, as though they'd been covered in blood.

"Papa, please. Please!" He gazed up at his father. Tears flooding his eyes.

"Darius."

His father turned and started toward his office.

"Papa," Roland whispered, rising from his stool. The next thing he knew, he was running, his heart pounding hard in his chest. He latched onto his father's arm. "Please. Anything else. I'll do anything else, just don't...don't take this away from me."

Darius glared at him, jerking his arm away violently. "My word is final."

Roland bit into his lip, forcing back his tears.

Adeline stood back, watching her husband and son, unsure if she should step in.

"Because you continue to act foolish and disobey me, there will be no more lessons. No piano playing of any kind. And you will *never* see that wretched girl again." Darius stared coldly, straight into Roland's eyes.

Roland shuddered. "You say you're trying to protect me, but you're smothering me! It feels like I'm being imprisoned in my own house!"

"Good. Then this is the perfect punishment. Perhaps now you'll think before deciding to disobey me. If you were one of my employees—"

"Well, I'm not. I'm your son."

"Roland, Roland sweetheart, you're shaking. Come, sit down." Adeline gently reached for his hand.

"I'm allowed to be happy. I'm allowed to enjoy the time I have," Roland snapped. "I deserve love just like everyone else."

"You don't know what love is! You're thirteen years old. By now, you should have realized that if you end up sick again, that's it. You're done. Your story ends!" Darius grabbed him by the shoulders. "There's no point in falling in love, getting married, going off to school! There's no point, Roland, because, for all we know, you could drop dead tomorrow, right now even! Why can't you get that into your head? Why?" Darius released his grip, watching the tears slide down Roland's face. "You were dead the day you were born," he muttered. "Your time here...it's all for nothing."

Roland backed away from him, his mother pulling him into her arms, stroking his hair, hushing him. He stared at Darius, barely blinking. "So, I'd be better off dead."

"Shh. No, no, that's not true. Papa's just angry, that's all. He didn't mean any of it," Adeline said.

Darius glared at her, then turned from them. He let out a shaky breath. "I have work to do," he mumbled, going into his office.

Roland remembered the click the door made as his father locked himself in the room, shutting him out once again. Looking at his hands, he lamented curling and uncurling his fingers, wondering if Darius and Lawrence's deaths had extended his own time. *He said he was going to get rid of the piano. But he never did. He never did...*

29

Micah shrieked as firm hands gripped his hair at the root and dragged him from the cell. He clawed at officer Nev, attempting to pry him off while the other three officers stood laughing.

Cato spat in his face. "Guess what today is?"

Micah struggled on the cement floor as the men held him down. "*Stai!*"

"I'm sorry, what was that? We can't understand you." Nev chuckled. "We don't speak mutt."

"*Doksot!*"

Nev yanked Micah's head back and glowered. "What did you call me?"

Micah clenched his teeth.

"Listen to it growl." Cato shivered, meeting his eyes.

"What's the matter, you scared of a little vermin?" Nev teased, flinging Micah into him. Cato jumped back, letting Micah fall flat against the concrete. "I think it just tried to bite me."

Micah propped himself up on his elbows and glared at him.

"Well, then it's a good thing I prepared a very special leash for our pet," a familiar voice spat.

Micah whipped his head around as Vincent Gray fastened the rope around his neck. He gagged as Vincent forced him up onto his feet.

"The judge said we—" Micah gasped.

"Oh, that? Merely a formality." Vincent grinned. "The newspaper headline will read that you and your sister attacked those farmers, causing the death of a sweet young baby and that as punishment, you, Lord Wolfe's abomination, were sentenced to death."

The men began to laugh as Micah tried to wriggle away.

"It wasn't that hard to buy off the judge either," Vincent added. "Just offered him your sister, and he was happy to let us proceed."

Micah's body went cold.

"What's the matter? No more fight left in you?" Nev peered over Vincent's shoulder. Cato and the other two men paced around them, smiles contorting on their faces.

Micah's throat tightened without the help of the rope.

Vincent yanked on the restraint. "Any last words, mutt?"

"I want to see my sister." Micah's legs shook.

Vincent pulled the rope again. "I said, last words, not last wish."

"Please," Micah sobbed. "I don't care what you do to me. Please, just let her go. She didn't do anything wrong. I'm the one who stole from your family, not her. She doesn't deserve this."

"You're vermin in Tavern. Mutts or not, rules are rules. Hung or burned. Choosing the noose for you is us doing you a favour." Vincent looked Micah in the face, giving him a little smile. "If you vermin just stayed out of Tavern, this never would've happened. Although, I suppose it's not your fault for being so stupid." He handed the rope to Nev and shook his head. "Bring him out."

Nev nodded.

Micah shivered, tears running down his cheeks as the thick rope rubbed against his skin. Burning into his flesh. He hung his head, his limp limbs heavy beneath him as Nev dragged him up out into the hall. The human eyes watched him, crawling across his skin as the officers forced him toward the doors.

Vincent unlocked it and stepped aside.

The sunlight stabbed Micah's eyes. The winter air pierced into his bare skin. *I was supposed to protect them.* He wheezed as Nev kneed him in the stomach and shoved him to the dirt. Micah rolled onto his chest and looked up at Vincent Gray, trying to draw in a deep breath.

"Looks like you're at the end of your rope, mutt." Vincent glanced over his shoulder. "I really will miss that sister of yours."

Micah lunged at him, eyes blazing. The rope slid from Nev's hands.

Vincent jumped back. "Grab him!"

Cato and the other two officers latched onto the rope and pulled Micah back.

"Hey, not so rough," Vincent scolded as the front gate opened. "Don't wanna break his neck. Yet."

Micah spun toward the gate as Judge Marston gestured to the men. Micah drew in a deep breath as they dragged him forward.

"Please, please let Zana go," Micah begged, reaching for the judge as Vincent shoved him forward. "Please, I—" Micah's eyes widened, the breath fleeing his lungs as he sank to his knees.

Dianna pushed the men off the battered boy and threw her coat around him. She glanced back at Theodore Wolfe as he held up his shivering daughter. She glared at Vincent, Nev and Cato, the boys she'd known in her youth. Their twisted expressions knotted her stomach. She barely recognized them or the tones in their voices.

"Nice to see you, Dianna." Vincent looked her over.

Nice? What's nice about this? Dianna slid against the ice as she tried to pull Micah up. "Get this thing off him." She said, glaring at Vincent.

"What?"

Micah fell from her arms against the cold earth.

"Get it off!" Dianna screamed, pulling at the rope.

Vincent knelt beside her, nodding slowly as he loosened the noose around the boy's neck. "You always did pity wounded animals," he whispered, lowering his head. He looked her in the eye, then glanced away again.

"What did you do to him?" Zana sobbed, clinging to her father.

Vincent helped Dianna up and cleared his throat. "You need to compose yourself. If anyone sees you showing sympathy to these creatures, you'll be labelled a—"

Dianna shot him a look, causing him to step back. "Either help me get him into the car or get out of my way."

Vincent turned to Judge Marston.

"Assist the lady," he said gently.

Theodore ushered his daughter into the vehicle while Vincent helped Dianna with Micah.

Zana sat beside her brother, shivering, resting her head against his. Silent tears coursed her cheeks as Micah wrapped his arm around her shoulders.

As Theodore climbed into the car, Vincent grabbed Dianna by the hand. "Listen."

Dianna pulled away from him. "They're just kids, Vincent."

"I've seen what those types of kids can do." Vincent lowered his voice. He peered over his shoulder at Judge Marston. "Once you leave with them, I can't protect you."

"When have I ever needed your protection?" She turned from him.

Vincent lowered his head. "You stay safe, Dianna."

Once in the car, Dianna wrapped the children in blankets. Zana was still staring at her, as she had been since being released from her cell.

She tried her best to ignore the smell, the bruises, the dried blood. *If this is what happens to half-vermin, I can only imagine what they do to full-blooded ones.*

Theodore remained silent for a time, then managed a smile. "I'm sure Nicholas will be happy to see you."

"Nicholas is alive?" Zana whispered.

Her father nodded.

Micah gave in to a sob. "It was all my fault. He was going to die. The man wouldn't sell it to me. He was going to die, Father."

Theodore nodded. "I understand. You must've been scared."

Micah rubbed his eyes and nodded.

Dianna watched Theodore shift around in his seat, his eyes fixated on his children. She'd expected him to wrap his arms around them and make a fuss like her own parents would have, but he merely sat there, looking at them as if they were strangers. She recalled the awkward way he held Zana when she ran into his arms. His actions seemed forced. *It's possible they haven't seen each other in some time. They were raised by their grandmother, after all.*

She shook her head and gave them a smile. "You must be starving," Dianna said quietly. "Roland is going to have a fit when he finds out I've gone behind his back."

"I'll be sure to thank him properly for taking care of Nicholas," Theodore said. "And, Miss Warren, I really can't express my gratitude."

"I never would have found your children if it weren't for my connections in Riversburg."

"Ah, yes. There's a large vermin population there."

Dianna nodded.

They arrived at the Crispin estate about twenty minutes later. Dianna thought her legs would turn to lead. Her entire body moved heavily, clunky. Roland was already angry with her. He hated her. She tried not to think about how he'd react to yet another little rebellion. She didn't even know how she would go about telling him.

Dianna forced her way to the front door and knocked, rubbing her hands together.

Roland opened the door and eyed her. He swallowed hard. "Dianna, I wanted to...who are they?" He stared at the bedraggled pair clinging to one another behind Theodore Wolfe.

"Don't be angry. I can explain."

Roland stepped aside, letting them in, his hand firmly gripping the door. She could tell by the way his knuckles jutted out that it took everything in him not to slam it shut. She held her breath as he quietly closed the door and turned to her.

"What is going on?"

Dianna smiled sheepishly. "This here is Zana, and this is Micah."

"Pardon?"

"They're my children." Theodore stepped forward.

"They're filthy. What happened to you? You look as though you've been mugged."

Rose and Nicholas peered into the room.

Nicholas' eyes widened. "Micah? Zana?"

Zana cried and ran to him. "I thought that something terrible happened to you. They kept saying they killed you. You've gotten taller. You look so nice. I'm so glad you're okay."

Nicholas wrapped his arms around her, gripped onto her shirt, and held her tight.

Micah smiled at him. "I heard these people found you."

Nicholas nodded, rubbing his eyes. "Where's Nyla? Isn't she with you?"

The brother and sister looked at one another.

"Nicholas...we, we were in jail," Micah said gently.

"They were in jail?" Roland snapped, racing over to Rose.

"Roland, may I make them something to eat? Rose, I'm sure I have a clean dress that Zana could wear. Would you help her to my room?" Dianna asked.

Rose nodded slowly and led Zana upstairs.

Roland took Dianna by the arm. "Can I borrow you for a

moment?" He spotted Lisa on the stairs and waved her over. "Lisa, the boy is freezing. Would you take him to the parlour? There should be a few blankets over there. I'd hate for him to catch cold."

Lisa nodded, leading Micah and Theodore into the other room. Roland smiled politely, then pulled Dianna into the office. She met his eyes briefly. *That's not the face of a happy person.*

Nicholas slipped between the door as Roland shut it behind them, curling up onto the chair behind the desk. He fiddled around with a pen, watching them.

Roland glowered. "Oh, you'd better start talking because I am this close to losing it."

"They were arrested for trying to get medicine for Nicholas. I found out, contacted their father and...they were being tortured."

"Why didn't you come to me?"

"If I went through you, then you'd have to deal with two more Nicholas'," she snapped.

Roland turned to Nicholas, who grinned. "Good point."

A knock came at the door.

Dianna let out a sigh of relief as Roland's face relaxed.

He opened it up and stepped out into the hall.

"T-thank you for..." Micah cleared his throat. "Thank you for saving my little brother, sir."

Roland nodded. "So then, what happens to Micah and Zana? Will they be returning home with you?"

Theodore nodded. "If they remain here, they'll be in constant danger."

"What about Nicholas?" Micah asked.

Theodore turned to Roland. "From what I understand, he's going to keep their necks from the noose."

Micah glared at them. "What does that mean?"

"Means I gotta stay and work for Mr. Crispin and Mr. Rissing— for now." Nicholas frowned. "Cause that's the only way they were able to keep me alive...knowing what I am."

Micah shook his head. "You're going to let him be a slave. Father, you can't."

"I have no way of protecting him." Theodore placed a hand on Micah's shoulder. "He'll be protected by the law this way."

"I don't intend to use him as a slave, I assure you. My job is simply to train him in our ways, and he'll help around the estate," Roland explained.

"Train him? Train him? He's not a dog. My brother is not a dog!" Micah growled, but it lost its ferociousness when he shivered, leaning against the wall. He shut his eyes, panting, trying to catch his breath. "I-I can't abandon my him. You know Zana would never agree to that. Father, there must be some other way."

"He isn't my child. I have no authority. He isn't even my property," Theodore whispered.

Nicholas looked away from his brother. "When I learn to write, I'll send you letters, and maybe we'll be able to visit each other."

"Nyla made me swear I'd take care of you. I swore," Micah sobbed. "I swore, Nicholas."

Roland and Dianna frowned.

"Micah, why don't you wash up...you can sleep in the same room as Nicholas tonight. There are some clothes about your size in a box in the closet. Dianna and I will make something to eat. Hopefully, it will hold you over until dinner." Roland sighed.

Zana followed the girl upstairs, going from one room into the next. She couldn't help but notice the way the younger girl watched her. She was thankful to get away from her for a few moments while she was in the bath.

When the dirt ran off her body, she found herself sobbing. *They're okay. My brothers are okay.* She scrubbed her face and rocked herself gently, watching the mixture of dried blood and dirt circle around her. She jumped at the knock on the door.

"Hi, um, it's me. Rose. I laid some clothes out for you. They're by the door."

Zana sank into the tub, nodding. "Thank you." She stared up at the ceiling. *How did Nicholas end up in a place like this?* She pulled herself from the tub, wrapped herself in a towel, and opened the bathroom door to find the girl fiddling with a ribbon in her hair.

The girl jumped. "You can change in my room." She gestured for Zana to go into the bedroom on her left. "It's the one next to Nicholas'...um, the nursery, I mean."

Zana nodded. When she entered the room, she found a simple green gabardine dress laid neatly on the bed. She unbuttoned the top of the dress and slid into it. She eyed the yellow bruises on her wrists, trying to tug the sleeves a bit further down. *Why do they fall at the elbow?* She rolled her tired eyes and opened the door. Again, the younger girl stood outside, fidgeting with the ribbon in her hair. Zana tilted her head as the girl entered the room and took her by the arm.

She sat Zana in front of the vanity and brushed out her long tawny hair. Zana could feel her eyes on her. *I thought I'd gotten used to humans staring at me.*

"All three of you have lovely long hair," she said quietly.

Zana stared at herself in the mirror, unsure of the human girl.

"Your eyes are the loveliest shade of brown." Rose sighed. "I would love to have brown eyes."

Zana forced herself to smile for the girl. "You find a lot of things lovely."

Rose blushed. "Yes, that's true." She pressed her lips together and continued brushing Zana's hair. "You don't really look like Nicholas."

"We wouldn't look alike." Zana pressed her thumb into the bruise on her knee. "We don't have the same mother and father."

Rose nodded. "He has brown hair like mine. Well, I suppose it's a bit closer to black and dark, dark eyes the colour of chocolate."

Zana played with the sleeves of the dress. "Are you afraid of me? Because of what I am?"

"Well, I've never met anybody who's been to jail before. But I have read books about pirates and all sorts of dastardly criminals." Rose said excitedly. "And you look much more like a princess."

Zana furrowed her brow. "I see."

Rose parted a few strands of her hair and tied a ribbon around them. "The green looks so nice on you."

Zana smiled.

"I have two brothers as well. Caspian and Julius. I'm the eldest. A pain, really, being the eldest of two younger brothers." Rose stopped and bit her lip. "I'm told I talk too much. I must be annoying you. I'll stop."

"No, I don't mind." Zana shook her head. "It's nice having somebody to talk to. I just don't really know what to say."

Rose's face lit up. "I bet you've been courted many times. You're so pretty."

Zana laughed and shook her head. "Only once."

Rose groaned. "There's a boy courting me. I don't have a mother or an older sister, so I don't really know who to ask about these things. There's nothing wrong with this boy, but I feel as though everyone wants us to be together and, well, he isn't exactly the type of boy I imagined I'd marry. He plans to marry me and assumes I'll say yes, but maybe I'll say, no, and I never want to see you again."

The two girls giggled.

"Boys are so strange," Rose said.

"Especially when they're sweet on someone."

"Has Nicholas ever been sweet on anyone?" Rose asked shyly.

Zana grinned. "He's always been a little bit slower than the other boys, but he's the youngest out of everyone in our pa—um our village."

"He's the youngest?"

"Yes, and he was very tiny when he was little. He always wanted to do what everyone else was doing. His father left him with us. He said he'd come back, but we never saw him again."

Rose grew quiet for a moment, twisting the ribbon in her own hair tightly around her finger. "My parents passed away five years ago. Three months after my grandfather."

"I lost my mother, too, so I understand. I thought that I'd lost Nicholas as well, but you saved him. I'm so glad. In my heart, I wanted him to be okay...but..."

A knock startled them.

"Come in," Rose called.

Nicholas propped open the door. "There's food if you're hungry." The girls nodded.

"You should eat something." Rose gave Zana's shoulder a gentle squeeze. "I can't even begin to imagine what you've been through."

Zana stood up and followed Nicholas down the stairs. Rose chased after them and tapped Nicholas on the shoulder. He turned to her.

"Your sister's so graceful. She's like a princess, isn't she?"

He smiled.

Doesn't she see all the bruises on my body? Zana blinked, utterly confused.

"Yes, she is."

Nicholas watched his older brother tear into his bread. He'd never seen Micah eat so fast or so aggressively. There was something about the way he glowered at the humans. It was like he wanted to rip into them with his teeth.

"How old are you?" Rose asked.

Micah glanced at her briefly and raised his brow.

Zana eyed her brother and spoke for both of them. "I'm sixteen, and Micah's eighteen."

Micah stared at Roland, his teeth grinding together. "Your father, he's—"

"Oh, Roland is my uncle," Rose said.

Micah turned to her. "He doesn't seem to like Nicholas."

"Well, I think they're both really stubborn. So, they argue a lot."

"I'm not stubborn," Nicholas snapped.

Zana shook her head. "Yes, you are, just like Micah."

Micah kissed his teeth.

"So, where is Nyla?" Nicholas asked.

Zana and Micah sighed.

"Nyla? That's your grandmother, right?" Rose watched the two Wolfe siblings go pale.

"Yes, she raised me." Nicholas smiled.

"We don't know where she is," Micah admitted. "As far as we know, she's probably dead."

Nicholas stared at him.

"She wasn't well. She couldn't have made it on her own. We never should have left her." Zana looked down at her plate.

Nicholas stood up, his chair scraping across the hardwood.

The adults turned their attention to the dining room table.

"Nicholas, is everything all right?" Dianna asked.

Nicholas backed away from the table, stumbling into the chair. He toppled over onto the floor.

Micah shoved another piece of bread into his mouth and turned from him.

Nicholas scrambled to his feet as Rose got up from her seat.

"Nicholas!" she cried.

He fled the room, and she hurried after him.

Micah remained in his seat, slowly forcing food down his throat. His sister glared at him but stayed by his side, keeping quiet.

Nicholas leaned against the bedroom door and held his breath. He clenched his fists, squeezing so tightly that his nails dug into his palms. He let out a whimper and shook his head violently, slamming a fist into the door.

"May I come in?" Rose asked quietly.

"Go away!" he barked, his eyes burning.

Rose sighed. His ears pricked as she made a soft thud leaning against the barrier. "I'm sorry, Nicholas."

He curled up into a ball and wept. Another set of footsteps mounted the stairs.

"Go downstairs and help Miss Warren."

Nicholas's ears twitched. *Mr. Crispin.* He slid toward the door, rubbing his eyes.

"I'm going to stay with Nicholas," Rose protested.

Roland sighed. The man always sighed, so he wasn't sure what it meant this time.

"I'll talk to him when he's calmed down. He needs a moment to himself. It's a lot to take in at once."

"He'll be leaving us..." Rose whispered.

Nicholas heard her fingers trace along the back of the door. He held his breath, following them through the solid barrier.

"He– he's actually under a contract so, he's staying," Roland said.

"A contract?"

"He works for Peter and I, and depending on how things play out, he'll be assisting Mayor Hood."

"But his family isn't from Tavern."

"They'll be leaving him behind."

Nicholas gripped his stomach. He wanted to vomit.

"That's...strange, isn't it?" Rose asked. "Uncle Roland, is there something you're not telling me?"

Nicholas could hear the honey in the man's voice. "Sometimes, it's better not to know."

Nicholas raised his head, rubbing his eyes roughly with the palms of his hands. It was dark outside now, with no sign of the moon hanging in the sky. Daylight always disappeared quickly during the colder seasons. He forced himself to his feet and watched as his hair dangled before his eyes. *This room will be my life now. Nyla's gone. Micah and Zana will be leaving with Uncle Theo. I have to look out for myself now. No one's going to protect me.*

The boy raised his head and brushed the hair out of his face. He found himself twisting the cold knob, propping the door open a little, and gazing out into the hall. His stomach growled. He tiptoed out into the dim hallway and glanced around as he made his way to the edge of the rotunda. Voices floated up from the parlour. He rested his chin on the wooden railing and shut his eyes. *Voices from the parlour after dark. This will be normal soon.*

A door creaked shut down the hall. His shoulders tensed as footsteps crept toward him. *Too large to be Rose's. Too light to be Mr. Rissing.* He spun around. "What?" Nicholas snapped.

"Didn't mean to frighten you," Roland apologized.

Nicholas lowered his head. "So, how long till I meet what's his name?"

"Before Thursday."

Nicholas glanced up at him briefly. "If, if I do a good job, will you teach me things like reading and business?"

"Why the sudden interest in education?" Roland asked.

"I want you to teach me." Nicholas shoved his hands into his pockets.

"Very well," he said, patting the boy's head.

Nicholas flinched, pulling away from the man. He eyed Roland, then frowned. "I'll do my best to make sure I don't mess up. I promise."

"Thank you, Nicholas." Roland headed toward the staircase. "It's nearly six-thirty. Dinner should be on the table."

He nodded.

"You should speak with Rose when you're up to it. She's worried about you," Roland mumbled.

"Yes, sir," Nicholas whispered. "I will."

30

Nicholas jumped at the heavy knock on the front door. He'd
been on edge ever since his family left.

"They have to leave as soon as possible," Miss Warren
had told him. "If word gets out they're staying here, it could cause a
lot of problems."

Nicholas peered down the stairs as Tabitha hurried to the door.
Mr. Rissing and Mr. Crispin left the office, papers rustling in their
hands. *Research. To show what's his name.* Nicholas smirked
whenever he referred to the mayor as "Sir such-and-such," or "Mayor
what's his name," for he knew his name was Kurtis Hood. He'd heard
about him enough. Still, it amused him whenever he imagined the
type of person the mayor might be to get two grown men such as
Roland and Peter so flustered and scared.

He popped his head up a bit higher and furrowed his brow,
watching the long flowing brown coat emerge from the frame of the
doorway. It was followed by a high-pitched greeting, and then
another larger coat entered.

"It's pretty nasty out," the man said.

"Thompson isn't with you today?" Roland asked.

"He's parking the car," a woman said.

Roland spotted the dark-eyed boy at the top of the stairs and gestured for him to come down. "Don't be shy." Nicholas stood and straightened out his jacket and pants. He'd promised to do his best.

"Let me take your coats." Tabitha helped the couple out of their jackets.

"Nicholas, this is Mayor Kurtis Hood and his wife Eloise," Roland said as Nicholas inched toward them.

"H-hello," Nicholas squeaked.

Kurtis eyed him carefully. "Seems to be healthy."

"He's improved immensely." Peter handed Kurtis a piece of paper. "We've been keeping track of his progress."

"How about we discuss this in my office?" Roland suggested.

Kurtis grinned and shook his head. "I'd like to visit first. It's been some time since Rose's party."

"Roland, you really must get Rose a fur of her own. She's a young lady now, and they're all the rage." Eloise turned to Nicholas. "What do you think? Should she not have one?"

"Is she getting married?" he asked.

"Not yet." Eloise laughed. "A woman doesn't wear fur only when she's married."

"Oh...I thought men gave furs to women they wanted to marry."

"What a peculiar idea."

"I parked the car near the stable, Father," Thompson said, opening the front door. He spotted Nicholas and smiled, removing his jacket. "You're up and about. That's good."

"You've met?" Kurtis questioned.

Thompson nodded. "Rose introduced us briefly. What's your name again?"

"Nicholas. Nicholas Slayden."

Thompson nodded. "Is Rose around?"

"She'll be down later, once she's finished her schoolwork." Roland clasped his hands. "Is anyone hungry?"

Nicholas nodded without thinking. His face flushed pink as Peter and Roland glared at him.

"Miss Warren and I prepared some light snacks. Rose has a pie in the oven. First, she's made on her own," Tabitha said, leading everyone into the parlour. "May I get any of you a drink? Wine perhaps?"

"I'd love a glass, thank you, Tabby." Eloise grinned.

Nicholas sat across from Thompson and eyed him. He was much taller than he'd remembered. Although, he didn't get a good look at him when they'd first met. He recalled all of the things Rose had told him about the boy and wrinkled his brow. There didn't seem to be anything wrong with him other than that he was a bit older than he'd originally thought. He barely remembered their first meeting.

Thompson caught Nicholas staring at him and grinned. He turned to Kurtis. "So, Father, are we going to wait for Rose before you begin your meeting?"

"No, we should probably begin without her. You and your mother will remain here until a final decision has been made."

Nicholas watched Kurtis eye the papers Roland had given him. He glanced up to examine the boy briefly. Dianna and Tabitha laid out the wine glasses, and the mayor turned to acknowledge the women, but his wife beat him to it.

"So, you've returned to Tavern, Dianna," Eloise said, crossing her legs.

Dianna nodded.

"Not sure why," Tabitha said under her breath.

Nicholas glanced at Roland, then to Dianna. The two of them had barely spoken to each other over the last couple of days. It made him uneasy.

Roland cleared his throat, squirming in his seat as he poured Eloise a glass of white wine.

"It was time I came back. Tavern is my home, after all," Dianna said.

Eloise held the wine glass between her fingers. "Where've you been staying?"

"Pardon?"

"I'm just surprised to see you *here*, is all."

Nicholas turned his head from side to side, trying to keep up with the conversation. There was more going on here than just polite conversation.

Thompson tapped his shoulder and gave him a smile. "My mother's not very fond of Miss Warren," he whispered. He pointed at Roland, leaning close to Nicholas' ear. "I'm sure Rose already updated you on their complex history."

"Not really."

Thompson raised his brow and watched as the three men rose to their feet. He chuckled softly, looking at the confusion on Nicholas' face. "I believe they're going to start the meeting."

Nicholas gave him a nod and climbed to his feet.

"Nicholas, wait in the hall." Peter glared at the boy. Nicholas glanced over his shoulder at Miss Warren and winced trying to force a smile.

Dianna gestured for him to go ahead. She picked up the tea tray. "Don't worry, I'll be with you shortly."

"Okay," Nicholas muttered before scurrying after the men and stood a sentinel by the door. He peered back into the parlour as the men went into the office.

"Roland told me you were leaving," Eloise said, turning her attention to Dianna. "Where did you end up moving to?"

Nicholas' eyes flickered as he adjusted his hair over his ears.

"When did he say that?"

"When he and I met for lunch."

Dianna straightened her back. "Well, Mrs. Hood, I haven't yet decided on whether or not I'll be leaving. Peter's recently requested that I say and help with Nicholas."

"You've been nursing him back to health." Eloise nodded, tapping her finger against the glass.

"I'd better bring this tray over. Besides, poor Nicholas is nervous as it is. He'll want me there." Dianna hurried out of the room. She stopped in the hall and gave Nicholas a weary grin.

"Thompson said his mother doesn't like you," Nicholas mumbled.

Dianna nodded. "I can tell. She and Tabitha are...never mind. How are you feeling?"

Nicholas chewed on his lower lip.

Roland opened the door and let them inside. He took the tray from Dianna and went back to the conversation.

"As you can see, sir, even just by looking at his rapid health increase compared to the average human, the creature is strong." Peter pointed to different spots on the paper. "What the vermin lack in knowledge they make up for in endurance, speed, and strength."

Roland nodded. "We believe it's because his specific pack practiced both hunting and agriculture."

Kurtis scanned the boy top to bottom and raised his brow. "He looks quite small."

"He's still young, sir," Roland pointed out. "Younger than your son."

"Ah, then he's not reached adulthood." Kurtis stood up and began circling the boy.

Nicholas shivered slightly. He didn't like being stared at, but this was what he had to do. Stand there and be quiet until spoken to.

"Do you read?" Kurtis asked.

"No, sir."

"Mmm...you've killed an animal before, yes?"

"I have," he lied, looking away from the man. He was good at catching animals. Before coming to Tavern, he'd tried sinking his teeth into a rabbit's neck, but it squirmed and squealed. When the blood pooled in his mouth, he spat it out. Micah scolded him for it. *Humans expect us to hunt. If Mayor Hood thinks I can't, then he'll think somethings wrong with me. It's better to lie.*

"What about a human?" Kurtis stopped in front of him. "Have you successfully taken the life of a man?"

Nicholas shook his head. "No. All I've killed are rabbits and foxes."

Kurtis leaned toward him. "But the desire to kill runs through your veins. You're a dangerous beast. Why should I spare you?"

"The boy is harmless," Roland assured him. "He could never do such a thing."

"What if he were provoked? I heard what happened with Dr. Gray," Kurtis snapped. "It was difficult for me to call this animal a boy in front of my wife. And to find out, now, that my son was around him. You've been careless, Roland. What if he attacked young Julius or even Miss Warren here?"

"Mr. Mayor, sir, I wouldn't ever hurt them." Nicholas tugged on his sleeve, lowering his head. "Whatever Mr. Crispin or Mr. Rissing tell me, I do."

"Without hesitation?"

Nicholas nodded. He knew it wasn't true, but it could be...

"Hmm. I'd like to speak with Nicholas alone. The rest of you can go. Leave the tray. Thank you."

The trio looked at the mayor, eyes wide.

Roland opened his mouth, shut it and nodded. "As you wish."

Peter turned to him, then to Nicholas. "But—"

Dianna gave Nicholas's hand a light squeeze as Roland opened the door.

"We're doomed," Peter mumbled sullenly.

Nicholas' shoulders shot up to his ears as the door closed behind him, and every single one of the human's who said they'd help him left. He stared at the mayor, watching the man take a seat in Roland's chair.

"Have a seat, Mr. Slayden." Kurtis gestured to the green and gold Recamier couch—it was low and small; backless, the headrest curving upward.

Nicholas sat down, listening to the legs of the seat creak beneath him. He held his breath.

"How old are you?"

"I'm *Sch*...um I'm four—"

"Speak up."

"*Schrein*."

Kurtis glowered, leaning forward in his seat. "And that is?"

Nicholas' tongue went dry. He lowered his head, pulling on the sleeves of his sweater. "I meant to say fourteen. I'm fourteen, sir."

Kurtis nodded. "Well, they didn't lie about you speaking our language well. How many languages do you speak?"

"*Va.* I mean two."

"Look at me when I'm speaking to you." The gruffness in his voice made Nicholas' ears twitch. He looked up. Kurtis stood up and made his way over to him. The mayor looked Nicholas over and shook his head. "I have no patience for meekness and very little patience for vermin. I want you to sit up straight, speak plainly, and stop fidgeting. I've seen Caspian manage it. I'm sure you, four years his senior, are capable as well."

Nicholas nodded, adjusting in his seat. "Yes, sir."

"How did you end up in Tavern? Did they send you to spy on us?"

"No...we were just trying to get to Murienne, and the only way there is through Tavern and Riversburg so—"

"Are all the vermin gathering in Murienne? It seems stupid to travel at this time of year."

"No, just us...we lost our homes and—"

"There is nothing more dangerous than a wild vermin. We don't even allow domestic ones in Tavern. Haven't since the war." Kurtis glared at him. "Roland is the son of a dear friend, but I won't deny that the boy is naïve. He sees a small sickly creature and decides to bring it home to train...as if you're some lost puppy. I've seen what you creatures are capable of."

Nicholas lowered his head.

"Look at me when I'm speaking to you."

Nicholas brushed his hair from his face, shooting Kurtis a dirty look. His eyes flickered.

Kurtis stepped back. "I've noticed in some of their notes it mentions your temper. A temper that Dr. Gray witnessed firsthand. It took a lot for me to persuade him not to hand you over to the police, you know."

"I'm sorry," Nicholas whispered.

"Are you?"

He nodded.

"So, if I were to do or say something you disliked, your first instinct wouldn't be to kill me?"

Nicholas furrowed his brow. "No, sir. That was a misunderstanding. Mr. Crispin explained my error to me."

Kurtis stretched out his hand and yanked on the boy's earring.

Nicholas yelped, biting down hard on his lip. He looked up at Kurtis.

"What is this?"

"My mother gave it to me," Nicholas growled, swallowing the sound. He kept his eyes on the man. *He's trying to provoke me. I can't let him.*

Kurtis let go of the earring. "Usually, domesticated vermin have their teeth shaved down to prevent any incidents. I'm still undecided about yours."

Nicholas watched him carefully. His eyes narrowed as Kurtis grabbed him by the jaw, and pushed his head back. *Doksot!* Nicholas jerked away, digging his nails into the seat.

Kurtis massaged his hand, glaring at him. "You've still got a lot of fight in you. We'll need to fix that." He rested his hand beneath his chin, fixating on Nicholas' jaw. "Open your mouth."

Nicholas did as commanded. For a brief moment, he thought he could hear the man's heart pounding in his chest. Nicholas's nostrils flared as Kurtis took a pen from off the desk and jammed it down his throat. He gagged. His eyes watering.

"Probably best to have these removed." Kurtis tapped the pen against Nicholas' fangs. He pulled the pen from his mouth and examined him. "What's wrong? Have I upset you?"

"No sir," Nicholas said hoarsely. He shook.

Kurtis dragged the pen through Nicholas's hair. "This'll need to go as well."

Nicholas bit into his lip.

Roland, Peter, and Dianna returned to the parlour and rejoined Thompson and Eloise. Rose sat with them now, her hands folded.

Roland sat beside her, nudging her gently with his shoulder. "You're awfully quiet today. Did something happen at school?"

Rose shook her head. "Is Nicholas all right?"

Roland's stomach dropped. He swallowed his nerves as best as he could. "We'll have to wait and see."

Thompson glared at the floor briefly, gritting his teeth.

Roland watched the lad as he dug his feet into the carpet. Peter gulped down another glass of wine. *How is him slurring his words going to help?* Roland looked over at Dianna, whose skirt shifted in measured beats. *Her legs are shaking.* He stood up and took the wine glass from Peter, placing it on the table. "Go comfort your cousin," he hissed in his best friend's ear.

Peter rubbed his hands together. "And who is going to comfort me?"

"Peter, please."

"I'm going out of my mind here, Roland. If that little prick has one misstep, we are—"

"Shh." Roland pulled Peter toward the old gramophone. "Go have some of Rose's pie if you must, but stop drinking. I'll talk to Dianna."

Peter nodded and sat himself down at the coffee table across from Eloise, who admired Rose's latest needlework.

Roland shoved his hands into his pockets and leaned up against the wall, nodding at Dianna. *It's been days since we've had an actual conversation...she's probably as scared as I am. It's silly trying to avoid each other. Nicholas doesn't need that right now. We need to be united.* He cleared his throat as she made her way over. "Are you all right?" he asked quietly.

She nodded. "Although, I don't think Peter's—"

"He has pie. He'll be fine."

Dianna rolled her eyes. "Yeah, the only person who finds food helpful in these types of situations is you." She shook her head and crossed her arms. "Well, at least you got him away from the wine."

I should apologize. I've been a jerk. I don't know why I was so cold to her. I should ask her to stay. Nicholas needs her. Roland ran a hand through his hair and sighed. "Dianna I—"

The group jumped as the office door swung open, crashing against the wall.

Roland swallowed hard.

Dianna latched onto his hand.

Kurtis entered the room and glared at Roland and Peter.

Peter lowered his plate. "Nicholas, what did you—"

"I'll hire him," Kurtis said nonchalantly.

The men's faces lit up.

"Thank you, sir," Roland said, bowing his head. "I promise, you won't regret this."

Nicholas hid behind the mayor, staring at his feet. Kurtis gestured to him. "Now, I believe you have something to tell everyone about your new pet."

Dianna let go of Roland's hand and stood back. A look of horror mingled with indignation threatened to spill something less than desirable from her lips.

Thompson chuckled. "Pet?"

Roland held his breath. "I'd prefer to speak to the children about this later."

"Either you tell the girl now, or tomorrow morning she'll have heard it in school."

Eloise raised her eyebrows as Rose turned to her uncle. "Tell me what?

"Kurtis, why are you so upset?" Eloise stood and approached her husband.

"Roland, tell her," Kurtis snapped.

Roland made his way over to his niece and took her by the hand. "Rose, Nicholas is...he's—"

"I'm a vermin."

The humans all turned to face the creature.

Thompson leaped to his feet and stood in front of Rose. "A vermin! An animal?"

Rose stared at Nicholas, her mouth hanging half-open. She pressed her lips together, suddenly remembering herself.

"Rose, don't you ever go near him again. He might hurt you or spread disease or—"

"May I please be excused?" she asked, turning to Roland, adding icy calm to her words.

He nodded, still eyeing Nicholas.

Rose hurried past Thompson before he could grab her. She looked Nicholas in the eye and frowned.

Roland watched Nicholas's expression darken as his niece fled upstairs. He could already hear her sobs.

"Roland, what were you thinking, having a vermin under the same roof as a young girl?" Eloise turned sharply and stepped toward him. "What if he hurt her?"

"I wouldn't ever hurt Rose. She's my friend," Nicholas said softly.

"Your friend?" Thompson laughed. "Vermin and humans are not friends. No, she's your mistress, and you're her dog."

Nicholas glared at him.

"You stay away from her," Thompson spat, grabbing the smaller boy by the collar. "'Cause if I ever catch you around her, I'll kill you."

Nicholas wriggled away and hurried over to Miss Warren. She

wrapped her arms over his shoulders.

Thompson smirked. "He's well trained, father. He keeps his tail between his legs."

"That's enough." Roland loomed over him, stepping between the boys. "I understand you're protective of my niece, but Nicholas knows his boundaries. There's no need to provoke him."

Thompson blushed. "I'm sorry, sir." He shot Nicholas a threatening glare. "It's just that I plan to marry her in a few years. I'd hate if something were to happen to her because she decided to befriend this beast."

"Marry her?" Nicholas choked. "But she doesn't even like you."

"Pardon?"

Nicholas gulped. "She...you...."

"What, then, does she like you?" Thompson crossed his arms, shaking his head. "Please, there is no way a woman of status would stoop so low."

"I never said she liked me." Nicholas glowered.

Thompson glared at him. "Change your tone, pet. My father is your employer now. I'm above you."

Roland grabbed Thompson by the wrist. "That's enough. You need to calm down."

"You let a disgusting vermin hang around my—"

"Rose doesn't belong to you," he snapped.

Thompson jerked away from him. "She shouldn't be living in the same house as this creature."

"Thompson!" Kurtis hollered. "Go get the car started."

Thompson nodded, shoving past Roland as he left.

"Nicholas will come see me immediately upon my return. Until then, he'll work for you.

"Yes, sir."

"Let's go, Eloise," Kurtis said softly, taking his wife's hand.

Eloise nodded slowly, getting up from her seat. She looked over at Roland and lowered her eyes, turning from him as Kurtis led her out of the house.

Roland's chest tightened. Eloise always had his best interests at heart, but now... now she couldn't even look at him.

Tabitha shut the door behind them.

"That either went very well or horribly wrong," Peter mumbled.

"I need to talk to Rose." Roland headed for the stairs.

"I need a bloody drink."

Roland glared at him as Tabitha gave his arm a little squeeze. He lowered his lashes, taking in a deep breath. "I shouldn't have kept this a secret from Eloise."

"You did it to protect her. I'm sure she'll understand." Tabitha gave him a kiss on the cheek. "Go, I'll keep an eye on Peter."

Dianna looked at Nicholas and smiled at him, gently brushing back his hair. "You did well."

Nicholas nodded.

"I wish you could've left with your uncle," she whispered.

"Me too," he sobbed, clinging to her tightly.

Rose sat down on her stool before her vanity and looked at the paleness of her face. She replayed the boy's words over and over in her mind, staring blankly at her own expression.

"Vermin." The word came out of her mouth like a curse. It tasted like bitter medicine, and when she sounded it out, her lips went dry. Still, she uttered it again, as if she were saying it to herself, calling herself the vilest creature in existence.

She whispered the word again like it was some dark secret.

Her heart skipped in her chest, and she turned from her reflection.

"Nicholas," she said, gripping the skirt of her dress.

This word didn't taste bitter on her tongue. This word made her lips turn upward into a smile. She could look at herself again, this time with a threatening glance. She gritted her teeth and glared hard into her own eyes.

"Nicholas is Nicholas," she snapped. "Not a human or a vermin, but Nicholas and that's, that!"

A quiet knock distracted Rose. She prayed it wasn't Thompson, although he rarely went anywhere past the parlour when he visited. There were only two places in the house where she could be alone, and her bedroom was one of them.

"Come in," she muttered reluctantly, picking up the novel on her vanity, trying to make herself look preoccupied.

Roland opened the door and shut it behind him. He gave her a slight smile and drew in a deep breath. "I know, I should have told you."

Rose lifted her eyes from the book. "When did you plan on making the announcement?"

"Once everything had been decided with Kurtis. Just, not so publicly." He pressed his back up against the door and groaned.

"Who knew about this?"

"Everyone...everyone helping with Nicholas, except you and your brothers." He sighed, his blue eyes avoiding hers.

She slammed the book shut. "How long have you known?"

"Since he came to stay with us. Everything happened so quickly. Nicholas, he's no danger to you."

"I'm aware."

Roland nodded. "It must've been shocking to hear."

She met his gaze. "What was shocking was standing there as everyone looked down on him. I'm not a little girl anymore. You can stop trying to protect me."

"To me, you are a little girl. Everyone keeps talking to me about you marrying Thompson and your reputation...about fur coats." Roland shook his head. "You're only thirteen. You still have some much life ahead of you."

"Marrying Thompson, ha. Who says I'll accept his proposal?"

"I'd like to think you would. He can care for you *and* your brothers."

"There are plenty of fine gentlemen in Tavern and beyond. Why does it have to be Tom?"

"Eloise was very close with your father."

"My father is dead. His opinion doesn't matter, and neither does yours. I can and will make my own decisions. I'm old enough now to be able to choose whether or not I'm ready for certain things."

Roland eyed her. "You'd better decide to change that tone. I didn't tell you about Nicholas because there are serious penalties for harbouring vermin. I wasn't going to bring my brother's children to the noose with me."

Rose got to her feet and glared at him. "So, now that I know I should treat him like a monster? I've shared some of my most intimate thoughts with him. He's become one of my dearest friends. Do you know how difficult it is for me to put on this mask every day? This last name is burned into my skin and follows me everywhere I go. I can't imagine Rose Hood or Rose Armstrong because even if I do marry, I can never erase the stain of a name like Crispin.

"People are afraid of you and say it the same way they say vermin or brute. To abandon you and my brothers with such a hateful name seems cruel. And the one person who sits and listens to me without much complaint is a vermin. Saying that makes my stomach turn! I'm supposed to hate vermin, but how can I hate him when I know what it's like to be hated?"

Roland stood there quietly as fresh tears streamed down her face. She struggled to catch her breath, forcing her lips shut so that nothing else would come out. She'd already said too much.

Her uncle let out a sigh and took her into his arms, rocking her gently. He kissed the top of her head and frowned. "I'm sorry, Flower," he whispered. "No matter what choice I made, I was bound to hurt someone. I'm sorry it was you."

Roland gave her a quick squeeze.

"I'm sorry too," Rose sobbed into his cardigan. She hugged him tightly, rubbing her face into his chest. He missed her. He missed just being her goofy uncle. He missed a lot of things, but that's what happened when the boy destined for death was the only one who lived.

Roland pressed his lips together.

The two remained like that, gripping one another until footsteps echoed outside the door.

"Roland, you in there?" Peter called.

Rose looked up at her uncle and rubbed her eyes. "I'm all right now. You have lots to do. I'll see you at dinner."

He nodded and went into the hall.

"Hood will return in about two weeks' time. So, we've got till then to prepare Nicholas for work. Do you know what sort of jobs he'll be doing?" Peter asked.

Roland rubbed the back of his neck as they walked down the hall. "Well, from what I know of our few conversations, it'll be labour-based. He'll probably run a lot of errands, perhaps even do some repairs?"

"I don't like not knowing. How's Rose?"

"I think she'll be okay. I don't want to press any further." Roland sighed. Life always seemed to hand him a dish of honey in one hand and a beehive in the other. "Where's Nicholas?"

"He's with Dianna in the parlour. She's teaching him a card game."

He nodded. "She'll be leaving soon, now that everything is over.

Peter smiled. "We'll see."

"What?" Roland stepped back, knitting his brow. His heart leap in his chest. *What made her change her mind?*

"The three of us, despite our arguments, do work well together... at times. And she is more familiar with vermin customs than we are— she's had practical experience. It's not over yet, Roland. The real challenge starts now. Hood's going to make our research public, and I can assure you, people aren't going to like it."

ABOUT THE AUTHOR

Ardin Patterson is a Canadian voice actress and author with a passion for storytelling. She is a Trent University Graduate, who spent her years there geeking out over Shakespeare, hanging with her friends at The Trend, and going to bookstores every weekend. When she isn't telling stories or lending her voice to little mice, princesses, and spunky teens, Ardin can be found playing video games with her sister, singing, drawing, and of course reading.

Manufactured by Amazon.ca
Bolton, ON

27842992R00164